THE NIGHT OF YOUR LIFE

D1114290

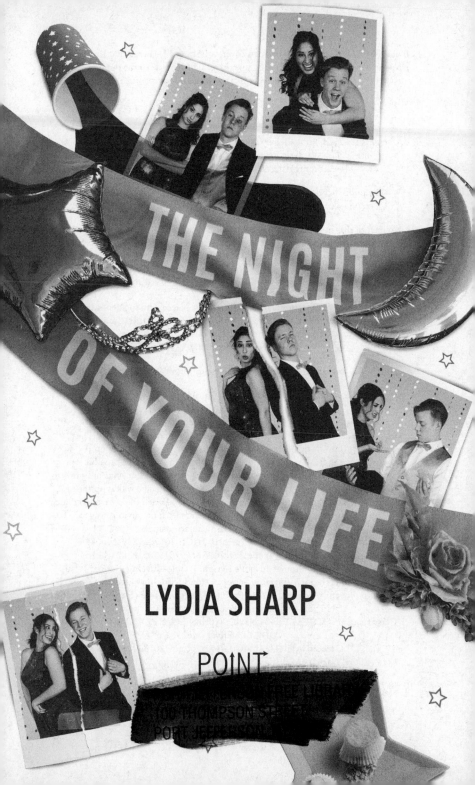

THE NIGHT OF YOUR LIFE

LYDIA SHARP

POINT

Copyright © 2020 by Lydia Sharp

All rights reserved. Published by Point, an imprint of Scholastic Inc., *Publishers since 1920*. SCHOLASTIC, POINT, and associated logos are trademarks and/or registered trademarks of Scholastic Inc.

The publisher does not have any control over and does not assume any responsibility for author or third-party websites or their content.

This book is a work of fiction. Names, characters, places, and incidents are either the product of the author's imagination or are used fictitiously, and any resemblance to actual persons, living or dead, business establishments, events, or locales is entirely coincidental.

Library of Congress Cataloging-in-Publication Data

Names: Sharp, Lydia, author.
Title: The night of your life / Lydia Sharp.
Description: First edition. | New York : Point, an imprint of Scholastic Inc., 2020. | Audience: Ages 12 and up. | Audience: Grades 7-9. | Summary: JJ is taking his best friend Lucy to the senior prom, but on the way there a near car crash suddenly points him in the direction of a possible new romance, and when he finally gets to the prom he finds that Lucy has been taken to the hospital and never wants to see him again; but when he wakes up the next morning he finds that it is prom day again—and what seemed like a second chance quickly turns into an endless loop of disasters with no obvious way to break the cycle and fix his relationship.
Identifiers: LCCN 2019029858 (print) | LCCN 2019029859 (ebook) | ISBN 9781338317275 (paperback) | ISBN 9781338317282 (ebk)
Subjects: LCSH: Proms—Juvenile fiction. | Time—Juvenile fiction. | Interpersonal relations—Juvenile fiction. | Conduct of life—Juvenile fiction. | Friendship—Juvenile fiction. | CYAC: Proms—Fiction. | Time—Fiction. | Conduct of life—Fiction. | Friendship—Fiction.
Classification: LCC PZ7.1.S484 Ni 2020 (print) | LCC PZ7.1.S484 (ebook) | DDC 813.6 [Fic] —dc23
LC record available at https://lccn.loc.gov/2019029858
LC ebook record available at https://lccn.loc.gov/2019029859

10 9 8 7 6 5 4 3 2 1   20 21 22 23 24

Printed in the U.S.A.   23
First edition, March 2020

Book design by Yaffa Jaskoll

TO MELISSA LINVILLE,
my very dear friend
WHO PASSED AWAY WHILE I
WAS WRITING THIS BOOK.
Miss you. Love you. Always.

Today is yours.

Don't waste it.

Go create your own fate.

 the NIGHT of the BROKEN MOON

Lucy is doing that thing with her lips again. I call it a twibble, a twitch too subtle to be a quiver or a tremble. She's trying not to let this get to her. She's failing to hide that she's trying not to let this get to her. I just haven't figured out what *this* is yet.

"So . . ." I lean against the doorway to her bedroom as Lucy finishes getting ready for school, pulling up sections of her hair to pin them back. If we talk, eventually the reason for her twibble will come out. "Did you get your prom dress yet?"

"Prom is *tomorrow night*, JJ," she says without looking away from the mirror above her dresser. She plucks another pin from the tray next to a bottle of lotion. "If I didn't have my dress yet, I wouldn't be going."

She also wouldn't be Lucy if she didn't plan every little thing ten steps ahead. But for this, I'm in agreement. This is senior prom. Our last big hurrah before high school graduation. Before our entwined lives go their separate ways. I picked up my tux last week, but she never told me when she got her dress. She hasn't told me *anything* about it, actually, not even the color.

1

"Can I see it?" I take one step toward her closet—

In a blink, she's across the room and blocking me. "No!"

"All right, all right," I say through a laugh. "I won't look." I keep smiling—it's not a big deal. But still . . . "What's the big deal?"

Prom is supposed to be a night of fun, nothing more. Nothing serious. We made a promise to each other at the beginning of senior year, that if neither of us had dates for prom, we'd go with each other. At the time I hadn't thought that would actually happen. It was likely I'd still be single, but before this past school year, Lucy never went long between partners. But now it's the day before prom, and we're both still dateless. The chances of that changing in the next thirty-six hours are close to nil.

"It's *not* a big deal," she insists.

"Then why can't I see it? I'm just curious."

"Your curiosity can hold out one more day." Her lips twibble again.

Okay . . . Is this about the dress? "Does it fit okay?" I ask.

She goes back to the mirror to finish her hair, her green-purple-blue-swirled tunic top swishing back and forth. "I didn't get too fat for it since picking it up, if that's what you mean."

"That's *not* what I mean. You're not 'too fat' for anything, now or ever. I mean I know it's hard for you to find clothes that complement your shape, and I want you to be comfortable."

Her dark-brown gaze catches mine through the mirror, and then another twibble. "Sorry, my brother is just . . . getting to me lately. He's on some new fitness plan, and according to his chart, I'm morbidly obese and one cupcake away from heart failure." She rolls her eyes, then mutters, "I've got a chart of my own I'd like to show him."

This again. God, I hate that guy. "You could out-yoga him with both hands tied behind your back. Don't listen to him."

"Trying not to." Her shoulders drop with a sigh. "Anyway, I've got everything sorted out. Shoes, accessories, hair, makeup. And the dress fits perfectly."

"Good."

"It is good." She smiles unconvincingly, the corners of her mouth barely lifting. Even in the weak lighting of her bedroom, I notice her skin is already getting darker with the longer, sunnier days. She drinks in sunlight as if it's water and she completely dehydrated over the cold months. In midwinter Lucy appears almost as white as I am, but by midsummer she turns a radiant golden brown, while I become a very attractive shade of burnt and peeling. She stabs the nest of dark-auburn curls on her head with another pin. "And we've got enough to worry about today," she continues, then sucks in a breath, the rest of her freezing in place. "Did you remember to bring Marty—"

"He's in my car," I assure her. "Everything's ready to go. Except you."

Most school days I find Lucy and a to-go cup of coffee waiting for me in the kitchen downstairs. It's only on the twibble days that I have to venture up to her room because she needs more time. Is she nervous about our presentation with

Marty today? Is that what this is all about? Yesterday she was fine. Today she's on the brink of not-fine. But we've been practicing. It's flawless, everything set, down to the pauses for breath. Because Lucy is flawless, perfect as always, and so is all she does. I'm the one who's likely going to flub something up.

Oh. Maybe that's it—me. I have a tendency to stress her out sometimes. Okay, more than sometimes, but never on purpose. She's a perfectionist, and I'm whatever is the opposite of that. A disorganizationist? A go-with-the-flow-ist? A hot-mess . . . ist? So we clash. We have spats. And then we get over it. That's just us. Complicated, but it works. We are a well-oiled machine made of broken parts.

Without Lucy to keep me in order, I'd probably fall apart. Spontaneously self-destruct. I don't remember how I kept it together before I met her almost four years ago.

"I'm ready now," she declares, and grabs her messenger bag, then slings it over her head to crisscross over her chest. I turn to walk out and she falls into step behind me as we head downstairs. "There's a spot on your glasses," she says casually. "Left lens. Upper right corner."

I remove them, use the bottom of my shirt to wipe away the offending spot, and slip them back on. "Anything else?"

We reach the bottom of the stairs and she looks me up and down. Her assessment pauses at my "distance-raptor over time-raptor equals veloci-raptor" T-shirt.

Twibble. "Good choice. That's one of my favorites."

I know. That's why I wore it. "Glad you approve."

"You *appear* ready," she says, "but if you're not feeling ready, tell me now. We have only one shot at this. One chance to nail this thing that counts for half our final physics grade. *One chance.*"

"You don't have to remind me there are no second chances." With this project, or anything. "Everything's going to be fine. We got this, okay?"

"What do you got?" her dad shouts from the kitchen. "Unless it's a cold, you better share!" He laughs, throaty and robust, at his own joke. The sound of it tugs a grin out of me, even though I've heard that joke from him a million times. Yeah, I hate her brother, but I love her dad.

Lucy sighs, heading across her living room. "Nothing, Papà, just school stuff. *A dopo!*" She waves goodbye to him as she passes the kitchen on her way to the front door.

"*Ciao*, Lucilla!" he calls back to her. "JJ, don't forget your coffee!"

"*Va bene.*" My Italian is borderline embarrassing with my blah Ohio accent. But every word I know of it, I learned from Lucy and her family. When I'm around them, it just comes out.

She glances over her shoulder at me. "Grab your coffee, let's go. We're running late."

"We're running right on time."

"I meant we *will* be running late if we don't leave now." She snatches her rainbow-striped umbrella from the front closet and then she's out the door, into the grim haze of a steady spring drizzle.

"My mistake." I grab the to-go cup of coffee she left for me on the kitchen counter, say hello and goodbye to Signore

Bellini—conveniently the same word in Italian for both—and meet Lucy in my car. Same as I always do, every school day of the year.

But today feels different, even with the routine. Because today is the day before the day I've been looking forward to since the start of freshman year. Tomorrow is our senior prom. So today, nothing can go wrong.

"Something's wrong," Lucy says, staring down at Marty like he's suddenly grown a fungus. Marty is the time-travel device we made for our science project and about the size of a football, an amalgamation of plastic, metal, and wires.

I know he's on because the steady hum of his motor buzzes in the silence of our physics classroom. Lucy flips the switch again, the one that should send our test subject—a bright purple Sharpie—back to ten seconds ago, before she pulled it out of her bag.

Nothing happens. Again. And I have no idea why. What's different now?

Marty is a crude device and can't send anything further than ten seconds, but it worked in our trials. It's a starting point. And it *worked*. After weeks of exploding markers and melting crayons, we finally got it to work without "killing" the subject, just a few days ago. We'd move the test subject from a specific location, to Marty, and then watch it disappear—only to reappear ten seconds later, as if it had gone backward by ten seconds and then took those ten seconds to catch up with itself in the present. Or at least that's what we concluded was happening, because that's what we'd wanted to happen.

The fact we were slightly delirious from too much sugar and too little sleep that day—night?—didn't make it into our official data log. But we couldn't have both had the same hallucination at the exact same time, multiple times in a row . . . I don't think?

Someone cracks their knuckles. Another person lets out a bored yawn. Mrs. Ruano checks her watch, then makes a note on our score sheet. We're running out of time.

Lucy laughs nervously, a forced grin plastered on her face. Through her teeth she whispers to me, "What did you do to it?"

"Nothing," I whisper back, analyzing what I can without taking Marty apart. I really want to take him apart right now. Let him think about what he's done while I dissect him, slowly and methodically, piece by piece. Everything looks good on the outside, though. I don't get it. "Why do you assume this is my fault?"

Never mind. I was the last person to have Marty in my possession, and I'm usually the one who screws things up. Usually meaning always. The last time she saw this, it worked. We celebrated. We fantasized about getting rich and famous from this thing. This thing that can't even *tell* time now, let alone manipulate it.

"Don't start an argument, JJ, just help me." Her tone is on the verge of panic.

Okay. We got this. *Deep breath.* Time to improvise. I lift the

Sharpie and twirl it like a mini baton. We have to move it every ten seconds or our model proves nothing. But also, I'm distracting the class so Lucy can troubleshoot without twenty pairs of eyes on her. I start spouting off whatever scientific anything I can think of, as if it's a step-by-step of what we're doing. Like this was all planned.

"In our quest to understand how the universe works, we study the basic building blocks of our existence—matter, energy, space, and time . . ."

Lucy catches on fast, and in my side vision I watch her frantically flipping switches and discreetly popping panels open. She pulls a hairpin from her head and uses it to tug on a wire, muttering something under her breath in Italian. Probably cuss words.

Even if she can fix this, we're going to need consolation ice cream later.

Lucy releases a mouse-like squeak, and I flick a glance at her. She's wide-eyed, pulling another pin out of her hair, which loosens a curl. *The bobby fell inside*, she mouths, and tucks the loose hair behind her ear. A blue spark flies, and she yanks back her hand. Then, when it's clear we didn't accidentally create a bomb, she tries again.

Make that triple scoops. Chocolate, vanilla, and strawberry.

In a last-ditch effort to give Lucy a few more seconds, I pull the basic definition of *science* out of my butt and hope Mrs. Ruano doesn't call me out on it. ". . . the use of evidence to construct testable explanations and predictions of natural

8

phenomena, as well as the knowledge generated through this process—"

"Time's up," Mrs. Ruano says.

"Wait, I almost—" Lucy protests, but Mrs. Ruano raises her palm toward us.

"Back to your seats, please."

With a grimace, I grab the infernal thing off the counter and shove it into my backpack, then follow Lucy's swishing tunic top to our table in the back of the class. Her lips are far beyond twibble territory. They're trembling, likely from holding in whatever she wants to vent about what just happened.

Mrs. Ruano studies her notes for a moment before lifting her head and saying, "It was a good idea and very well researched. You lost some points for presentation, but to be honest, I wasn't expecting it to work. Time travel just isn't possible. Neither is speeding up time, slowing it down, or stopping it altogether. Scientists have been trying to do it for centuries—you aren't the first to fail at it and you won't be the last." And on that inspirational concluding note, she calls up another pair of students to the front of the class.

Triple scoops, whipped cream, and a cherry on top. I don't even like cherries, but after this, I need one or five.

Lucy's leg bounces, her frustration seeking any physical outlet it can find. She's upset and has every reason to be. That one section of hair that came undone has to be bothering her, too. I know she'll fix it as soon as we're out of class and she can get to a mirror, but part of me wishes she'd just let herself be undone for a day, not worry about the little things. Part of me wants to tell her it's okay to be a mess sometimes, but the rest of me, the logical me, keeps my mouth shut. Because when Lucy has it in her head to do something—or not do something—there's no changing her mind. It's a done deal. *Finale.*

I hand her the bright purple Sharpie, and she uses it to write on her spiral notebook, then slides the message over to my side of the table.

We failed.

I write back: *We didn't fail the project. The project failed us. It was perfect until the very end. I bet we still get an A.*

Slide.

Sigh.

Scribble.

Slide.

Until we know for sure, she wrote, *what's the plan?*

She's asking *me* for a plan? Has she met me? All I know how to do is improvise. I mean, I'm the guy who chose what college to attend by putting all my acceptances on a dartboard, blindfolding myself, and taking my best shot. With Lucy already approved—a long time ago—for a geosciences program in Italy, nothing I chose in the States would keep us any closer. They were all the same to me, so. University of Texas, here I come.

If she wants to know my "plan," I guess it's that we'll figure out what went wrong later, but for right now, for this project, for this grade, for this class, for this school year, that was our only chance. We're done. There are no repeats and no do-overs. So tonight?

I write: *Ice cream.*

On Fridays I tutor math-challenged students after school and Lucy gets a ride home from her cousin Chaz. We'll meet at my place for ice cream later and watch the stars come out. The rain is gone now, and the sky is clear. There's a meteor shower tomorrow night—actually it's been going on for days already, but it'll be most visible tomorrow—so we might catch some falling this evening.

Jenna, the girl I've been tutoring for the past six weeks, bites her lip and furrows her brow in concentration as she tries to solve an algebraic equation. This is stuff I learned freshman year. It comes easy to me. But I don't hold it against her that the only reason she's going to pass algebra her senior year is because I helped her out at the last minute. Jenna could write an article for the school newspaper, drafted, revised, edited, and polished, in six minutes flat. She helped me with an essay a couple of months ago, so I've been returning the favor.

I've known her from a distance for a few years. Now, the more time I've spent with her in closer proximity, the more she's wormed her way into my thoughts when we're *not* together. Meaning, I like her, what I know of her so far, and I'd like to know more. As her boyfriend? Maybe? I honestly don't know if what I feel for her is romantic attraction or just that we get along really well. But the only way to find out is to try. Go on a date. Take a chance. It takes me a while to get to this point with someone, where I even want to give it a try to see if there is a difference. And I think maybe I could be at that point with Jenna now, if only she were free for me to even ask her.

She has a reputation for being the life of all the parties—the ones I never get invited to but always hear about, the ones that are reserved for Beaver Creek High elite. She's got this vintage-movie-star look going on, with platinum-blond hair, a practically porcelain-white complexion, winged eyeliner, fire-engine-red lipstick, and I don't recall her ever wearing clothes that are considered "modern fashion." It works for her. Very well. Jenna is one of the most popular girls in the whole school, let alone the senior class, but she's also one of the nicest.

There is only one thing that kept me from asking her to prom. One six-foot-three thing with a chiseled physique, a British accent—which may or may not be as fake as Jenna's hair color—and a smile that gets him virtually anything he wants. Blair is sure to be voted prom king, and since Jenna is his girlfriend, she'll likely wear a crown tomorrow night, too. He probably rigged the ballot with just one wink at the right person.

Jenna's concentration breaks when her phone buzzes next to her paper, rattling the tabletop. The teacher supervising our session tells her to put it away so we don't disturb the other tutoring groups around us—even though they're "whispering" louder than any phone would buzz—and then she goes back to reading her paperback with the kilt-wearing Highlander on the cover.

"Sorry," Jenna whispers to me, and scowls at the message on her phone. "It's Blair. He's . . . Nothing." Her expression unnaturally brightens. "It's nothing." She sets the phone on her lap and goes back to trying to solve for X.

She's received texts from Blair during our tutoring sessions before, but this is the first time she hasn't sent him a reply. Something happened. Something bad. *Something that's none of your business*, a voice says in the back of my head. *Don't get involved.*

But a louder voice in front says, *This is your chance. Take it. You won't get another one.*

Her phone buzzes again. She glances down at it and sighs.

"What's the problem?" I say.

Well. That was *brilliant*.

She lifts her blue gaze from her math paper to me. "I'm still working on it. Sorry, I'm a little distracted today."

"No, I didn't mean the algebra problem. I meant with you and *Blair Bedford*." I say his name with the best British accent I can muster, which is even worse than my Italian, but she smiles. Okay. Good recovery. "I'm serious, though, are you all right? We can take a break from this for a minute if you need to vent."

I try to not sound too eager, but also like it's not a bother, and I come off sounding bored.

Why am I so terrible at this? It's no wonder I never get past a first date. I spend so much time getting to know a person before feeling anything in the realm of wanting to ask them out—and then my awkwardness kills any chance of continuing.

Either Jenna didn't notice or she doesn't care. She sets her pencil down and straightens, then turns to face me, keeping her knees together so the phone doesn't fall off her lap. It's buzzing again. "Go away," she hisses at it, and then to me she says, "So Blair and I were supposed to go out to the movies last night. That new one that just came out with that guy who was in the one from last year with the girl who used to be in that one Disney show? You know the one."

"I know the one. All the ones."

"And I was really looking forward to seeing it at the midnight showing," she goes on, "be one of the first so I could write a review for it in time for our final edition of the paper before school lets out. And why not make a date of it, right? So I told Blair about it, weeks ago, and we planned to go together. But then . . ." Her mouth twists. "I swear this isn't me being petty."

I flash my palms. "No judgment here. Just listening."

"Okay." Sigh. "He's been, I don't know, acting weird lately? I thought it was me overreacting, because I'm all stressed out about graduation and getting ready for college and trying not to fail a math class that I'm in with a bunch of freshmen—and prom. We've got everything planned, and I've been looking forward to it, you know, just this one night where I can relax and have fun and not worry about all the things I've been worrying about."

"Yes. *Exactly*. I get that." What I don't get is how this connects back to the movie?

"See. Even you understand."

Even me?

"But Blair's all whatever about it." She leans back in her chair, crossing her arms with a huff. "And I broke up with him last night."

Wait—what? This is way worse than I thought. Or better? They're not together anymore. I thought I'd be listing reasons why she should break up with him, or at least consider it, but she's already done the deed, without so much as a watery eye the day after. The spine on this girl is amazing. She dumped the guy everyone in this school pines after, two days before prom. But . . . why?

Still in shock, I give her a minute to finish the story, but she says nothing. "Uh . . . okay," I start. "Can we back up a few steps? I think I missed something. What happened at the movie?"

"Nothing. That was the problem. And it's a problem we've had before. I'm tired of it."

"Mr. Johnson, Miss Davenport," the teacher says, eyes never leaving her romance novel, "work quietly."

"I'm not following," I tell Jenna, keeping my voice low.

With a slide of her thumb, she opens something on her phone, scrolls a bit, and then shows it to me. It's a text conversation between her and Blair, with yesterday's date.

Jenna, 4:06 p.m.: Do you want to do dinner before the movie tonight?

Blair, 5:12 p.m.: I just ate. What movie?

Jenna, 5:14 p.m.: The movie we've been planning to see since forever ago. You're still going right?

Blair, 7:47 p.m.: Not sure if I'm free

Jenna, 7:48 p.m.: We just talked about this yesterday! What changed?

Jenna, 8:03 p.m.: It's at midnight. Will you be done with your whatever by then?

Jenna, 11:32 p.m.: I guess we can meet there?

Blair, 12:01 a.m.: Something came up

That's the end of it. I hand her the phone, not sure how to respond without using gestures and language that would get me suspended.

"Something always *comes up*," Jenna says. "According to *Savvy Teen*, that's one of the top three signs your guy is cheating on you. So I dumped him before he could dump me. And you know what? I'm not even sad about it. I feel free. I should have done it a long time ago. Sometimes, I guess, the only solution to your problem? Is to take yourself out of the equation."

"Nice analogy. Very math-y."

"Thank you." She holds her chin up and grins, but it quickly fades. "Now I have a different problem, though . . . I don't have a date for prom. I'm in *charge* of the *prom committee*. I worked hard, for months, doing fund-raisers and making sure it will be the best senior prom Beaver Creek has ever had. After all that, I can't just not go! And he's been sending me texts all day about how it only took him five seconds to replace me—"

Of course it did. He already had someone on standby.

"—and how ridiculous I'm going to look showing up alone," she finishes.

"He's garbage, Jenna."

"A steaming six-foot-three pile of *rubbish*," she agrees, with

16

a spot-on British accent at the end. Even better than Blair's. "But he's also right. If I show up to prom alone, and he shows up with Farah freaking Justice on his arm, everyone's going to assume *he* dumped *me*."

"Then don't show up alone," I say without thinking. "I can take you."

Her eyes go wide and her mouth drops open a little. So much for not sounding eager.

"Are you—" She glances around nervously. "Are you asking me out?"

"No, uh. Not like that. We could go as friends? Acquaintances. Whatever you want to call us. No pressure. Just a stress-free night of fun." Because I'm already Lucy's prom partner, and I'm not going to pull a Blair and leave her stranded. So Jenna and I can't make this a date, or a "going out," or anything else that wouldn't be considered platonic. No matter how much I want to try a new kind of relationship with her.

Her shoulders drop as she smiles, releasing a breathy laugh. "Okay. Sure! Why not?"

Yes. YES. Okay. Act casual. "What color is your dress?"

She doesn't hesitate. "White and sparkly. Spaghetti straps and a crisscross front. Long hem with a vertical ruffle all the way down one leg. It's a 1978— Actually, here, I have a picture of it on my phone, do you want to see?"

"No, that's all right." I'm sure it looks better in person. When her face falls, I add, "I was just . . . wondering." Wondering if she'd tell me what Lucy refused to, and she did. So I'm *still* wondering why it's such a big deal to Lucy that I not know

17

anything. It's just a dress. If she wanted to see my tux, I'd show her. "I'll pick you up at seven thirty . . . ish," I tell Jenna. "I gotta get Lucy, too."

"Who's— Oh, Lucy your friend Lucy. Bellini, right? The one with the big, um . . . nose . . ."

Lucy does have a larger-than-average nose. Definitely bigger than Jenna's, which is slim, pointed, and petite, Hollywood pretty like everything else about her. But I like Lucy's nose. It fits her. It's different. "Something wrong with that?"

"No, of course not!" Jenna backpedals. "It's great. I mean she's great. The more the merrier." Flashy smile. "We'll all have fun!"

"That's the idea. Nothing serious."

We exchange numbers, and she rattles off her address. I tap it into my phone, trying not to let a goofy grin take over my face. Remind myself we're going as *friends*, like me and Lucy— except this is nothing like me and Lucy, because Lucy is my best friend and Jenna could be my girlfriend. Potentially. We're just going to have fun tomorrow, though. I don't want Lucy to feel like a third wheel. But maybe, hopefully, after prom night Jenna and I will *keep* having fun. As a couple. It could happen, right? Anything could happen.

Jenna's phone buzzes with another text message. She rolls her eyes but reads the text anyway, then starts gathering her things. "That's not him this time, thank God, it's just my ride. I have to go. Thanks for helping me, JJ."

"You're gonna ace that test on Monday."

"Right, yeah. That, too. But I meant with prom." She stands, slinging her backpack over one shoulder. "I'm not going to let Blair ruin everything. He can kiss my sax." She picks up her saxophone case from the floor and grins. "Call me cheesy, but that never gets old."

I'm dead. She's too adorable. "Okay, cheesy. See you tomorrow."

"Seven thirty. *Ish*." Another smile and she walks out into the hall, her high-heeled Mary Janes echoing loudly in the after-school quiet.

Now I let the goofy grin take over my face, and fire off a text to Lucy.

Me: You're not going to believe what just happened

"I can't believe it," Mom says. "The meteor shower peaks the same night as prom? What are you gonna do, sneak out to watch it in between dances?" She tilts the can of Reddi-wip so the nozzle is pointed downward and adds an illegal amount of whipped cream to each of our sundaes, then I top them with the cherries, and they're done.

"No," I say through a sigh. I haven't missed a meteor shower since I was nine. Each of them is different and beautiful in its own way, like snowflakes, or sunsets. "It'll be too light by the building to see anything, anyway, even if I can sneak out and take a look."

This year, the Eta Aquarids—the fallen crumbs of Halley's Comet—are expected to be especially bright and active. You can see them anytime after sunset, but that doesn't mean I'm going to miss them just because I'll be having the night of my life *inside* when it all starts. While most people have made plans to attend an after-prom party of some sort, Lucy and I are going to the bluffs to watch the meteors at their peak visibility. Mom doesn't know that, though. Because when she was my age, Whip's Ledge was where people went to make out. So if I told her, she'd accuse me of trying to seduce my best friend.

It's just not like that with Lucy and me. Never has been.

And I'm glad. Because all of Lucy's exes are no longer in her life, but guess who still is—me. Being her best friend instead of her boyfriend is the better side of the deal.

Going to the bluffs was Lucy's idea, anyway, not mine. There are other places we could watch the meteor shower, but she insisted Whip's Ledge is the best, and we deserve the best on prom night. I couldn't argue with that. Her plans are always better than anything I could think up.

"Well." Mom shrugs. "There will be other meteors. You only get one senior prom."

Shayla, my runt of a little sister, skips into the kitchen, grabs her sundae, and exits back to the living room, where Mama, our other mother, is already setting up a movie for Shayla to watch with her middle school friends. Mom starts to follow her, while I grab the last two sundaes and then kill the lights in the kitchen.

"Keep the lights on," Mom says, pausing at the archway to the living room.

"We need the lights off to see the stars."

"Not with you and a girl out there alone. Keep the lights on."

"Why? It's Lucy." We've been over this before. "Nothing like what you're thinking will happen is going to happen."

"She likes you, James."

"I like her, too. That's kind of a requirement for being friends."

She eyes me up and down, the glow of the TV from the living room at her back giving her pale face an eerie, shadowy visage. "Are you still sure you aren't gay? Or ace? Aro? It's a whole spectrum, you know, and it's normal to not have it all figured out at your age. Has anything changed since the last time we talked?"

"Nothing's changed." We've been over this before, too, and Mom gets carried away with the labels sometimes. If there's a particular label for me, I don't know yet what it is, but I've been going with "straight" so far, and that seems okay. I very much want to be in a romantic relationship with someone, and eventually, with the right person at the right time, I want the physical things, too. With a girl. I'm sure. I just don't fall head over heels for someone as hard and fast as other people seem to. What does that make me? No clue. And I don't feel like hashing it out with Mom right now; it'll go all night. So I settle on, "I can't be queer just because you want me to be."

She nods. "You're right. I blame your father."

Now she's just messing with me. My father was an anonymous sperm donor. She knows nothing about him besides what was on a medical chart. "You also can't blame someone for something just because they aren't here to defend themselves."

"True," she says, "but your straightness had to come from somewhere and it certainly wasn't me. And since Lucy also isn't gay—"

"She's not straight, either, though, she's bi," I remind her. Not that that's relevant here.

"There is potential there. Keep the lights on," she says in her Mom Voice. That's it. Argument over. "Don't make me pull the Do It Because I Said So card."

I flip the switch up with my elbow, and with a victorious grin, Mom makes her exit.

So do I, in the other direction, through the sliding patio door to join Lucy on the back deck. It's too chilly tonight for outdoor ice cream, and everything is still damp from the rain earlier today, but once we have a plan for something, we don't deviate. Mostly because that's what makes Lucy happy, and when Lucy's happy, I'm happy.

But now she's kind of miffed at me for asking Jenna to prom with us. It has nothing to do with Jenna and everything to do with me. Lucy and Jenna aren't friends, but they also aren't not-friends. I'm the one who messed it all up. I changed our plans at the last minute, and Lucy doesn't deal well with change. One thing out of place might as well be all of them out of place. I know I should know better than to make plans without her input. She's the planner, not me. When I make plans, this is what happens. So now I'm getting the too-calm-to-really-be-calm version of Lucy that's unnerving. I'd rather she snap at me. Nitpick me. Tell me off for being impulsive. *Something*.

I hand her a sundae, and she silently accepts it, her gaze focused on the pink-orange horizon. The sun is sinking. It'll be dark soon—it'll be tomorrow soon. But as much as I'm looking forward to that, I'm not ready for today to be over yet. The time I have left to spend with Lucy keeps getting shorter and shorter.

The only bad thing about prom is that it's at the end of senior year. The end of senior year means the end of high school. And the end of high school means things are going to change in a way *I* don't want them to.

But for now, I'm here. She's here. We're together.

"Talk to me." I settle onto the patio swing next to her and start pushing us gently.

Lucy focuses too intently on eating her sundae, wrapped in a fleece blanket with different phases of the moon depicted on it. She gave it to me as a gift a few months ago, but I think she's gotten more use out of it than I have. After a couple of bites, she says, "Talk to you about what?"

"Ah. Okay." I pop the cherry into my mouth and pull away the stem. Swallow. Flick the stem so it sails across the deck and into the grass. A lingering tartness tingles my cheeks. "We haven't played this one in a while. Remind me of the rules? Am I supposed to pretend to believe you really don't know what I'm referring to, and then explain it all, and then get blamed for bringing it up and starting an argument? Or is that a different game?"

"JJ . . ." She sighs.

"Lucy . . ." I mimic her sigh dramatically.

"I just need time to process and then readjust the plan in my head, okay? After that I'll be fine. There's nothing else to say."

I take a bite of ice cream, making sure to get the chocolate, vanilla, and strawberry all in one scoop. The chill makes me shudder, and I move all the way up against Lucy and the blanket. Warm. Soft. Cozy. *Perfection.* "Will you be fine by tomorrow night at, say, seven thirty?"

She laughs, then her tongue darts out to catch a rogue blob of whipped cream on her lip. "That's oddly specific," she says after swallowing. "Any particular reason you chose that day and time?"

"Nah." I shake my head and take another bite of ice cream. "Totally random."

"Liar."

"Blanket thief."

Another laugh and I know we're good now. That's the magic of ice cream. And our friendship.

"Scooch," she says, and I slide all the way to the other end of the swing's bench. She shifts so she's lying across the length of it and leans her head against my ribs, staring across the expanse of my backyard to watch the sun finally go to bed. One by one the stars timidly start to twinkle all around us.

It's mostly quiet out here, with eleven acres between my house and our closest neighbors, but every so often one of the horses in our barn putters a sigh through its flappy lips or knocks against a bucket or something. We finish our sundaes and set the empty cups on the deck. With my hands free now, I drape one arm along the top edge of the bench and Lucy lets her head drop back onto my legs, staring straight up at the sky.

Her nose is strikingly beautiful, like the rest of her, the perfect complement to her big brown eyes and her pillowy plump lips. Jenna may be pretty and smart and fun—a trifecta, for sure—but she has no clue about what makes a good nose on a person.

I tear my gaze from Lucy's face and tilt my head back to look up into the black.

"Spica," she says, starting our game. Name all the visible stars. I guess it's not a game, though, because no one wins or loses. We just keep going until one of us declares *game over*.

"Jupiter," I say.

"Not a star."

"Yeah, but from here it looks like one."

"JJ."

"Fine. Ursa Major."

"That's a constellation."

"It contains stars. It counts."

"Game over."

"That was fast," I say through a laugh.

"You changed the rules." Her tone is annoyed, but she smiles. "You're chaos personified, you know that?"

"Thank you." I keep us swinging gently, like a rocking chair, and her breaths get slow and even. Relaxed. The moon is bright and swollen tonight, but not full.

"Look at that fat gibbous."

Lucy feigns offense. "What did you call me?"

"You know I was talking about the moon," I say, giving her a playful bump of my leg, and her head bounces softly. "Besides, if I ever called you the moon, it would be a compliment."

"Please, enlighten me." She curls up her legs and releases a wide yawn. "How can a lifeless, dusty, crater-filled ball of cold rock be a compliment?"

"Challenge accepted." But it's not a challenge at all. "The moon is a light shining in a dark place."

She snorts. "Cliché."

"I wasn't done yet. The moon is a loyal, steadfast, dependable companion to the earth. Always in flux but entirely predictable. And even when it's not full and appears broken, it still has enough strength to pull the tides."

I look down to see her reaction, see if I should keep going on about the wonders of the moon and how she compares to it. She isn't looking back up at me, but her lips twibble.

I must have said something wrong. "Lucy—"

She flinches, pointing toward the midnight-blue horizon. "Did you see that?"

"No. What—" A streak of white flashes across the sky. Quicker than a blink, it's gone.

"There's another one!" she squeals.

"I saw it!" Excitement bubbles in my chest. I almost missed it, though. It wasn't that bright, or that high. "I'll get my telescope. We can see them better—"

"No." She reaches up to put a hand on my arm. "Stay. Please? I'm comfy. We'll see them with the telescope tomorrow night. Right now, let's just . . ." She pulls her hand back inside the folds of the blanket. "Stay," she repeats, as if she's afraid I might actually deny her request.

Never. What the moon wants, the moon gets.

"All right," I say. "Let's play a new game. We'll both make a wish on the next one, and then see whose comes true."

She hums in amusement, the sound vibrating softly against my thigh. "Do wishes on falling stars come true? Wouldn't the fact that they're falling and disintegrating cancel it out?"

"Good question." I pull my cell phone out of my pocket and ask Google. Just as the search results pop up, there's another flash in my peripheral vision. Lucy squeezes her eyes closed tight, making her wish.

"I missed it."

"I didn't." She opens her eyes again, smiling. "What does Google say?"

I tap the link to the top article, then skim through it. "Hm. It doesn't cancel it out."

"Good."

"Not necessarily. According to this website, if you wish on a falling star, you'll receive the opposite of whatever you wished for."

"Oh . . . Oops."

"What did you wish?"

"For Marty to work, eventually, so I can . . ."

We never talked about this. All those weeks building the device together, we never admitted our personal reasons for wanting it to work. It was just a school project, a way to get a good grade—until it was more than that, because we started to hope. Or at least I did. I didn't realize Lucy had, too.

"So you can what?" I press.

"Go back to five years ago and see my mom. Convince her

not to leave us. Then we could have a second chance at, maybe, having a relationship of some kind. Even if she wasn't the greatest mom. That would be better than nothing."

"Lucy . . . I want that for you more than anything. But—"

"There are no second chances," she says with me.

"Yeah."

"And I just nailed that coffin shut tight with a backwards wish on a falling star. Marty will never work now."

I shove my phone in my pocket, then push us into a gentle swinging motion again. "You know that stuff isn't real. It's superstition. It's people trying to find explanations behind things that can't be explained, because they're just coincidence."

"I know." Her voice is too quiet, though. Disheartened. This isn't the note I want to end the night on. We were laughing a few minutes ago. We had ice cream. We had magic. We can turn this around.

"Okay, let's make a wish on the moon, just to be safe. It's so big I bet it trumps all the stars, falling or not."

"You're full of it," she says, "but okay. Just to be safe." She looks up at the broken moon, then closes her eyes, and so do I. My other senses immediately heighten, focusing on the smell of rain lingering in the air, the sound of the swing hinges creaking, the sugary taste of ice cream still on my tongue, the feel of Lucy's warm body wrapped in fleece pressed against me . . .

I know what I want, and even though it can't possibly come true, I think it anyway.

I wish we could stay like this forever.

the NIGHT of the BLACK HOLE

Lucy hasn't said a word to me all day, but as expected, her text comes through at seven thirty on the nose.

Lucy: Where are you?

Me: Leaving soon

I slip my phone back into my pocket and look up, into the mirror hanging off my closet door. Back to the task at hand. Maybe the twentieth time's the charm. But within seconds, my fingers get tangled and the thing around my neck looks like it needs to be put out of its misery.

Whoever invented bow ties can go straight to—

Something bright, blinding white, flashes outside my bedroom window, snapping my head in that direction. What the . . . ? The whole room vibrates. Shudders. Like an earthquake. In Ohio? It's been known to happen but extremely rarely. The windows rattle, my reflection in the mirror blurs, and Marty vibrates across the top of my bookshelf where I left him after school yesterday. He lets loose a few blue sparks, and I rush to stamp them out on the carpet. Piece of trash, why didn't I just dump him yesterday?

Then, as quickly as it all started, it stops. I run to the window and look outside. Nothing seems different. Same acres of lush spring grass and our long gravel driveway that leads to the country road. No power lines have come down. What made that light, then? It was too bright for a meteor, even a big one, and it's not dark out, anyway, even though it will be soon. They're not visible yet.

Everything's quiet. Even the horses out back aren't whinnying like they're scared and confused. Weird. A large fly buzzing too close to them would set them off. Why wouldn't an earthquake?

Never mind about the horses, I need to check on my parents and sister. I turn to rush out and do just that, when—

"Knock, knock," Mom says from the other side of my bedroom door. "Are you decent?"

She sounds fine.

"Yes, come in." I yank the strip of blue fabric out from around my neck, practically choking myself in the process. "Did you feel that earthquake?"

Mom's reflection approaches mine in the mirror. "No, what? We don't get earthquakes here." She catches sight of the bow tie in my fist, and without a word, she takes it from me and starts fastening it around my neck like a pro. In three seconds flat, she's done.

That's my mom, top student at YouTube University. Just about everything she knows, she learned from the internet. We watched the how-to videos for bow ties after picking up my tux, but apparently she's the only one who retained the lessons.

"You feeling all right?" she says. "You look nervous."

"I'm not nervous, I just ... You sure you didn't feel any vibrations?"

Her blue-gray eyes narrow and study me from beneath her brunette bangs, but then Shayla comes blazing into the room, effectively cutting off any lingering fears I had that anyone got hurt. If they're both okay, and so are the horses, then Mama likely is, too. Maybe I *am* just nervous about tonight. Or overexcited. Too frustrated with the bow tie. Enough to see and feel things that aren't there? I don't know.

"Look at you all fancy!" Shayla squeals, and I can't help but laugh. "Dance with me, JJ."

It's not a request; it's an order, one I know better than to disobey. She grabs my hands and starts doing this jump-skip-fairy-sprite-forest-dance thing, her medium-brown cheeks bunched up with a huge grin, humming through her teeth like a ventriloquist, probably some song she just made up, while I stand in place, wondering what I'm supposed to do. I opt for twirling her around me a few times, then sweep her up into my arms, and she begs me to toss her onto my bed. She's so tiny, she weighs nothing.

Shayla may not share my genetics, but she is 100 percent my baby sister. Mama was newly divorced and newly pregnant when she became my riding instructor, and that's how she met Mom. Not long after Shayla was born, they got married. At the time, we had to travel to a different state for their marriage to be legal. I was only six, so it was like going on a vacation. I got to be the ring bearer. And that was the last time I wore a tux before tonight.

Shayla's curtain of long black braids swishes, then splays out on the bed as she lands with a little bounce. "I can't *wait* until my prom." Her big brown eyes go bigger, widening toward Mom, and she pops up onto her knees, making her way across the mattress. Dragging the blankets along behind her. "Can I wear a tux to my prom, too? But a pink one? With roses embroidered on the sleeves? And sequined high heels? And a giant rose corsage on my wrist?"

"Of course you can," Mama says, entering the room. "You can do whatever you want, baby girl." Shayla jumps off the bed, shouts in victory, then runs off down the hall and thunders down the stairs. She's a human tornado, always has been, appearing just long enough to let everyone know she's a force, then disappearing again.

So Mama *is* okay, and no one seemed to notice anything weird going on. It's like the earthquake, bomb, or whatever it was never happened.

Did it?

Mama whips out her phone. "Can I get a few pictures before you leave?"

Pictures, fantastic. I was hoping we could avoid this part. That's blackmail material for every stage of my life after this. "Okay," I concede, "but just a few. I'm already running late, thanks to a bow tie malfunction. I was supposed to pick up Lucy"—I pull out my phone to check the time—"four minutes ago. You know how she is."

"Look here and smile," Mama says. "Yes, we know how Lucy is, and that's why we love her. She's good for you. You're good

32

for *each other.*" Mama laughs, snapping again and again, changing the angle of the phone in between, telling me to "vogue" and "strike a pose" like it's still the 1990s and she's the teenager here. She's enjoying this way too much. "I wish we could get the both of you together. Can you ask her dad to take some pictures of you together for us?"

Sigh. "Sure."

"Look at him, Danni, our little boy is all grown up." Mom's voice cracks like she's about to cry. God help me, that's worse than the pictures. If she cries, then I'll start crying.

"Please stop making a big deal of this. It's just prom," I say, as if I haven't been looking forward to this for years. Seeing Shayla talk about prom with stars in her eyes . . . that was me when I was a freshman. Prom seemed so far away then. How is it here already? How is high school almost over?

Suddenly it all feels surreal. This tux I'm wearing. Mama snapping pictures and Mom getting emotional. Imagining Lucy in her own room right now, making last-minute finishing touches while she's waiting for me to pick her up. Wondering what her dress looks like. Finally getting to see it.

My heartbeat kicks up a few notches. This is really happening, right now and never again. *Live it up, JJ, you only get one senior prom. Carpe noctem—seize the night. You can worry about what happens after . . . after.*

"And soon you'll be graduating," Mom is saying, forcing me to think about the very thing I don't want to—graduation. Moving on. Living half a world apart from my best friend, who's been right here with me through all of high school. I try to shake it off as Mom continues, "Then college and a career and, knowing you, you'll probably start a colony on Mars and we'll never see you again except through a telescope. It's bad enough you're moving to Texas, but at least we can take a plane there once in a while. We can't do that if you're in outer space."

"Fine. I promise I won't start a colony on Mars unless you can live there, too."

"Thank you," she says, like this was an actual serious conversation.

Mama finally wraps up her photo shoot, and I check myself in the mirror again. Hair is good . . . enough. Floppy is in style now, right? Bow tie effectively tied. Contacts instead of glasses. Converse instead of dress shoes. Tickets—no, Lucy has the tickets so I wouldn't lose them. She's got me covered. All I need to do is grab my car keys and I'm good to go. Unless I'm forgetting something . . .

I'm probably forgetting something. If Lucy were here, she'd tell me. She forgets nothing and notices everything. That's part of why we're good together, like Mama said. We balance.

"Remember the rules," Mom says.

"I know, I know. No drugs, alcohol, speeding, getting anyone pregnant, or being a juvenile delinquent."

Mom crosses her arms. "You forgot the most important one."

"What's that?"

"Have fun," Mama says with a smile.

My shoulders drop, and I smile back at her. At both of them. I pull them up against me in a none-too-gentle group hug, then kiss each of them on the top of their head. "Love you, love you. I promise to have more fun tonight than I've ever had in my entire life."

"Well, maybe not too much fun . . ." Mom says, a warning in her tone.

"I'm going to have exactly zero fun if you guys don't let me go."

They both drop their arms and back off. Mama tugs Mom out of the room. "Come on, Lex, time to cut the cord." Then to me, she says, "Be safe, JJ."

"I will. Don't wait up for me." I usher them out of my room and downstairs.

"Don't be out all night," Mom volleys back.

"I won't," I promise. Just half the night. Or three-quarters, if things are going really great and I "accidentally" lose track of time.

At the bottom of the stairs, they go through the kitchen and out to the backyard to feed the horses. Shayla's probably already out there refilling water buckets. I usually help them, too—many hands lighten the load, as Mama would say—but not tonight. I make it all the way to the front door and get as far as grabbing the doorknob before I remember, with a frustrated groan, that my keys are still sitting on my nightstand.

Rushing upstairs, I pat my back pocket—got my wallet. Okay. Good. And I put the telescope in my trunk last night, after Lucy reminded me, so we wouldn't have to come back here to get it before heading out to the bluffs later. I stretch across my bed and snatch the keys off my nightstand, hoping that was my flub of the night. Everything I do has one screwup, that's just me. Sometimes it's big, sometimes small. At least I got it out of the way early this time, and all it did was make me a little bit more late. Nothing too major.

As I skitter down the stairs, my phone chimes. A new text.

Lucy: On your way yet?

Me: Yes I'll be there in ten

More like fifteen, but she doesn't know I haven't actually left.

Lucy: Are you texting and driving?

Lucy: Don't answer that if you are!

Well, now what? If I answer her, then she knows I'm not driving yet. If I don't, she might think I got in an accident from texting and driving. I take the neutral middle road with a quick thumbs-up, then pocket my phone, hop in my car, and crunch tires down our driveway, out to the country road. It's clear and the asphalt is dry. No imminent dangers. My promise not to speed echoes in my mind, but I'm late and Lucy's stressing about it. She had this planned so we'd get there right before dinner is served at eight. That's almost impossible now, even if I didn't have to pick up Jenna, too. This night is supposed to be fun for us, and it won't be fun if Lucy is stressed the whole time.

I press the gas pedal down farther. The engine revs, then shifts gears. I'll be there in ten.

Only three minutes have passed before Lucy's texting me again, the chime ringing out from my hip.

"This better be an emergency—" I twist to get into my pocket, inadvertently pushing harder on the gas pedal, just as a big curve in the road approaches way too fast. I know this road, I know this turn, so I should know better. It's not just a sudden curve but also a steep descent. The phrase "chaos personified" is actually flashing through my mind in bright neon lights when a series of things happen all at once, but also, weirdly, in super-slow motion.

I untwist and yank my hand out of my pocket, still holding my phone but then quickly releasing it, and the thing goes flying toward the passenger seat. I hear it knock against the window. *Clunk!*

Grabbing the steering wheel with both hands, I hit the brakes and manage to keep control of the car as it hugs the sharp bend at no less than fifty miles an hour, all while wondering how exactly am I not dead? Momentum pulls me hard to the right as I steer left and my seat belt locks.

And just as I safely reach the other side of the bend and the bottom of the slope, and my brain remembers breathing is necessary, something big, orange, and billowing in the spring breeze—a dress? in the middle of the road?—flashes by my windshield. I swerve hard to the left again and slam the brakes even harder. Tires squeal and someone screams. Someone on the road? Or was that me? Then the front end of my car dips on the left side—I overcompensated and hit the ditch—and I swerve to the right again, pulling back up onto the asphalt just as everything comes to a screeching halt.

I'm facing another ditch, and beyond that, trees. *Facing* it. Which means my car is sitting across the road in both lanes. Afraid I just survived one accident only to die in another, I move the car forward, back, forward, and back a few times until I'm parallel on the shoulder. Then I put it in park and try not to pass out from shock.

The sudden silence makes my labored breathing sound like a roaring lion.

My heart . . . where is my heart? It leaped right out of my throat and now I can't find it.

In another second, it returns with a vengeance, beating so hard against my chest I think I might puke. *Do* not *puke on your tux, JJ, it's rented.*

Okay. Lesson learned. I am never speeding again. My parents were right to make that rule—aren't they always right? And I'm shutting off my phone completely whenever I'm in the car. What a worthless reason to possibly die. I'm lucky, and I shouldn't be this lucky after doing something I knew I shouldn't have.

"Hello?" a female voice calls from somewhere. "Hey, are you okay?"

I didn't imagine it. There really was a dress in the middle of the road. That means . . . oh God, I almost hit a *person.*

I can't get out of the car fast enough—because I don't want to puke on my tux *or* my car—fumbling to open the door and then stumbling over my own feet until I reach the ditch. I bend over just in time. Not much comes out, because my stomach is empty, but it still burns my throat. I skipped dinner at home because we're supposed to eat at prom.

Prom.

Lucy.

I instinctively reach inside my pants pocket but find nothing.

"Where's my phone?" I mutter. Then I remember it's still in the car. Why did I think that simply forgetting my keys was my flub of the night? This . . . *disaster* within *five minutes* of leaving my house is much more my style. I swallow back acid. Straighten. Turn—

And I'm face-to-face with dark-brown eyes and dark-brown skin. Bright fuchsia lipstick on full lips. The girl I almost hit? Glancing down confirms it. She's wearing a formal dress, strapless with a big billowy skirt, in Creamsicle orange. It has the faintest shimmer reflecting the lowering sun's warm glow. Her thick black spiral curls are swept up in an elegant twist. She looks like she walked off a Hollywood red carpet. If this wasn't prom night, I would wonder what celebrity awards ceremony could possibly be held in nothing little Beaver Creek, Ohio.

"Are you okay?" she repeats. "That was so close. I'm sorry, I didn't see you coming."

"*You're* sorry? No, no, no, *I'm* sorry. I almost hit you! Are *you* okay? You seem okay, but are you okay? Why are you out here walking . . . ? Is something wrong?" This is a rural road with no sidewalks. Pedestrians don't exist unless it's someone getting their mail.

"I'm fine. But my car? Not so great." She gestures to the cream-colored Volkswagen Beetle with a black convertible top on the side of the road, its hood propped up, which I didn't even notice until she jacked her thumb toward it. "When I came down the curve, I think the engine blew. There was smoke everywhere, and now I can't get her to start again." She lets out a long sigh. "She's old and tired, but I don't want to accept she's done for good this time. I made too many memories with this old girl."

"I'm sorry, uh . . ."

"Melody," she says. "But you can call me Mel."

Oh. That wasn't what I meant, I was just at a loss, but: "I'm James. You can call me JJ. Do you need help with this?"

Her brows shoot upward. "You think you can fix it?"

"Uhm. Heh. No, actually. I live on a farm. I know horses better than cars. I mean, I know the basics, like how often to change the oil, and, you know, it's beneficial to keep the gas tank full, that kind of stuff . . . Pathetic, right?" I flash a smile to shut myself up. The longer I go on, the more ridiculous I sound.

"That's okay." She returns the smile, except bigger and better. "You're allowed to be a guy and not know how to fix a car. I'm pretty sure she's a goner, but thanks for offering."

"Oh. Well, the least I can do is give you a ride, then. I swear I'm a better driver than what you just saw. That was a fluke, never happened to me before, and I've driven this road a million times. It's the one I always take to get to my best friend's house." My best friend who is likely plotting my murder as we speak. "Anyway. Do you want a ride? You look like you might even be going to the same place as I am."

She eyes me up and down, understanding flitting across her expression like she just now realized I'm wearing a tux. "Yeah, if you mean senior prom? For Whitman Academy."

Whitman. Wow. Melody goes to a private school. We probably would have never crossed paths if not for this almost accident. "I'm on my way to prom, too," I say. "For Beaver Creek High."

Her mouth twists. "Too bad we both have prom the same night." She holds up her skirt a little and starts walking back toward her car.

I'm right on her heels—which I can now see are the same orange color of her dress, at least four inches high, and she walks in them as effortlessly as if they were Keds. But then I stop at my car and reach inside, across the driver's seat, to retrieve my phone from the passenger seat. Just the one missed text, but it's almost ten to eight. Ten minutes until they serve dinner at prom.

"Lucy really is going to murder me," I mutter under my breath, then open the text and lean against the side of my car. The text is from Jenna, though, not Lucy. Crisis averted. For now. "What do you mean too bad?" I say absently, reading.

"I just thought maybe us meeting like this was fate or something," Melody says. "But we're headed to two different places, and— Oh."

When I look up to see what stopped her, she's standing by her car.

She plunks down the hood of her Bug. "It was nice meeting you, JJ, even if it was . . . a little scary at first. But you can go now. I'm going to call a tow."

"What?" I missed something. She wants me to leave?

"Your girlfriend. Or boyfriend. Or partner." She points at my phone, tapping the screen of her own with her opposite thumb. "Are they waiting on you to pick them up? You don't have to make them wait longer because of me."

"Yes—I mean no. I don't have a girlfriend. Or boyfriend. Or anyone like that. Just a friend and a . . ." Whatever Jenna is to me.

Melody isn't listening anymore. She's talking to the tow service.

I glance down at the text again.

Jenna: Lucy said you're running late?

It's 7:49. This text came in at 7:43. Lucy must be worried if she's already telling Jenna that I might be irrevocably late in picking them up less than five minutes after I said I was on my way. But given the circumstances, Lucy won't fault me for making her wait if it helps someone in need.

"How long until the tow truck gets here?" I ask Melody after she disconnects her call.

She checks an imaginary watch on her bare wrist. "Any year now."

That's what I was afraid of. "It'll be dark soon. My parents would disown me if I didn't offer to stay to make sure you were safe. And if I'm going to stay until the tow gets here, I might as well give you a ride to your prom, too. But it's up to you."

She eyes my seven-year-old cranberry Honda Civic. Not exactly a chariot, I know. But Lucy's never complained about the ride, not once, except to tell me when it's due for a wash. And if Lucy likes it, it can't be that bad.

"It isn't much to look at, but it's gotta be better than a tow truck, right?"

"That's very nice of you, JJ," Melody says. "You seem . . . genuinely nice. Honest. But what about your friend?"

42

I hold up my phone. "Taking care of it. Just need to send a few texts . . ."

> Jenna: Lucy said you're running late? I can get a ride from Autumn Mitchell. She rented a limo.
>
> Me: Yeah sorry was held up. Almost got in an accident but OK. Can you guys pick up Lucy too? I'll just meet you there
>
> Jenna: Okie dokie! Glad you're OK ☺

I give her Lucy's address, then go back to my other text conversation.

> Me: Jenna's going to pick you up. I almost got in a—

No. Don't tell Lucy that. She'll just worry. I can tell her when I see her later, when she can see with her own eyes that I'm all right. I shouldn't have told Jenna, either, but I can't take that back now. Hopefully Jenna won't say anything about it.

> Me: Jenna's going to pick you up. You get to ride in a limo! ☺ fun right?
>
> Lucy: What happened? Where are you?

Distraction technique, failed.

> Me: Helping someone with car trouble. Waiting on a tow then driving them to their thing then I'll meet you there. See you soon
>
> Lucy: OK sounds good.

I don't even get the phone to my pocket before it chimes again.

> Lucy: Do you think you'll miss dinner completely?
>
> Me: I hope not I'm starving
>
> Lucy: I'll see if they can save you a dish.
>
> Me: Grazie

Wait. Something doesn't feel right. She's too agreeable.

    Me: Do you need anything?

    Lucy: Don't worry about me

Don't worry about her? I don't know if I can do that. I worry about Lucy because Lucy worries about *everything*. But she seems all right, so if that's what she wants, then I'll try this not-worrying-about-her thing. I pocket the phone and look up at Melody. "We're all set. No problem."

"Impressive," she says, nodding. "You're very go-with-the-flow. I like that."

She likes that. My grin spreads even wider. "And you're very say-exactly-what-you're-thinking. I like that."

"It's unanimous, then. We like each other." She flashes a thousand-watt smile.

"So . . ." I take a few slow steps toward Melody, something between a stroll and a strut. "What should we do to pass the time?"

"Time is the most abstract concept in the universe," Melody says, then takes a sip of water from a bottle I pulled out of my trunk. Lucy insists I keep emergency stuff in there like snacks, water, a first aid kit, a heated blanket, an extra phone charger, flares—the works—just in case, I don't know, I get stuck on the side of the road or something. Which had never happened once before tonight, so, another thing I owe Lucy for, another reason I'm thankful she's in my life. I'll just add it to the countless others that have piled up over the years. Though technically my car isn't the one broken down. Melody turns in the passenger seat to face me squarely. "There's no way we can know for sure if time exists anywhere but in our minds."

This is a conversation I never thought I'd have with a person. Melody goes to a private school that specializes in the arts—and apparently that includes philosophy. I don't do well with abstract concepts, though. My comfort lies in things that are tangible, provable . . . factual. Even the time-travel device for our physics project was based on hard science, so it should have worked. We didn't construct Marty out of wishes and dreams. But there's something about the way Melody presents her theories that keeps me intrigued and thinking . . . *maybe*. Maybe this different idea of hers could be true.

But it takes zero point zero seconds for me to shoot this particular idea down flat.

"That's impossible," I tell her. "We age. Animals and plants age. The *planet* ages—we can see evidence of it. Wrinkles. Decay. Fossils. Tree rings. Those are all physical indicators of the passage of time. It's a real thing."

If it wasn't real, I wouldn't be losing my best friend this summer—and there's more proof right there. Summer. The changing seasons. That wouldn't happen if time didn't exist.

"Or it's a fake thing someone made up to explain a real thing they didn't understand," she counters, and I shoot her a let's-not-go-there look. "Okay, okay, just hear me out—have you ever accidentally lost track of time?"

"Occasionally." If occasionally means regularly.

"Did you actually lose *time*," Melody says, "or did you lose what you were supposed to do with that time?"

"I—" Hang on. I sit back and think. "Okay, that still doesn't explain wrinkles, but you might have a point. A tiny one. Barely microscopic."

"How generous of you." She laughs and the sound is like her name, a melody.

This girl. Did she really just get me to almost believe there's a slight possible chance that time only exists as a relative theory of the mind? She totally did. And maybe that's partly because there's a slight possible chance I want it to be true. If time isn't real, then nothing changes.

Melody says fate brought us together, but I don't believe in fate. I say it was coincidence, but she doesn't believe there are any coincidences in life—according to Melody, everything happens for a reason. I don't care who's right, though, I'm just glad we met.

"Well, even if it is only in our minds," I say, "we've been sitting here for nearly an hour and a half and no one has shown up." It's almost nine thirty p.m. Prom ends at eleven. I've not only missed dinner—peanut butter crackers and cheap bottled water don't count—but also half of the event I've been waiting all my high school years to attend, no big deal. And Lucy hasn't texted me once, not even to ask where I am. *Don't worry about me*, she said.

With concerted effort, I push Lucy out of my thoughts. She's fine. If she wasn't, I'd know. Someone would tell me. Everyone knows we're best friends.

Nothing I can do now to change how late I am, anyway, or how she is or isn't reacting to that. If there's one thing I know for sure about time, it's that it doesn't move backward. "Who did you call for the tow?"

Melody glances at the clock on my dashboard, her eyes widening. "Shoot, I didn't realize how late it was." She picks up her phone from her lap and starts swiping and tapping. "They closed at nine—those jerks stranded me? Every other place is closed, too. What am I gonna . . . I can't just leave my car here all night."

"Or maybe you can," I say, and step out of my car. Look around. It's pitch-dark, no streetlights out here, and the moonlight is scattered by branchy treetops only just starting to grow new leaves. But there's a mailbox next to a patch of gravel not far from Melody's car. That has to be someone's driveway; I just can't see the house past all the tree trunks. It's probably pretty far back. Melody's car is small, though. As long as the person who lives here doesn't mind, it's our best option. This is going to suck, pushing a car in a tux, but good call on the Converse instead of dress shoes.

Melody stays in the car while I take the long, scary trek down a gravel driveway that cuts through a dank, dark forest— made a little less scary by the flashlight I had in my trunk, *thank you again, Lucy*—and find someone home who is okay with us leaving a car on their property. The guy who answers is older than dirt, though, and in a wheelchair, so I'm pushing this thing on my own. I've never been into sports or working out, because I get enough at home. Riding horses works my

47

legs and core. Shoveling manure and tossing hay bales works my arms and shoulders.

You don't need a gym membership to build muscle, Mama says. Just own a horse or two.

I remove my vest then unbutton the sleeves of my shirt and roll them up while Melody gets in her car and puts it in neutral. "Okay," she shouts out the driver's side window. "I'm ready!"

I'm not weak, but this taxes me. Even a small car is still a car. Bigger than me. A giant chunk of metal. My feet slip in the gravel, and I work up a nasty sweat. Inch by inch, I push it halfway down the drive. We decide that's far enough and park her Bug off to the side, partially in the trees, then call the tow and leave a message so they know where to pick it up tomorrow. I offer to hold Melody's hand to help her walk back to the road. Heels plus gravel could equal a broken ankle. I don't want to end this night in a hospital.

She takes my hand, and as soon as our feet hit the road asphalt, she lets go but keeps walking. I follow her to my car. My pits are wet. My muscles are sore. My white hands are smudged with black and my black pants are smudged with white, and who knows what those marks are even from. I really don't understand cars.

The scent of Melody's floral perfume hits me when I get back into my car. Lucy's not going to like that. She's extremely perfume-averse; it gives her a headache. I roll down all the windows an inch or two. Once we're both in and buckled, I say, "It's late. Do you still want to go to your prom, or should I take you home?"

She sits quietly for a moment, and her stomach gurgles loudly. Then she looks at me, her smile lighting up the night. Her lipstick has faded, but her hair is still perfect. "Neither," she says. "Let's go eat some real food."

Not a bad idea. But: "I don't have much cash. Do you?"

"None. I didn't think I'd need it tonight."

Okay . . . "Do you consider Taco Bell real food?"

"I don't even think Taco Bell considers Taco Bell real food."

"By the time we get into town, though, it's the only place that'll be open. That I can afford," I add.

"Okay, new plan. Let's not go eat some real food. Let's go eat some Taco Bell."

"Eating at Taco Bell in a sweaty, dusty tux," I say through a laugh. "This is really not how I imagined my prom night."

"Me neither. But that's life, right? You have to expect the unexpected." She shrugs. "At least we'll have a good story to tell our friends tomorrow."

"Yeah." My smile dies when I wonder what's been happening at my prom without me. Does everyone think I ditched them? Not just Lucy and Jenna, but Chaz and Marcos and all the people I might not see again after high school. This was our last hurrah before graduation.

I got to meet someone new, a great new someone who I don't regret meeting, but I also lost a lot—more than just time. Melody was right about that much. I lost a once-in-a-lifetime experience tonight. You only get one senior prom.

I start the car and check my phone. Nothing new. Lucy's most recent text is still the same: *Don't worry about me.*

Okay. I'm not worrying. *I'm not.* If she needed something she would let me know, just like she always has for years. She must be fine. *Everything's fine.* I'll get something to eat, then drop off Melody and pick up Lucy and we'll go to the bluffs. Just like she planned. Sort of. But with a detour along the way. It's only 10:17, the night isn't even close to over yet.

Melody's stomach gurgles again, and so does mine. "They're gonna start fighting each other if we don't feed them soon," she says. "Is something wrong?"

"No." Carpe noctem, *JJ, just go with it.* I will . . . after I send this one text to Chaz.

> Me: Sorry I'm missing everything. Is Lucy OK?

If I can't check on her directly, then I'll check on her indirectly. But I don't expect Chaz to text back right away, so I turn off the sound on my phone for now—not driving with it on ever again— and then we're on our way to a formal Taco Bell dinner.

"Nothing's wrong," I assure Melody. "Just trying to decide whether I want a taco, a burrito, or nachos."

"You should have gotten the nachos," Melody says, handing me a napkin across the sticky table.

"Thanks." I take the napkin to wipe the blob of sour cream, hot sauce, and guac that squirted out the end of my taco like bird poop, right down the middle of my white shirt, miraculously avoiding my blue satin vest. I was doing great until the last bite. Why does the *last bite* always end up on my shirt—and only when I'm wearing white? "But I don't think I would have fared better with anything else on the menu," I tell Melody. Because it's sadly true.

A fitting end to this unexpected night with her. I don't even care that I'm a mess, though. Having Melody as a friend now is worth the extra cleaning fee I'm going to be charged for this taco stain.

We finish eating, then talk for a while longer—Melody goes on a little too long about the compatibility of our star signs and I go on a little too long about the chemical reactions inside actual stars—before heading back out to the parking lot. Melody shivers, and I notice her bare arms are covered in goose bumps. I pull my tux jacket out of the back seat of my car, the only part of my wardrobe that's still clean because I haven't worn it, and drape it over her. She slips her arms through and thanks me, tugs it tight around herself.

"Such a gentleman," she says.

"Don't go spreading it around," I tease. "I've got this reputation as a loser to uphold. Took me years of carefully ignoring the needs of others to curate."

"If anyone asks, I'll tell them you let me freeze— No, no, better yet! You completely ignored me from the beginning, just left me on the side of the road and kept right on driving."

"That means we never even met. Excuse me, person getting into my car, who are you?"

We continue bantering like this on the ride to her house, until she says, "Turn right up there," and suddenly, just like that, our time together is up. Where did the night go?

She lives in a new development full of houses twice the size of mine, built on what was a working cow farm for centuries until about ten years ago. It's just after eleven o'clock now, and I've officially missed my senior prom, spent the whole night with this wonderful girl instead. Really, though, I shouldn't have expected anything to go according to plan tonight—nothing ever does if I'm involved. Especially without Lucy to make corrections when things veer off course. After I park in Melody's driveway, she takes off my jacket and hands it over to me.

"This was fun," she says.

"Yeah. It was." And now it's over.

"I like you, JJ."

"I like you, too." I turn in my seat to face her. "I thought we established that already."

She smiles and it's like I'm staring at the sun. But then it dims. "I mean I like you as a friend. Just to be clear. I didn't want you to think it might be something else."

"Oh. *No.* No, I'm not—I wasn't thinking that. Sorry if I gave that impression. Sometimes I don't realize . . ."

My words trail off because I don't have an explanation. It's different for me than most people. I am usually only thinking "friends" and believe I'm doing "friend things"—like being nice to people stranded on the side of the road, or joking around, or offering a girl my jacket if she's cold—and they mistake it for something else. For a lot of people, it means something else. It means you're flirting. I know this. I just don't know why it's different for me, why I don't see it that way and why I need so much more time before taking one step down that path with someone. Everyone around me seems to have it all figured out. Dating looks easy for them. They meet someone they like, they do stuff together, they fall in love. Sometimes immediately. That's how quick it was for Marcos and Chaz.

"It wasn't anything you did," Melody says. "I just never know how people are going to react. I know I should be up front to prevent . . . well, exactly this conversation we're having right now." She laughs a little. Like she's nervous. Why would she be nervous? "But this is hard for me," she goes on, "especially with new people. I'm not totally out yet. And I shouldn't assume you would even be interested, but most guys I've met—" She shakes her head. "Let's just say they're not like you."

She's not . . . out . . . "You're gay."

"Lesbian. Yeah." She looks away, toward the window at her side. Fidgets, like she doesn't know what to do with her hands. "You still okay with being friends now that you know?"

"One hundred percent okay with it."

Her laugh is breathy, laced through a sigh of relief. "Thank you."

"My moms are lesbians," I mutter. "You'd think I would have inherited better gaydar."

She stares at me blankly, like she's waiting for me to say more.

"What?" I ask.

"Oh my God . . . you aren't kidding? You have two gay moms?"

"I do."

"You're so lucky!"

That tugs a smile out of me. "This isn't the reaction I usually get when people find out."

She laughs louder this time. "I told you it was fate that we met, didn't I?"

"Yes. Yes, you did." Doesn't mean I believe in fate, but she did say that.

"There's no one in my family like me who I can talk to about . . . certain things. I wish I had someone like your moms . . ."

"I'm sure they'd be happy to meet you, if you wanted."

"Really? Do you think they'd mind?"

"They wouldn't mind. Talking is one of their favorite things to do. So is being gay. And talking about being gay, especially with other gay people. Yeah, it's . . . definitely okay."

She snatches her silky ivory clutch purse from off the dashboard and pulls out her phone. "Give me your number?"

"Sure." I grab my phone from my pocket, swipe it to life—

And I'm greeted with a bunch of new text notifications. Oops. I forgot I turned everything off for distraction-free driving. That's what I get for trying to learn from my mistakes. I quickly exchange numbers with Melody and we say goodbye. Once she's in her house, I scroll through the texts. Most are from Chaz. One from Jenna. None from Lucy.

Wait a minute. None? I double-check my ongoing text conversation with her.

Lucy: Don't worry about me.

Chaz is Lucy's cousin and one of my closest friends besides

her. If Chaz sent the most, but Lucy sent nothing . . .

My stomach churns, and I can't blame it on Taco Bell. I tap open the first text.

> Me: Sorry I'm missing everything. Is Lucy OK?

> Chaz: Where are you? Prom's almost over and I lost Lucy

He *lost* her? How . . . ? What does that even mean?

> Chaz: Found her. GET HERE

> Chaz: She's convinced you're dead. Are you?

Why would she— *Jenna.* I flip to Jenna's new message, a sickening dread coiling in my gut.

> Jenna: Lucy disappeared. She asked if I heard from you and I said no not since you texted me that you were in an accident and then she was like not breathing normal? She said she needed to get some air and now no one can find her. Everyone is looking for her and for you and I hear sirens. Gotta go.

No, no, no, no, sirens might mean an ambulance. I hope I'm wrong. But she said she wasn't breathing normal . . . What if that means— Please let me be wrong.

> Chaz: PICK UP YOUR PHONE

I put my car in drive and peel out onto the road, my phone still in one hand, scrolling through more texts until I see one that brings my worst fears to life.

> Chaz: If you get this they took her to—

"No!" The word erupts from me with volcanic force, sounding equal parts roar and plea. Lucy was taken away in an ambulance. That text was sent ten minutes ago. A lot can go wrong in ten minutes. Earlier tonight, a lot went wrong in only ten *seconds*. I toss my phone onto the passenger seat, do a sharp U-turn, tires squealing, and floor it, speeding in the opposite direction of Beaver Creek High.

Inside the emergency room, the waiting room isn't very full—a woman with a coughing toddler, an elderly guy who seems to be sleeping with his eyes open, a kid holding their head back with a bloody tissue pressed against their nose—so it's easy to spot among them a couple of very out-of-place-looking teenagers in a vintage prom dress and sporty tuxedo.

It's Jenna, in her sparkly white dress and platinum-blond hair that's been styled in long loose curls. The tall guy standing next to her isn't unfamiliar, either. Her ex, Blair Bedford. She turns toward him, and he pulls her into an embrace. Are they . . . back together now?

"Jenna," I say through panting breaths. "What happened, is Lucy okay?"

She and Blair both turn to face me. Jenna's makeup is smudged all around her eyes and Blair's tan chiseled jaw ticks. "Look who finally decided to show up," he says, and just hearing that British accent makes every muscle in my body coil tight. What right does he have to judge anyone after what he did to Jenna?

She steps away from him, then right up to me, staring hard with watery blue eyes, her glossy red lips trembling. "I've never been so scared in my life," she says. "I thought she was going to die and it was my fault. I was the last one she talked to before she—" Her breath hitches like she might cry. "Where have you been all night?"

"With a girl from another school," I start.

"*What?*"

I hold my palms out in surrender. "It's not what it sounds like, I swear. I only just met her and she was alone and it was getting dark, so we—"

"What is wrong with you!" she shouts. That gets Blair stepping toward us, and I'm not positive he won't kill me with his bare hands, right here in front of all these witnesses.

"I'm sorry, Jenna, and I promise I'll explain after I see Lucy—"

She smacks me so hard across the cheek my head whips to the side. For a moment, I actually see stars and my ears ring. Jenna may be willowy and graceful, but she's not weak. I've taken punches that hurt less. Blair isn't the one I should have been worried about.

And maybe I deserved that, but I don't have time for this drama. I bend over and push my palms against my thighs, willing the sting on my cheek to fade. The carpet is gray, I notice, as if it matters, and the whole room just got eerily quiet. Not even a cough or a sniffle.

"Let's go," Blair says, his voice sounding distant even though I can see his shiny black shoes near my Cons and Jenna's strappy heels and polished red toes. "I'll take you home."

Good. I can't deal with them right now. Once I can see straight again and get my bearings, I bolt to the check-in desk. "I'm here to see Lucy Bellini, can I see her, is she okay?"

"Are you family?" the receptionist says.

Family. I glance around the waiting room, but I don't see Chaz or anyone else from Lucy's family. Are they already back there with her? "No," I say. "We're friends."

"Then you'll have to wait until the patient is ready for visitors. Have a seat, Mr. . . . ."

"Johnson. James Johnson. Tell her it's JJ. Tell her I'm not dead."

She doesn't even nod or blink. "Have a seat, Mr. Johnson, and turn off your phone while you're in here."

"Gladly," I mutter, and actually consider tossing it in the trash can. That thing has been the root of all evil tonight. Worse than Marty yesterday.

As if I could just sit and wait, though, not knowing what's happening with my best friend. I pace along a wall away from the chairs full of people staring at me.

After a few minutes, the main entrance to the ER slides open, and Lucy's dad walks in briskly, his thick salt-and-pepper hair disheveled and his bushy brows set in the deepest furrow I've ever seen.

"Papà." I trot over then keep pace with him as he steps up to the check-in desk. "Thank God you're here. They won't let me see her. Tell them I'm family."

"Family?" he says, and shakes his head. "Family doesn't do what you did."

Oh no, not him, too. "I can explain—"

"No. Chaz tell me everything." With a shake of his head, he talks to the receptionist for a minute, then turns back to me while she's checking his ID. "Wait out here and be good, JJ. You cause enough trouble already."

He might as well have just kicked me in the face. I'm losing everything tonight—prom, my best friend, my potential girl-friend, the man I think of as a father—it's all slipping through my fingers.

The receptionist gives Signore Bellini his ID, then leads him out of the waiting room. My hands curl into fists, and I slam one down on the check-in desk. That did nothing but hurt me, and now someone's baby is crying. Fantastic. Even babies hate me. I'm still full of frustrated anger and need some kind of release. And my eyes are dry and itchy from these contacts—wearing them was just another bad decision I made tonight—but I don't want to leave even for the minute it would take me to get my glasses or eye drops from my car. I go back to pacing along the wall and thinking about what a horrible friend I was tonight.

But what could I have done differently? What was I supposed to do, just leave Melody on the side of the road in the dark? No, it's a good thing I stayed with her, because the tow truck never showed. And we had to eat; we missed dinner. None of those texts came through until late, anyway. Up until then, I have to assume Lucy was fine. Maybe. So if I had just remembered to turn my phone back on when we got to Taco Bell, this wouldn't have happened. I could have texted Lucy—or better yet, I could have called her, let her hear my voice—and none of this would have happened. We'd be at the bluffs right now, watching the meteor shower, just the two of us . . . comfortable. Happy. *Safe*.

If ever I needed a second chance at something, this night is it. I'd go back to the beginning, to before I even left my house, and do this whole thing over. But that's more impossible than Melody's theory about time not actually existing outside our heads.

"JJ," Chaz says, stopping me in place as he appears right next to me. I didn't even notice him walk across the room. His tux is the same style as mine, except it's clean, and his vest and bow tie are wine red, I assume to match Marcos's outfit, but . . . Marcos isn't with him. Odd. Those two are practically inseparable. They've been dating for as long as Lucy and I have been friends. Since freshman year. Since before Chaz came out as a trans boy, changed his name and corrected his pronoun, stopped wearing makeup and started wearing a binder. Their relationship is so sweet and pure it's almost unreal, and I'd be lying if I said I wasn't jealous of that.

"Where's Marcos—" I start, but Chaz says at the same time, "Lucy's gonna be okay. They're pretty sure she had an anxiety attack. She blacked out for a bit, but she's okay."

I sigh so heavily I nearly collapse. Chaz puts an arm across my shoulders, steadying me. "Glad you're not dead, bub. I was seriously starting to wonder. What happened to you?"

"I will tell you everything—later." I glance at the wall clock. It's pushing midnight. How long was I pacing in here? "Can I see her now?"

He steps back, shaking his head, and a section of his floppy brown hair falls over his eyes. He sweeps the bangs across his forehead, his white skin with the same warm undertone as

60

Lucy's, and tucks it behind his ear. "Uncle G's talking to her. Letting her know he just saw you, so you can't possibly be dead."

"Good."

"No, not good. None of this is good, JJ. Why didn't you just send her a text?"

"She told me not to." Kind of.

"Why didn't you reply to me, then?"

"I had to turn my phone off. But as soon as I got the messages, I dropped everything. I didn't— If I'd known she was . . ." Sigh. "I didn't ignore anyone on purpose."

"I believe you. Okay? It's all gonna be okay. I know you wouldn't do anything to hurt her. And how could you have known it would escalate like that? I've just never seen her so bad before . . . except that time when we were twelve, before we all moved out of the city, when her mom—" He looks away for a second, and everything Lucy told me about the worst moment of her life before I met her comes rushing back. Then Chaz locks his blue-green eyes onto me, pulling me into the here and now. "It was just . . . scary. She looked like death. They want to keep her under observation and run more tests to make sure it wasn't something more serious. I guess it's standard when you have chest pain and then, you know, you don't breathe for so long that you pass out." He pauses, studying me. "JJ, you look terrible. Uncle G's here. She'll be okay. You should go, get some sleep, and come back tomorrow."

"No, I'm staying."

"You sure?"

"Yes, I need to see her." My eyes burn and water, and I

absently rub at them. For a second, my vision blurs. "I'm not leaving until I see her. I'll wait until morning if I have to."

His mouth twists. "What if she doesn't want to see you?"

"Don't say that."

"Look, I'm sure you had a good excuse for all this, but you know how she is. No excuse is justified when she's mad, and this . . . Now that the fear is gone, she's pretty mad."

He has a point, but I can't even fathom that kind of rejection from Lucy, let alone how I would handle it. "Chaz, if you hadn't been there—"

"But I was, and it turned out all right. Full stop. Don't start with the what-ifs; don't go down that road. It leads to no place good." Chaz pats me on the shoulder and squeezes. "I gotta go make sure Marcos made it home all right. I left him at prom so I could hop in the ambulance with Lucy. See you tomorrow, bub. We'll catch up."

I glance at the clock again. "Technically today. It's midnight."

"Okay, then, see you today." He grins and I know we're really okay. No bad blood between us because of this.

Chaz leaves and I have my pick of empty seats in the waiting room. With my adrenaline fading, I'm suddenly very tired. It doesn't take long for me to drift off, but what seems like a few seconds later, someone is shaking me awake.

"JJ," Signore Bellini says, his thick accent tugging me out of sleep. "You want coffee?"

"Coffee . . . what?" I rub my eyes until his face and the clock on the wall come into focus. It's after one in the morning. Ughf, I hope that smell isn't me. Stretching, I lift my arms and—it *is* me. Sweat and Taco Bell are a bad mix. "Lucy's okay?"

He nods but still hasn't smiled. "She want to talk to you now. Go before she change her mind. I will get coffee. Long night ahead." He turns and walks out. Where he plans on getting coffee at one in the morning is a mystery, but maybe that's not the point. He's giving me some time alone to talk with Lucy. I can't not take this opportunity.

Her dad must have told the receptionist it's okay for me to see her now, because all I do is walk up to the check-in desk and she escorts me to the back corridor without a word. Lucy's not in a room, just an area large enough for a bed and a chair and a medical cart, sectioned off from the others like it with a thin curtain. It's white with little blue flowers all over it. Entirely too cheerful for what happens here.

The lights are dimmed and her eyes are closed. Half her dark auburn curls are piled on top of her head and the other half hang down in a cascade over her bare shoulders. She's wearing dark red lipstick, which makes her mouth seem ten times its usual size—I could see those lips from Mars, like a homing beacon leading me right to her. I step up to the bed as quietly as I can and just look at her for a minute, listen to the steady *beep-beep* of whatever machine she's hooked up to that tells me she's okay. She's alive. Her heart is beating at a regular pace and her breaths are slow and steady like they should be.

I can't see her dress except a black strap that comes up from the front and wraps around the back of her neck. Her shoes are under the chair, a pair of midnight-blue pumps with short, sturdy heels. Not like Melody's or Jenna's. Lucy's never been one to wear "ankle breakers," as she calls them. Always practical, safe, and thinking ahead.

And she ended up in the ER anyway.

When I sit on the plastic chair next to her bed, it creaks, and she flinches. Her eyes flutter open. She blinks and her brow furrows, staring straight ahead.

"Lucy, I'm here." I reach over and take her hand, and she turns her face toward me.

It's clear the very second she recognizes me. A brilliant smile takes over her face, even though her eyes are still sleepy. "Hey, you," she says, her voice low. "Nice bow tie."

I swallow hard and can't meet her gaze. I don't deserve that smile. I don't deserve *her*.

"Your dad said you wanted to talk?"

"I do, but I'm really tired," she says. "It's been a long night." Her smile drops, and she lets go of my hand. Reality just set in. She turns her face forward again. "I'm so embarrassed, JJ. Everyone saw me . . . pass out."

"I should've been there. I should've told you what happened."

Her face drifts toward me. "What did happen? Jenna said you were in an accident."

"I was *almost* in an accident. You know that nasty curve on Huffman Road?"

She nods and I continue the story, every bit of it, pouring my heart out like I'm at a confessional. Every once in a while her eyelids flutter like she might fall asleep again, but then she snaps back to attention.

When I get to the part about going to Taco Bell, she stops me. "All right, I got the point. I don't need to hear all the details of your fabulous night with this amazing new girl, while I was sitting around the whole time just watching the door, waiting for you to walk in . . ." She flicks a glance at the stain on my shirt. "Looks like it got messy at some point."

"It wasn't—" I start, but she's done listening.

"It's fine."

Which in Lucy Language means "not even close to fine," because she is the ruling queen of Opposite Land, her native country.

"You changed plans, you went with the flow." She shakes her head at herself. "I should have known you would do something like that. I shouldn't have jumped to assuming the worst."

"And I should have . . ." Checked on her anyway. Listened to my gut. "I shouldn't have turned my phone off."

"We both made mistakes, I guess."

I try a smile, but it feels weak. "Forgive?"

That's how this works with us. We make mistakes. We forgive each other. We go back to the way we were.

"I . . ." Her lips twibble and my heart rate kicks up a few notches. "JJ, I don't think we—" Another twibble and she presses her lips firmly together, takes a moment to breathe. "I'm not sure it's good for us to be around each other, if all we ever do is stress each other out."

"What are you— You don't stress me out. What are you talking about?"

"You know what I'm talking about."

I do. I was hoping I misunderstood.

"We're too opposite," she says. "And it only creates problems."

"So what do you mean, like, you don't want me around *right now*?" I bite my lip and nod. "Okay. I'll leave you alone to think, or whatever you need to do, for the weekend. And then I'll—I'll pick you up for school on Monday and we can talk, when you're feeling better."

"No. Not just a day or even a week." She swallows hard, closing her eyes briefly. "This was going to happen anyway, you know? Us splitting up. I'm going to Italy; you're going to Texas. How do you think that's going to work? We can barely go one day without arguing about *something*. Or just . . . annoying each other. And that's without half a world of distance between us." She still isn't looking at me.

"We have phones," I say. "And email. Social media. We talked about this. We agreed to keep in touch." I'm missing something. Something else happened that she's not telling me.

She shakes her head. "I'm no good for you, JJ. We're no good for each other."

"That isn't—" Something catches in my throat. "That isn't true."

"It's something that's been true for a while," she says. "I just didn't want to believe it. But tonight proved we'd both be better off away from each other. Why try so hard to keep something together that's always falling apart? We should cut this off now, not drag it out, if this is where it's leading eventually anyway."

My eyes are glued to the floor, trying to find where my heart fell to, but I can't find it. It's gone. And the black hole it left in my chest is painfully sucking in the rest of me. I'm on the brink of imploding.

"Please don't push me away." I can't keep the tremor out of my voice. "This night was just a mistake—a big string of mistakes I'll never do again." I dare to look up, meet her deep brown gaze. Her eyes have welled with tears and I'm pretty sure this is what dying feels like. "Give me another chance."

Even as I say it, I know that's not going to happen. There are no second chances. That's been our mantra for years. For Lucy, it gave her reason to always plan ahead. For me, it gave me reason to always go with the flow. Our viewpoints were completely opposite—like everything else about us—yet neither of them kept us from getting screwed tonight.

Her lip trembles so much her cheeks ripple. The heart rate monitor beeps a little faster. "I—I think you should go," she says. "I'm tired. Let me sleep." As if her words weren't enough to make her point, she rolls over in the bed so her back is facing me.

The top of the blanket falls, exposing her bare upper back. I'm never going to see her dress, and out of all the things running through my mind, that particular thought is what crushes the last bit of hope I'd been holding on to that this night would end okay. My throat tightens and my head feels like it's been hit by a sledgehammer from the inside out and my dry eyes burn even more as moisture pricks them. I tug the blanket up over her back so she doesn't get cold. Why is it so cold in here? My hands are shaking.

Signore Bellini peeks in from the other side of the curtain, then steps around it. When he sees Lucy with her eyes closed, he silently holds out a to-go cup of coffee from a gas station. "You good now?" he whispers. "You staying?"

"No, she doesn't— She doesn't want me to." I leave him. Leave Lucy. And try to breathe, but it's difficult when you no longer have air. For the past almost-four years, Lucy has been my air. Her dad catches up to me in the waiting room and offers me the coffee again.

"Don't drive tired," he says. "Don't drive upset. Be safe." He lets out a long sigh, as if contemplating whether to say what he's thinking. "Lucilla can be . . . like her mother. She need patience. I was not patient with Viola when she need me to be. So she had no patience for me, and she left. Don't be like me. *Capisce?*"

"*Sì,*" I tell him, but I don't understand, not really. I take the coffee, wincing at the heat but also welcoming it, and promise to drive safe.

But when I get to my car, even though I'm sort of awake enough, I can't get rid of the "upset" part. So I sit. And dump this bitter coffee when it goes cold. And take out these moisture-leaching contacts. And cry, mentally kicking myself over and over. And go nowhere. And the clock keeps ticking. There are only a few hours until dawn. I promised my parents I wouldn't be out all night.

Now I *am* too tired to drive, but I have to get home before my parents wake up with the sun to feed the horses. I put on the pair of glasses I keep in my car as an emergency spare—another

68

insistence of Lucy's—and leave the ER lot, covering a mammoth yawn with one hand and steering with the other. Nodding off more than a few times.

What am I supposed to do?

I can't lose her, not completely. She's right; our split was inevitable. But not like this. Not forever. And part of me was hoping . . . maybe not at all. Maybe something would change at the last minute—isn't that how things usually happen for me? For us?

"How am I going to get her back?" I ask whatever higher being might be listening. I need all the help I can get with this.

I'm about halfway home, my headlights highlighting a mist floating above the road, when . . . a groundhog lumbers into the path of my car out of nowhere, like it has all the time in the world, then freezes, just staring at me through the windshield, as if it's daring me to hit it. Or maybe its life is flashing before its eyes. Either way, that ugly rodent is large enough to do some damage if I hit it.

Instinctively I swerve, and without any sound—no screeching tires, no *thud-thump* of an impact, not even a whispered curse under my breath—the whole world disappears and I slip into a cold black void.

the NIGHT of the PARALLAX

My reflection in the mirror blurs as the floor vibrates, my bedroom window rattles, and a bright white light flashes behind my eyes. What the—

Blue sparks fly in my side vision, and I whip my face in that direction. Marty is fritzing. Again? Should have tossed him in a dumpster after school on Friday, the useless piece of junk. I rush over and stamp out the sparks that landed on my bedroom carpet, then check the bottom of my Converse for any scorch marks. Nothing. Good. Now, what was I doing?

I step in front of the mirror hanging off my closet door. My tux is perfect, crisp and clean, and I can see clearly without my glasses. But I swear I took out my contacts last night . . . and wasn't I driving? I don't remember coming home. I don't remember anything after almost hitting that groundhog. Was I that tired? I didn't even change my clothes.

But they're clean. The taco stain is gone. The dust from Melody's car is gone, and my pits don't stink. My bow tie isn't around my neck; it's crumpled in my fist. Just like it was when

I was getting ready for prom last night . . . My head swims. *Was it last night?*

The clock radio on my nightstand reads 7:31 p.m. Did I sleep all day? I pull my phone out of my pocket. Same time on there, but it's showing yesterday's date. Saturday. The day of senior prom.

Okay . . .

If the last night I remember as last night wasn't really last night, that means I never actually met a person named Melody? That also means Lucy didn't have a massive anxiety attack. That means she didn't spend the night in the hospital. That means—

I open my ongoing text conversation with her and find the most recent messages.

Lucy: Where are you?

Me: Leaving soon

That means it was only a bad dream.

I fall back onto my bed, melting with relief, and stare up at the galaxy of glow-in-the-dark star stickers on the ceiling that have been there since I was ten. It felt so real. I remember it like it was real, not fuzzy and jumpy like a dream, can remember way too many details—the floral scent of Melody's perfume, the conversations we had, the panicked texts from Chaz, Lucy breaking up our friendship, and the deep regret in her dad's eye when he said, *Don't be like me.* But it couldn't have been real, because here I am in my room, getting ready for prom again.

No, not "again." This is the first time. The real time.

"Knock, knock," Mom says on the other side of my door. "Are you decent?"

"Yeah, come in." As I get up off my bed, I shoot Lucy a quick text just to be sure my worst fear—losing her—didn't really happen.

Me: You need anything?

Lucy: Don't worry about me.

The back of my neck tingles. In my dream, that exact text from Lucy caused a lot of trouble. No way I'm *not* going to worry about her, especially with those images so fresh in my mind, but that's a strange coincidence. *Shake it off.* I pocket my phone and look up to find Mom staring at me.

"Is that Lucy?" she says.

"Yeah, I was supposed to be picking her up *right this minute*. You know how she is."

She smiles at that and sweeps her bangs to the side. "Yes, I do know how she is. But she's good for you. You're good for each other."

I'm no good for you, JJ, Lucy's voice says in my head. *We're no good for each other.*

"Funny," I tell Mom, mentally downing all the red flags that just popped up. "Mama told me the same thing yesterday." Didn't she?

Please don't push me away. Give me another chance.

STOP. It didn't happen.

"Well, we can't both be wrong," Mom says. "You know the old saying, two moms make a right."

Sigh. "It's two *wrongs*, and they *don't* make a right."

"I was making a pun, James." She narrows her eyes at me. "You usually love my puns. Are you feeling okay? Your eyes are all red. Have you been crying?"

"I feel fine." Sort of. A little dazed. "It's just my contacts," I assure her, and myself. "They dry me out." Not usually this fast, though. Didn't I just put them in?

"Maybe you shouldn't wear them tonight," Mom suggests. "If they're bothering you already . . ." She takes the bow tie from my hand and fastens it like an expert in only a few seconds. I watch her in the mirror and try to commit her moves to memory. I can't go the rest of my life relying on my mother to knot my ties.

As soon as she's done, I thank her and head to the bathroom, nearly colliding with my sister, the human tornado, in the hallway. "Look at you all fancy!" Shayla says, and grabs my hand. "Dance with me, JJ."

"Hang on a sec." I tug away from her and shut myself in the bathroom. Shayla grumbles something on the other side of the door, and I'm pretty sure that request for a dance is now null and void. Her feet pounding too loudly down the steps confirms it. She's mad I brushed her off. Whatever, I'll make it up to her another day. I swipe both contacts out of my eyes and drop them into the case of solution. Lucy says I look better without glasses, though she's never told me why. I can't wear them that often and tonight is special. I wanted to look nice for her. But my eyes really are bloodshot. It's not happening.

I apply a few eye drops, slip my glasses on, and check my phone: 7:35.

When I return to my room to grab my car keys, Mama is there now, too, holding her phone up like a camera. Her brown eyes are shining and her smile stretches from ear to ear. "Can I get a few pictures before you go?"

"I'm already late." I trot around the end of my bed and snatch the keys from my nightstand. "I'll ask Lucy's dad to take a few if we have time, but if I don't get there soon, Lucy—"

"It's all right, go," Mama says, still smiling, but the spark has fizzled. "Don't leave her waiting. Have fun, JJ. You look great."

"Thanks, love you, bye," I say in a rush, headed out the bedroom door.

"Remember the rules!" Mom shouts to my back. As I take the stairs, her voice drifts farther and farther away until it disappears. I don't need to hear what she said, though. I know the rules. No drugs, alcohol, speeding, getting anyone pregnant, or being a juvenile delinquent.

I hop into my car and buckle up, turn the key, and . . . pause for a second. That smell. What is that? It's not unpleasant, and weirdly familiar. I sniff harder, leaning toward the passenger seat. Perfume. Very subtle, like someone who was wearing it sat in here. But the only other person usually in this car besides me is Lucy, and perfume makes her sick. It reminds me of the perfume Mel— No. She doesn't exist, and therefore neither does her scent. I'm just remembering the fantasy of her so strongly that my brain thinks the smell is real.

The clock on the dashboard reads 7:36 p.m. I'm six minutes late and Lucy hasn't sent another text to nag me. That's really not like her. I check my phone, just in case I missed it.

Nope. Nada. Nothing. Her most recent message is still: *Don't worry about me.*

Maybe she's so mad she's giving me the silent treatment, like she did the other day when I told her Jenna would be coming with us to prom. The other day? No, that was yesterday. Last night. We had ice cream sundaes and made a wish on the moon. She mentioned her mom for the first time in months. Normally that's a topic she avoids . . .

I should ask her about that. Another day, though. Tonight is supposed to be fun.

Gravel spits out from under my tires as I tear down the driveway—

Wait, no speeding. *And shut off the phone*, a little voice reminds me. Done and done.

Once I turn onto the asphalt road, I progress at grandma level. Even if it was just a dream, I remember my almost accident as clearly as if it happened only minutes ago in real time. Imagination or not, that was one of the scariest moments of my life. It started with a text, getting distracted, not paying attention. In a word, preventable. Lucy will just have to be mad at me for being late—wouldn't be the first time. But like Mama says, better late than dead.

Dead Man's Curve lies ahead, a steep, sharp, downhill turn on Huffman Road between my house and Lucy's. Aptly nicknamed, since there are numerous stories of people dying in magnificent crashes here. I've driven this curve countless times before, usually without a second thought as I ease off the gas and gently but firmly apply the brake, but today I'm extra cautious. I slow to a crawl. Images flash in my head—a billowing orange dress that glows in the setting sun; leaning over a roadside ditch, feeling acid rise in my throat; a classy little VW Bug, cream-colored with a black convertible top, the hood propped up . . .

No way.

No freaking way.

I pass the Bug at the same turtle speed I used on the curve, even though the road is straight and flat now. But I'm not looking at the road anymore. My head is turned, staring out the passenger window, as the person behind the open hood comes into view.

A gorgeous Black girl in a Creamsicle-orange prom dress that glitters in the waning sunlight. Her spiral curls are swept up in the same elegant twist, and when the breeze catches her skirt, pulling up the hem, I see those same high heels that prompted me to hold her hand so she wouldn't fall on the gravel driveway . . . after I pushed her car into the woods . . .

I think?

She lifts her head from the car and locks her gaze onto me, her eyes narrowing when I hit the brakes, bringing my car to a whisper-soft stop. I was barely moving.

"Can I help you?" she says.

I don't hear it as much as read her lips, with the window closed. Her full lips painted the same fuchsia as before. I push the button on the driver's side door that drops the passenger-side window open. "Shouldn't I be asking *you* that?"

"Thanks, but I'm fine. I got this."

She grabs for something under the hood, juggling a few other items, and just as I'm reaching for my door handle to get out and offer a hand, a yellow plastic funnel goes flying out in front of my car. It bounces on the road and then rolls all the way into the ditch on the other side. With a growl of frustration, she sets down the other stuff and marches across the road, her dress billowing like a parachute in the breeze. She didn't even check to see if any cars were coming. She could have been hit by someone coming from the other direction.

Or from this direction . . . from me . . . if I'd been moving when she crossed.

That's exactly what happened. In my dream? In my future memory of yesterday? No, that makes even less sense. A different version of today? Maybe. I got here sooner this time. *Think.* I got here sooner because I left earlier so I wouldn't be late. But then I drove slower, losing some of the time I wanted to save, so when I got here it was a minute before she crossed instead of right *when* she crossed.

Am I really analyzing this like it's even plausible?

After picking up the now-dirt-covered funnel, Melody walks behind my car to get back to hers. She crossed the road again without looking, but she's safe. No screaming. She's safe because I'm not speeding out of control off that curve this time. *This time.* I'm starting to doubt this is déjà vu or a memory of a dream, though I have no logical explanation for it, either. My imagination gets far-fetched sometimes, but conjuring up a girl with that much detail and similarity to someone who really exists? Who I've never met before? No. Impossible.

But so is reliving the same day.

A retching sensation hits me out of nowhere. For no reason whatsoever I feel like I'm going to throw up. What the hecking heck? I pull my car up alongside the ditch in front of hers and stumble out, getting to the ditch just in time to lean over and spit out bile. I've been here before, staring at this same ditch and at the scuffed white toes of my Converse, feeling this same burn in my throat. My stomach is empty because I skipped dinner. I skipped dinner because I'm supposed to eat at prom—

The world goes silent, and my mind is suddenly crystal clear.

I *am* going to eat at prom. I'll be there. With Lucy. With Jenna. With everyone. I can make sure of it now.

There are no second chances, but somehow, miraculously, I have one. And I will not screw up the night this time. I'll figure out what caused this phenomenon later—Lucy is going to have a field day trying to explain this through science. I'll tell her all about it tomorrow. For right now, though, I have a disaster prom night to make sure never happens.

"Are you okay?" Melody says beside me.

I straighten too quickly, too eager. "Yes!" I blurt, and she flinches. "Yes, sorry, I'm okay. Everything is okay now. It's all good. We're good. Really good." I smile wide and watch her closely, searching for any sign she remembers me.

"Ooh-kayy." She gives me a funny look, then turns away. Heads back to her car.

"Mel, wait—"

She stops and spins to face me. "What did you call me?"

"N-Nothing." She has no idea. *Why?* Why is it just me who remembers? "I said, *No, wait.* Are you sure you don't need help with this? It feels wrong to just leave you stranded."

"That's very nice of you." Her shoulders relax. "But I won't be stranded. I'm about to call a tow."

"I know, but—"

"How do you know?"

Oops. "Lucky guess. It doesn't look like your Bug is going anywhere without one. What happened, you blow the engine? Those older models are notorious for that."

Her mouth drops open a little and it's a struggle not to smile. Everything I know about her car I learned from her, but she doesn't remember telling me any of it. This is ludicrous.

"Look," I say, "I can see you're on your way to prom. Right? So am I, but I don't think I've ever seen you at my school. I go to Beaver Creek High."

"Yeah, no," she says. "Whitman Academy. What's your point?"

"My point is: What if the tow never shows up? It'll be dark soon."

"If by soon you mean a half hour. Plenty of time for the tow to get here." She raises a brow. "Anyway, I'm still not following. Why does this concern you, exactly?"

"Because I can give you a ride."

She shakes her head, rolling her eyes. "Thanks, but you're not my type."

Mel, no, it's not like that. But how can I make her see . . .

"Too male?" I try.

She opens her mouth to retort, then snaps it shut. Studies me for a second. I've completely baffled her with that one. "Maybe," she says. "What of it?"

"Nothing. I wasn't flirting with you, anyway." I wouldn't this soon after meeting someone. Not to mention: "I know you're gay. And before you ask—both my parents are lesbians, so I have really good gaydar. It's not a big deal."

Actually, it is the biggest of deals. Because this whole situation is so impossible it's sick. Also, I'm lying. My gaydar is the absolute worst, even Lucy has said so.

Lucy.

Why hasn't she— Oh, for the love of— I forgot I turned my phone off to drive. Again.

I yank my phone out of my pocket and turn it on. Three new messages since I left home, from three different people. Lucy, Jenna, and Chaz. But Chaz didn't text me yesterday—I mean the other today—until prom was almost over, when Lucy was . . . *no*. That's not going to happen again.

"If you need to get going," Melody says, "it's okay. I appreciate the offer for a ride and the . . . extremely weird conversation"— she smiles at that and I almost relax, *almost*—"but you can go. Really. Have fun at your prom. I can take care of myself."

"I know you can, but hang on, I just need to . . ." I tap open the message from Lucy first.

Lucy: On your way yet?

That was only a few minutes ago. But a lot can happen in a few minutes.

Me: Yes. Do you need something?

Please reply, please reply, please—

    Lucy: Just for you to get here. Are you texting and driving?

    Lucy: Don't answer that if you are!

I lean back against my car, and a whoosh of air escapes me. She's okay.

    Me: Not driving. Had to stop. Will explain later. Be there soon

I'm vaguely aware of Melody talking on her phone, calling the tow, while I open the message from Jenna.

    Jenna: Lucy said you're running late? I can get a ride from

    Autumn Mitchell. She rented a limo.

Right, I remember her saying that before. If she got a ride from Autumn that would be one less stop for me to make.

    Me: Do you mind? Sorry. I got held up

    Jenna: No problem! I'll just meet you there. Is everything okay?

Don't mention a car accident.

    Me: Yeah I'll explain later

    Jenna: Okie dokie ☺

So far, so good. I tap open the final message.

    Chaz: You OK?

Hunh. So his message wasn't about Lucy, then. But Chaz never checks on me out of the blue like that, not without a reason.

    Me: Fine. Why?

His reply is immediate.

    Chaz: OK bub never mind.

    Me: No what's wrong? Talk to me

    Chaz: Had a bad vibe. It's gone now. Forget it. See you

    at prom?

Me: Yeah see you soon

Just another weird thing to add to the weirdness list for tonight. I pocket my phone and walk over to Melody, who is now sitting inside her car with the driver's side door hanging open and her legs dangling out, as if that isn't a fantastic way to get the door knocked off by a passing car and a double leg amputation. If Lucy saw her, she'd have no qualms about telling Melody exactly that, as bluntly as possible for maximum effect. That's how Lucy shows she cares.

The sun is lower in the sky now. It'll be completely set in half an hour. It'll take me about ten minutes to get to Lucy's house from here, then another ten minutes to snap a few pictures and get back on the road again, ten minutes back here . . . that's about a half hour. Perfect.

"Something wrong?" Melody says, looking up at me. I catch the scent of her floral perfume when the wind blows. The same perfume I smelled in my car, because she was *there*. If that's still there with me, and all the memories . . . maybe something about me is still with her.

Instead of answering her question, I say, "My name's JJ."

You know this. You know *me*. I know you, too. Your name is Melody, but you go by Mel, and oh by the way, we spent a whole night together. We went to Taco Bell instead of prom and you were excited to meet my parents. You're amazing, intelligent, creative, and bold. You made me think in ways I've never thought before. *Just remember me, Mel, please.* I need to know I haven't lost our friendship to this, whatever it is.

But even hearing my name doesn't spark any recognition in

her eyes. The same as with everything else, it's like yesterday—the other today—never happened. In some ways that's good. A blessing, even. A miracle I don't deserve. But with this . . . with Melody . . . it feels damning.

"Okay," she says. "*JJ.* Why are you still here?"

Because we're friends, even though she thinks I'm a stranger, and friends help each other. "I'll leave in a second, but I just want to make sure you'll be okay."

"That's very nice of you," she says again. "You seem . . . genuinely nice. Honest. But what about your prom? Whoever you were texting . . . girlfriend? Boyfriend? Partner? Are they waiting on you?"

"Yes, I'm going to pick up my friend for prom. She lives about ten minutes from here. So how about if, after I get her, I come back this way and see if you're still waiting on the tow, and if you are, I can call Triple-A—they never not show up—and give you a ride to your prom. If you're okay with that? It's up to you, but my car's gotta be better than a tow truck, right? And I'll have someone else with me, another girl, so you don't have to worry about me kidnapping you or anything like that. I just . . . I don't feel right leaving you on the side of the road. In the dark. Alone. It's against my upbringing. My parents would seriously kill me."

"Your lesbian parents," she says with a smirk, like I made all this up.

I pull my phone out and find a picture of them and me and Shayla all together, then show it to her. Then, just to cover all my bases, I show her the veritable millions of pictures of me and Lucy on my phone, too. "My best friend in the whole world. Her name's Lucy. She'll vouch."

"Okay, I believe you." She sighs. "But it's fine. The tow will be here any minute."

"Then you'll be gone when I get back and it won't matter."

"True," she says.

"Everything happens for a reason, right?" That perks her up. I knew it would—I heard that line from her. "So let's just see what happens."

What happens is I'm going to call AAA as soon as I get to Lucy's house, to save us some time, because when I get back here, Melody will still be waiting for her tow. Unless I'm totally wrong about this. And if I am, I'll just keep improvising. But I'm pretty sure that if I can help get Melody on her way, then Lucy and I can be on ours, and the rest of the night will be fine. For everyone.

"Okay, JJ," Melody says. "Now go. Never make a girl wait on you. Get out of here."

"About time you got here," Lucy's brother says in greeting, stepping aside to let me in their house. No *ciao* or *how you been?* The feeling is mutual.

"Hey, Nico." I hardly give him a passing glance. "Is Lucy—"

I stop dead in my tracks and my jaw stretches toward the floor. She's standing in the middle of the living room, right in front of me, in *that dress*. That dress she refused to show me. That dress I'm finally seeing and finally understanding what the big deal was. That dress I can't take my eyes off of.

"That dress is . . . Lucy, it's . . ." My brain fails me and there are no words, only the biggest smile I've ever felt on my face in my entire existence of almost eighteen years.

The same black strap I saw on her at the hospital wraps up from the front and around the back of her neck, no other straps, leaving her shoulders bare except where her dark auburn curls brush over them. The rest of the dress is a black night sky speckled with stars and splashes of colorful nebulas. Pinks, purples, blues, oranges, yellows, and reds. It flows loosely over her curves, all the way down to her midnight-blue pumps with the sturdy heels.

It's a *galaxy*. It's a galaxy in the shape of Lucy. That dress, on her, is the most beautiful thing I've ever seen.

And then I get it. I get why she didn't want me to see it until now. Lucy is a science geek, but not in the same way I'm a science geek. She's much more grounded, her favorite field being geophysics, while my focus is always up in the stars. I'm the one who's into astronomy, not her.

So that galaxy dress . . . is for me. She picked it out because she knew I'd love it. She wore it because she knew I'd love it. And she told me it didn't matter what color accents I chose for my tux— because anything would match that dress with every color on it—so I chose blue . . . for her. Blue is her favorite color. This shade of blue, especially, blue as a robin's egg. She says it's her favorite color on me because it's the same color as my eyes. She says wearing this color makes my eyes glow even brighter blue than usual.

Everything we did, we did for each other, without knowing what the other was doing.

If that doesn't make us the best of best friends, I don't know what else would.

"You like it?" she says, her tone hesitant and unsure even though my smile is still stretching so far my cheeks ache.

Miraculously, I find my voice again. "It's perfect, Lucy. You just look . . . *perfect*."

"Well, I wouldn't go that far. Perfection is an unreachable standard." She's blushing. Lucy never blushes. "But *grazie*. And you look good, too," she adds. "Good color choice. I like it." Her gaze stays on my glasses for a beat and her lips twibble.

I was right. She was hoping I wouldn't wear them tonight. God only knows why. How can I know a person for almost four years and still be mystified by them?

"What, no corsage?" Nico says. "Did you forget, *coglione*, or are you just that cheap?"

"She didn't want one," I say at the same time Lucy says, "I told him I didn't want one," followed by rapid Italian and an expression I'm thankful isn't directed at me. Lucy and I talked about the corsage, even if we didn't discuss the dress. I can see now she picked and chose what to tell me and what to keep to herself so this moment, likely this whole night, would all go according to her plan. Of course she did. I wouldn't expect, or want, anything less from her.

"JJ!" Signore Bellini exclaims as he reaches the bottom of the stairs. "You made it! Look at you, *polpetto*. He clean up nice, eh, Lucilla? And you . . ." He puts all his fingers to his lips, then

86

kisses them and pulls them away, spreading them into the air. "Sopraffino."

She rolls her eyes, as if his praise is just so cumbersome. But I know on the inside she thrives on it. She gets it double from him because he knows she gets zero from her mom.

"Papà," she says, grabbing a small glittering purse the same midnight blue as her shoes, "we're running late. Give JJ your talk so we can go."

"What talk?" That sounds suspiciously parental and slightly terrifying.

Nico laughs as he heads upstairs, spouting off something in Italian so quickly I can't pick out one familiar word. But judging by the glare Lucy gives his back, I'm sure it had something to do with the fact I probably look like I just messed my pants.

Signore Bellini ignores the whole exchange, leading me to the kitchen to give us some privacy. "Tonight is special," he says, his voice low. "But don't make it *too* special, *capisce*?"

"*Sì*." Yes, I hear him loud and clear: *Don't do anything inappropriate with my daughter.* Nothing to worry about there. Lucy and I aren't like that. We never have been and we never will be. Our friendship is good. The best, even. At least it was, until . . .

Why try so hard to keep something together that's always falling apart? We should cut this off now—

No. That was a fluke. A bad reaction to a bad situation. She doesn't really want that.

"You almost an adult," Signore Bellini goes on. "But not yet. Be a child tonight. Have fun. Make nice memories, dancing, laughing, those things. Plenty of time for other stuff later."

"Papà, hurry up, we need to go!" Lucy shouts from the living room.

Her dad sighs. "Lucilla not so patient sometimes."

"She's not? I didn't notice."

He barks a laugh. "She just excited for tonight. She want it all to be perfect." His smile lingers for a moment then he sobers. "If she not patient with you, you be patient with her. Then it all work out."

"Right." He said the same thing to me last night—the other tonight. "Got it."

"Good talk." He claps a hand on my shoulder. "Now, *muoversi*. Before she come over here and drag you out."

"Going," I say through a laugh. I take two steps away, then turn back to him. Give him a big bear hug and welcome the generous way he returns it. For a few dreadful moments last night, I'd thought I lost his presence in my life for good, too, by screwing things up with Lucy. Tonight isn't just a second chance with her. It's a second chance with him.

"*Grazie*, Papà." I pull back before my gratitude for this man overwhelms me.

"For what?" he says.

"Everything."

Lucy steps into the kitchen, pulling my attention away. "Ready now?" she says.

"Ready." It's quarter past eight. We should be at prom already, eating dinner. Playing our own geeked-up version of Trivial Pursuit, while Chaz and Marcos and Jenna, and who-ever else has the misfortune of sitting with us, try to shift us into a normal conversation. Lucy has a very concrete idea of how it's all supposed to go tonight. She has an itinerary in her head, and she just mentally checked off "picked up by JJ." The next item on the list is "go to prom" followed closely by "eat." She's got to be as hungry as I am.

So I wait until we're inside my car and buckled up before dropping my improvisation bomb on her. But then she speaks first.

"What's that smell?" She sniffs the air. "Perfume. Was there a girl in here? I thought you said Jenna was getting a ride from someone else."

"She did. You can smell that?"

"That sounds guilty," she says with a laugh, then fiddles with the clasp on her purse. "So who is she, do I know her?"

"No." *Not yet, but you're about to.* "She goes to Whitman Academy."

"Ooh, a rich girl. You're stepping up in the world, Mr. Johnson."

I shake my head. "It's not like that. We're friends. I mean barely. We just met. You know how I am." Lucy's one of the few people who doesn't make me feel wrong for it, or who doesn't try to force me to explain something I don't totally understand about myself.

"I know," she says. "I didn't mean that you were dating already, but maybe, potentially, down the road . . . Anyway, whatever it's like"—she places my right hand on the gear shift—"you can fill me in on the way."

Subtle as a volcanic eruption. I put the car in reverse and

back down her driveway. At the end, I turn onto the road in the opposite direction of our school.

"Wait—JJ—" Her face snaps toward me. "Where are you going?"

"We have to make a couple of stops first. The girl wearing that perfume might need our help."

Lucy handled the news about as well as I could have expected—meaning not well at all—but after the ten minutes it took to drive from her house to Melody's car, she agreed we were doing the right thing, despite the inconvenient change in plans. Once her anxiety over my improvising recedes, her logic returns, and no way would she just leave someone stranded in the dark.

Only a quickly vanishing blush is left on the horizon. I flip my headlights on as we near the bottom of Dead Man's Curve, and Melody's Bug comes into view. She's sitting in the car. Good. And she closed the door this time.

I park alongside the ditch on the opposite side of the road as her car.

"Why didn't she call a tow?" Lucy says, unbuckling her seat belt.

"She did."

"Well, if it's on its way, then—"

"It's not on its way."

"How do you know?"

"I don't know. I mean I do know it's not coming, but I don't know how I know."

90

She sighs a sigh that in Lucy Language means "you're making a whole lot of zero sense."

Whatever, I know what I meant. And besides: "Do you want to sit here all night waiting to see if I'm wrong?" Been there already and it ended in disaster. Not doing it again.

"No," she concedes. "It's just weird. Like you think you're psychic or something."

"I'm not psychic." I also don't have the words to explain any of this right now. I turn to look at her squarely and, with great effort, keep my eyes on her face and off *that dress*. That dress that I can still see in my peripheral. That dress that looks like a literal picture of heaven . . . What were we talking about?

"Why are you staring," Lucy says, "do I have something on my face?"

"No. I was just thinking." *Think, JJ*. Right. Melody. She's waiting on a tow truck that isn't coming. "Can you get out of the car with me?"

"Yeah," she says. "Good idea."

We exit the car and cross the road together. As we get closer, Melody steps out of her Bug. "JJ," she says. "I wasn't sure if it was you, it's . . . getting dark. And my tow never showed up."

"Yeah . . . I see that." One side of my mouth lifts into a smirk, but I have no good reason to be this cocky. It wasn't because of anything special or skillful I did that I knew her tow wouldn't show up. Really I'm just glad she's okay. Anything could have happened in the half hour I was gone, even in daylight. We're in the middle of nowhere. Weirdos are everywhere.

"Yeah, you were right," Melody concedes. "So now what?"

"We wait for the tow," I say. "I mean the one I called. It'll be here any minute. And then we can drive you to your prom. Unless you don't want us to?"

"No, I . . ." Melody scratches at her brow. "I can take care of myself, but I can also admit when I could use some help." Her gaze shifts to Lucy. "You must be the best friend. Lucy, right?" Lucy nods. "I'm Melody. But you can call me Mel."

Lucy grins. "Mel, you're lucky JJ found you and not some weirdo. Well, not luck. That doesn't really exist. But, as a figure of speech. I just meant it was a good thing."

"Maybe it was fate," Melody suggests.

I watch them expectantly, wondering if this will lead to the same conversation Melody and I had last night. Wondering what Lucy would think of it, if she could be swayed like I was, even if only for a fraction of a smidgen of a second.

Lucy's mouth twists. "It was a very well-timed coincidence that worked in your favor."

That's a no. And also a *no surprise*, followed by relief. I don't want any surprises from Lucy tonight. I want her just the way she's always been. No changing her mind about us.

"Are you thirsty?" Lucy asks Melody. "JJ keeps bottled water in his trunk." She thrusts an open palm toward me, and I instinctively hand her my keys, then she and Melody cross the road together, toward my car, chatting away like old friends. In the growing dark and the distance yawning between us, they become fluid shadows.

Amber flashing lights approach from down the road. The

tow truck. *Yes.* Lucy and Melody are sitting in my car, smiling, safe. This night is going much smoother than it did before. I didn't mess anything up on purpose last time, but yeah, I screwed up. So tonight I improvised. And now, everything's going to be okay.

"Okay, it should be the next driveway on the left," Melody says, reading the map on her phone.

I turn left onto a smooth asphalt drive and we pass through an open set of metal-barred gates, then we're greeted by a large stone building with the kind of landscaping that's so perfect it has to be fake. Sculpted shrubbery, climbing vines, beds full of flowers in all different shapes and colors. I recognize the tulips and daffodils, but the rest I can't name. Lilies maybe? An elegantly painted sign reads: FROST CENTER FOR FINE ENTERTAINING. The drive circles around close to the building, where I guess I'm supposed to drop Melody off, right by a giant fountain statue of a mermaid wearing a couple of shells for a top.

A *mermaid.* We've officially entered a fantasy world.

"Wow," Lucy says, staring wide-eyed out her window. "This is so . . . bougie."

My thoughts exactly. "I didn't think places like this existed in Beaver Creek."

From the back seat, Melody catches my gaze in the rearview mirror. "Technically, this is outside Beaver Creek city limits. And even more technically, Beaver Creek is not a city."

Which reminds me we're way out of our way here; we've got a bit of a drive to get back to Beaver Creek High. Probably twenty minutes, or more, because I am *not* speeding. So . . .

"I'm hungry," I say. "Lucy, are you hungry?"

"Maybe."

That's a yes.

She turns her face slowly from the window to me. "Depends on why you're asking."

"By the time we get to our prom, they'll have put the food away. Do you wanna . . . ?"

It takes all of one second for her to figure out where I'm going. "Eat here? Are you serious? We can't just walk in there and ask for a plate. You have to have tickets for these things. And for a prom this fancy, you probably have to provide a birth certificate, show proof of US residency, and agree to a DNA test."

"Not all that," Melody says on a laugh, "but you do need tickets." She glances at the building, where her prom has already started. We're the only ones out here right now. "Once I'm in, I could meet you at a back door. There will be plenty of food here; Whitman doesn't do anything small. No reason for perfectly good food to go to waste when you two are perfectly capable of eating it."

Lucy turns to face her. "I can't believe you're encouraging this."

"Encouraging what, being generous?"

"It feels more like stealing," Lucy clarifies. "This isn't our prom. People paid to get in here. It's not right if we get in for free. If we get caught we'll be in trouble."

"We'll just eat, then go," I tell her. "I don't want to miss our prom, so if anyone notices, we'll be on our way out anyway. What kind of trouble do you think we'll get into? No one from

94

our school is here. No one even knows our names, except Mel."

"And I'm not gonna out you," Melody says. "Think of this as my way of paying you back for helping me. I owe you guys."

The more I think about it, the more logical it sounds. The food here has got to be a zillion times better than what we'd be getting at our prom, and it's for heck sure better than not eating at all if we get there too late. I'm not hitting Taco Bell two nights in a row, or my after-prom at the bluffs will be spent on a toilet instead. And maybe this is another part of my second chance, getting two proms in one night because I completely missed the original. The first prom here, and then another one later, at Beaver Creek High.

My mind is made up, and so is Melody's. We're in sync just like we were last night. Except tonight, everything's clicking into place with Lucy here, too. And once I get to our prom, everything else will be as it should be, with all the right people. Melody gets out of the car and says, "I'll meet you around back in a few minutes."

After she's disappeared through the front doors, I park the car and turn the key. The engine quiets. Lucy doesn't move.

When I turn to look at her, her lips twibble, and that's all it takes to *un*make up my mind.

"If you really don't want to," I say, "we can leave. I won't force you into something you feel that strongly about avoiding. I'll go meet Mel just to tell her forget it."

Her nostrils flare slightly as she forces air in and out of her nose, staring ahead into the dark lot full of cars and trucks and limos. Then her stomach gurgles, sounding like a couple

95

of cats about to either fight to the death or make a litter of kittens . . . and she cracks a smile.

"I've been outvoted by my own body," she says. "This is so typical of you, you know? Nothing can ever go according to plan with you; I don't know why I even try."

Why try so hard to keep something together that's always falling apart?

"That's why we're good together, though," I say, countering my memory of something she said that only I remember. "That's what my parents said. We balance each other out."

She shakes her head noncommittally, still smiling, and pulls out her phone.

"What are you doing?"

"Letting Chaz know we're running late. Well, more late." She finishes the text and slides the phone back into her midnight-blue clutch purse that matches her shoes. "Let's go."

I meet her around the car and walk her across the lot, arm in arm, with *that dress* flowing behind her in the breeze. *That dress* she picked out for me. Her hip bumps against me softly with every step, and all I can smell is her shampoo. I don't even know what to call its scent. It's just "Lucy's shampoo." The same-scented shampoo she's been using for as long as I've known her. Whenever I smell it, my whole body relaxes, because I can only smell it when I'm close to Lucy.

"You sure about this?"

She looks up at me with a dark-lipped smile, just before we slip around the side of the building. "I can be spontaneous, too, sometimes."

96

Lucy from last night, the other tonight, would beg to differ. So which Lucy should I believe? The one who pushed me away for doing what I do best—improvising, going with the flow—or the one who just agreed to be my partner in crime?

All we ever do is stress each other out.

No. She's not thinking that now. She didn't mean it before, either. She was just upset.

My brain keeps jumbling together what's happening tonight and what happened the other tonight, making it all feel like a parallax. Viewing the same thing from the same vantage point but seeing it at two slightly different angles, like when you close one eye, then open it and close the other. You're looking at the same thing, but it shifts. And when I put the two nights together, look at it with both eyes open, rather than having them blend into one fixed clear image, I'm left with a distorted memory of events and details that don't add up.

"Another?" I ask Lucy as she sets an empty cupcake liner onto her plate sprinkled with chocolate crumbs.

"I think we'd better just go," she says, though she's eyeing the dessert table like a lioness about to pounce on a gazelle. "Or I might talk myself into staying here all night."

"I might already be considering it. There are only four empty cupcake liners on my plate. If I don't eat more, it'll burn off too quick when I start dancing. I need my strength, Lucy."

"No," she says sternly but through a smile. "Chaz and Marcos are waiting for us. Jenna, too, for you," she adds, her gaze dropping to her twiddling thumbs.

"Yeah. Jenna, too. I didn't forget." I also didn't forget how Blair was holding her so protectively last night. How she leaned herself into him for support, even after she'd dumped him for plenty of good reasons. How he drove her home after she'd slapped me. How none of that would have happened if I'd been where I was supposed to be. I know we need to get going. Not just that; I *want* to leave. I want to go have fun at *our* prom with *our* friends.

But: "This place is just . . ."

"A dream, for people like us," Lucy fills in. "I know."

The food, as expected, was a glorious experience, in which I consumed a steak so perfect I swear I saw God with every bite. And the hums of pleasure coming from beside me were proof that Lucy's chicken Florentine was just as heavenly. It's an Italian dish, so of course she made a comment about how much she's looking forward to eating at her new school. Italian food made in Italy—you can't get more authentic than that.

I'm happy for her. I really am. I just don't want to think about it tonight.

After Melody let us in, she pointed out an empty table where we could sit. It was actually a service table of some sort, tucked away in a corner, but with two teenagers sitting there in a tux and a fancy dress, the servers assumed we should be fed. *Servers*. I'm pretty sure the food at our prom was "served" buffet style, like horses feeding at a trough. Everything here for Whitman's prom is kind of unreal. From the food to the overly formal, wedding-like decorations to the live band instead of a deejay . . .

"One dance before we go?" I say. Might as well get the full Whitman experience. One dance here won't keep us from spending most of the night as we'd planned. When will we ever be in a place like this again?

But Lucy shakes her head. "I'm too full. And we should leave now anyway, before someone notices we don't belong here."

"Fine, okay," I say through a defeated sigh. "You ready, then?"

"Yeah, I just need to freshen up first."

I nod, and she clacks her midnight-blue pumps with the sturdy heels down a corridor, to the restrooms, leaving me sitting alone on the edges of the main room, watching everyone dance and have a generally good time. Including Melody. She's surrounded by a circle of friends now, friends she was willing to ditch last night. I mean the other tonight. To be fair, though, I ditched my friends, too. So I get it. We're both the same in that way. We just go with whatever happens and find a way to make it work.

Still, I wonder what Marcos and Chaz are doing right now without us. And Jenna. Does she think I let her down? I was supposed to be her plus-one. Well, plus-two, with Lucy.

While Lucy's in the bathroom, I shoot a quick text to Chaz.

Me: Done with dinner leaving now

Chaz: OK see you soon

Melody approaches the table just as I'm putting my phone away. Her forehead is glistening and the rest of her is glowing. Happy. This is where she's supposed to be tonight, not talking to me in my car, waiting for a tow that will never show up.

"You leaving?" she says. "Where's Lucy?"

"Bathroom. Then, yeah, we're leaving. Thanks for this, Mel. It was good. Really good."

"And see? Nothing bad happened." She waves a hand. "No one cares. They're all too worried about their own selves to even notice anyone else—" Her eyes widen as she glances over her shoulder, then she sighs and rolls her eyes. "I'm sorry for whatever is about to come out of this troll's mouth. Just ignore him and I'll handle this."

"Um . . . okay." I follow her gaze to a guy coming off the dance floor and straight for us in the corner. He's blond and beefy, his chest as solid as a brick wall, with a crew cut and sparkling cuff links at his wrists. His cheeks are reddened, most likely from the drink in his hand that I doubt is "virgin," and his smile is more like a leer. Everything about this guy has me on high alert.

"Melody!" he booms, even though he's two feet away now, at most. "Babe. I've been looking for you all night. What're you doing over here with . . . Who're you?" He slinks an arm around her waist, and she immediately removes it.

She's not out. He thinks I'm a threat just because I'm male and he wants her. Fantastic.

"Don't you have some primordial ooze to crawl back into?" Melody says. "Someone let you out early."

Her jab doesn't faze him. "Is this guy your date from another school or something? You told me you didn't want a date for prom. Did you lie to me?"

My muscles tighten and I try to relax them. *Just ignore him,* she said. She'll handle it.

"I didn't lie," Melody says. "He's not my date, he's my friend. And I don't owe you an explanation. He's leaving now, anyway, so—"

"Awesome. Let me show you out, *friend*." He grabs me by the collar, like I'm a kitten that's wandered off from its mother, pulling me up and out of my seat, then dragging me across the room so fast I'm tripping over my feet. Melody shouts something, but her words are lost in the blasting music and the din of the crowd.

"Let go of me!" I don't think; I just start throwing elbows. One of them finds his jaw. I actually hear a crack on impact, and I'm sure I broke his face.

But then my elbow throbs and a million pinpricks sting down the length of my forearm, all the way to my fingertips. It was me who cracked. He's made of concrete, and yeah, I've got muscle, but compared to him I'm a six-foot branch. Thin and easy to snap.

He drops me just short of the exit, tossing me forward at the same time, the force of it knocking my glasses off. They hit the polished hardwood and some jerk kicks them aside. Everything blurs. A colorful blob has gathered around—a crowd. They're here to see a fight. Before I can plan a block, let alone an escape, Tank Boy rears back a fist and punches, sending me sprawling against the crowd. They so helpfully step away, and I slide to the floor like syrup. My eye throbs and swells shut. Now I *really* can't see.

"Who is that?" a girl says. "Is he with someone? How'd he even get in here?"

The questions and murmurs continue as the crowd dissipates, then Melody appears in front of me. "Oh my God, JJ, are you okay?"

I offer a weak smile. "What were you saying about nothing bad happening?"

Chaos personified, Lucy would say. I can't even be surprised by this.

"That looks bad," Melody says, helping me to my feet. "You want some ice?"

"Yeah. Thank you. I'm sorry. This is . . ."

"Not your fault," she fills in. "Brock and I . . . have a history. I'm sorry you got mixed up in it, but you should probably leave. People are talking now. I can get the ice and meet you outside?"

"Okay." My ears are buzzing. My elbow is tingling. My whole face hurts. I can barely make out there are doors ahead of me. I push through the exit, into the dark, cool night air, unable to decipher anything clearly but the giant mermaid fountain. So I follow the sound of trickling water until I find the edge of it, and sit.

The mermaid stares down at me. Her expression is equal parts innocent and judging. This place really is a fantasy world, inside and out. I should have known better than to try to fit in somewhere I was never meant to be. And now, somehow, I have to drive. There's an extra pair of glasses in my car, but my one eye is swollen shut. I'm sure that'll work out just fine. Right. But what else can I do? We have to get to our prom and Lucy doesn't drive. At least not legally. She does know how, she just hasn't had a reason to get her license yet, not when I'm always available to take her anywhere.

Well . . . she's about to get some unexpected practice, and hopefully we won't get stopped by any cops. I need her to drive us to our prom now.

She's really not going to like this. But it's the best improvisation I can think up.

I attempt to text her, and that plan goes nowhere fast with my eye problem. So I call her instead. She picks up before the end of the first ring.

"JJ?" she says through the phone. "Where are you?"

"Outside. By the fountain. Where are you?"

"On my way. I came out of the bathroom and you were just *gone*, so I was looking for you and then I found Melody instead and she gave me some ice for you." Her words are breathy, and I can hear the music in the background. She's still inside. "Why do you need ice?"

"I got punched in the face."

"What! Why?"

"This guy . . . he just hit me."

Something on her end clunks at the same time I see the front door open in my side vision. "For no reason?" she says. I hear her through the phone and also in person. She's close.

"It's a long story."

"Of course it is." She sighs. "All you had to do was stay where you were and wait for me. Why was that too hard?"

As her breaths pant through the phone, I hear her shoes

clacking against the sidewalk. Closer and closer. Until she's right in front of me.

"That looks really bad," she says, more subdued. "Does it hurt?"

"A lot."

She hands me a small plastic baggie full of crushed ice.

"Thanks." When I hold it against my eye, it stings. I let out a hiss.

"How are you gonna . . . ?" she starts.

I don't need her to finish. I fish the keys out of my pocket and hold them out to her.

"JJ."

"Please?"

"I can't drive."

"Yes, you can. I'm the one who can't right now."

"What if we get pulled over?"

"We won't," I assure her.

"You don't know that."

"I know we don't have a better option."

She takes the keys with a resigned sigh and sits next to me on the lip of the fountain, close enough that her body heat warms my side. And I start to relax. But then she says, "Why did I think we could have a nice prom night together without anything going wrong?"

"This was a total fluke," I counter. "How could I have possibly prevented someone from punching me for no reason?"

"Easy," she says. "By not being here in the first place. But it's not like we can go back in time and try again for a perfect prom night. There are no second chances."

Except I *was* given a second chance, and it still came to this. I'd take a punch to the face over Lucy in the hospital any day of the week—*every* day of the week if I had to—but she doesn't know what happened before, so to her, this is probably the worst-case scenario. I'm half-blind and bleeding, and she, a non-driver, has to drive us to prom. In the dark. On winding country roads. And hopefully not land us in a ditch or hit a deer or something. Really, cops are the least of our worries.

"Stay here," she says, and stands. "I'll pull the car up."

"Okay." Not arguing with that. Since we were late, almost all the spots were taken. It's a long trek to my car, all the way across the lot, and I don't trust my vision right now.

As she walks away, all I can do is shake my head. Why did I get a do-over just to steer it wrong again? Is that how it will always be with us?

We're too opposite, and it only creates problems.

Lucy didn't want to have dinner here. It was my idea, and she just went along with it. She wanted us to drop Melody off and leave. Yeah, we were both hungry, but we would have arrived at our prom in twenty minutes, tops. Has anyone ever died of starvation in twenty minutes? *Have they, JJ, you colossal screwup?*

Looking back, the answers are clear. I wish I could see those things in the moment.

"I tried," I say to no one. And at least this time she didn't break up our friendship over it. At least I didn't lose her. We'll be okay. We're still going to prom. We'll still have our after-prom. Everything will be fine; I'll just see only half of it.

With my good eye, I notice a small dog, or a cat, or something is walking toward me. I turn my head to look and . . . it's not a dog or cat at all. It's a groundhog.

Out here? In a parking lot? At night?

Headlights snap my attention the other way, and I catch Lucy's silhouette in the distance. The lights shine brightly, coming straight up from behind her . . . like they don't even see her.

Is that person drunk?

This is prom night. The possibility is high.

"Lucy!" I shout at the top of my lungs.

She stops. *No.* "What?" she yells back.

The car has room to go around her. She's probably assuming it will. And maybe I'm wrong, thinking it won't—*please let me be wrong*—but I start running toward her. The closer I get, the better I can see the disaster unfolding.

"What is that?" she says. "A woodchuck?"

She takes a step toward the groundhog, making shooing motions, and the thing freezes. In the middle of the lane, just like last night when I almost hit one on the road.

Just like last night . . .

I understand the parallax now. The events of the two nights have merged into one fixed image that's crystal clear. I'm going to lose her again, but differently this time.

Tonight proved we'd both be better off away from each other.

Lucy said this was preventable, and she was right. We

shouldn't have been here in the first place. Then I wouldn't have gotten mixed up in Melody's "history" with that human tank, and he wouldn't have punched me, and Lucy wouldn't have had to drive us anywhere, and she wouldn't be in this parking lot right now, just as this mindless person is behind the wheel.

Still, I try to stop the inevitable. Because *I can't lose her.*

I run faster, pumping my legs as hard as I can. "Lucy, *move!*"

The oncoming car swerves to avoid the groundhog—because that's more visible than a person?—and swerves right toward Lucy. Definitely drunk. Tires screech and squeal loudly. Lucy's screaming and I'm screaming and the groundhog's mouth drops open like it's screaming, too.

But the crash never happens. Lucy, the car, the pavement, *the whole world* disappears and I slip into a cold black void.

the NIGHT of the SOLAR FLARE

With a scream still in my throat, I'm no longer outside in the dark, my feet aren't moving, and I'm staring at my blurred reflection in the mirror hanging off my closet door, a bright white light flashing behind my eyes and the walls vibrating. I look around, get my bearings, and find my balance. I'm back in my room, getting ready to fasten my bow tie, which hangs limply in my hand.

It's happening again. The same night repeating.

But that means Lucy is okay. Right? We're back to square one, nothing bad has happened yet. Please, please, *please* let this mean she's okay—

Marty lets loose a few blue sparks from where I left him on my desk Friday after school, and the vibrations ease off. I stamp out the sparks in the carpet, then check the bottom of my Cons for scorch marks. Nothing. Good. But the piece of . . . junk . . . is . . . fritzing . . .

My thoughts slow. I stop and stare at the thing as realization hits me. Is *that* the reason for this? Could it be possible it's actually working? Kind of. Marty's obviously broken, but he did *something*. He manipulated the passage of time—not just manipulated but totally twisted it back on itself into a loop. More than once now.

Oh my heck. It's working! Lucy is going to *flip. Out.*

As soon as I figure out how to tell her, that is. How am I going to explain this when no one else seems to be affected by it? I'm the only one who remembers anything from the previous days. I . . . I could potentially be stuck in this loop forever, and no one would know because who would believe me?

But I'll worry about that later. For now, it's a good thing. It's given me a chance to make sure Melody makes it to her prom *and* I get to my own prom, too, with Lucy and Jenna. No sidetracks, just drop Melody off and go. Or . . . I could save even more time if I call in a reliable tow for her, then stay out of it. She doesn't need me to drop her off. But then . . . we'll never meet. We'll never have a chance at our friendship. Is getting to my prom *on time* worth losing that?

I'm the only one who'd be losing anything. She would never know the difference. So I don't know what the right answer is with Melody.

Lucy, on the other hand . . . easy. Just get us to prom the way we're supposed to.

I pull out my phone. The last message from Lucy is the same as it was at the start of the previous nights.

Lucy: Where are you?

Me: Leaving soon

I'm not going to screw this up again. I adamantly refuse to let *anything* go wrong tonight. But first—

Me: Leaving soon

Lucy: Is something wrong with your phone? The same text came through again.

No, I just had to be sure she's really okay.

Me: Weird. I'll restart it. See you in a few

"Knock, knock," Mom says on the other side of my door. "Are you decent?"

"Yeah, come in." I pocket my phone and step back up to the mirror. *What the— Oh no.*

Mom steps up behind me, and I catch her reflection in the mirror. Her eyes widen with horror. "What happened to your face!"

My left eye is an ugly shade of purple. Not swollen and bloody like before, though, and it doesn't hurt anymore. Like it's had time to start healing already. But it's been less than a half hour, my time. *My time.* As if that even makes sense. Everything else reset, though, why didn't my face?

"I . . . uh . . . clumsy," I try. "When I was cleaning stalls earlier, I hit myself with the manure fork. It was . . . I was over-excited about tonight and wasn't thinking. I got clumsy." I force a grin. "You think anyone will notice?"

"Yes!"

"I was kidding."

"I could put some makeup on it," she offers.

"Thanks, but no. I'm running late."

She sighs then, and notices the slip of fabric hanging from my fist. "Did you forget how to tie it? After all that time we spent learning on YouTube."

"No, I . . . well, yes, I did . . . before . . . but I think I remember now." I ignore her arched brow and give it a try. My fingers fumble a bit, but then I get it.

I got it. This is the first of many things that will be different tonight.

"There ya go," Mom says with a smile as big as mine. "Much better." Then her gaze drops and her smile falters again. "Is that a stain on your shirt? How did you manage to do that, James, for goodness' sake, what is with you today?" She shakes her head. "I'll see if I can get it out, hold on."

The stain from Taco Bell is back, though not fully. It's more like a shadow of a stain, which is probably why I didn't notice it until she pointed it out. But it's definitely the same blob shape I remember from the first night with Melody. And that's not the only thing—I'm wearing my glasses. I should be wearing my contacts if the night is resetting at this point.

Just when I think I've got it figured out, something changes. I need someone to talk to about this, bounce my thoughts off of, and come up with a theory. I need Lucy.

And that can't happen if I don't get myself together and get moving.

My eyes aren't dry and burning this time. She likes when I wear contacts. Yes, I can do that for her. One of my eyes is discolored and bloodshot, but it's the thought that counts, right? I step into the hall to cross from my room to the bathroom, and Shayla bumps into me.

Let me guess, she wants to dance?

"Look at you all fancy!" she squeals, but then she sees my

face and it's like watching someone receive news that their dog died. "What happened—"

"Nothing, it's fine."

"Then let's dance." She grabs my hands.

I indulge her because I made her mad last time and I haven't done anything real with her in days, even if in her mind she just saw me this afternoon—but only for a moment. I have to get out of here. Melody and Lucy are both counting on me, though they don't know it yet. Satisfied with our impromptu hallway dance, Shayla thunders off again, a human tornado on a mission to who knows what. Okay, what was I doing?

Contacts, in. Eye drops, in. I'm dressed. Lucy has the tickets. What's left? Keys.

After I run into my room to grab them and turn to leave again, Mom stops me at the doorway. "Let me dab that stain a little." She sprays. She dabs. She grunts. "Maybe just keep your jacket on."

"Will do. Gotta run." I kiss the top of her head.

And then Mama shows up with her phone held high. "Can I get a picture before you— What happened to your eye?"

Sigh. I'd better get used to this question tonight. "Nothing to worry about. It doesn't even hurt." And I've lived this twice before now; you'd think I would remember her photo shoot was coming.

"Okay." Mama frowns at her phone. "Oh, I already have some pictures. Never mind."

Huh. That's new . . .

Mom peeks at the phone. "Ooh, those are nice! Looks like

you had a fun photo shoot without me." She pouts at me, then looks at the phone again. "Wait . . . your eye looks normal in these? When did you . . . ?"

I stare back and forth between them, trying to think on my feet. That's what I do. That's what I'm good at—improvising, going with the flow. Making things work when the unexpected happens. But right now, absolutely no plausible explanation I can offer, real or fake, is coming to mind. Everything is supposed to reset, not carry over from night to night. And those pictures aren't even from last night; she took them on the first night, the original night. Same with the Taco Bell stain. So . . . some of this stuff is sticking—which is strange enough by itself—but not every time?

And I won't know what will stick or not stick until it either happens or doesn't happen. This could get interesting.

"Go on, JJ," Mama says. "Don't keep Lucy waiting. You know how she is."

"Yeah, I know how she . . ." Wait, this is backward. I said *You know how she is* the last two times—I think?—and then they said—*Stop*, it doesn't matter who said what. I need to go. Things will be different this time. It'll be better. I'm making sure of it.

I can still have a fun senior prom, even with a black eye and a stained tux. I can still have the night of my life.

Mom opens her mouth to add something, but I say it before she can, spouting off all the "going out" rules as I rush down the hall and downstairs.

"Remember to get a picture of you and Lucy together!" she shouts after me.

Oh, right, I did forget to do that yesterday—the second today? I've got to start keeping track of these, and numbers will be the easiest way. Numbers are always logical and make sense. Numbers will keep me focused in all this. So tonight is number three. And as Mama likes to say, third time's a charm.

My third approach toward Dead Man's Curve on the third attempt of the same night, I turn onto Huffman Road after letting a cream-colored black-top convertible Volkswagen Beetle pass at the intersection. That's Melody. I got here early. She's driving a little over the speed limit, and I keep a few car lengths between us because I know she's about to have an incident. Even at this distance, I can see her head bebopping to whatever's playing on her radio. She has no idea what's coming.

Her brake lights glow red as she approaches the curve, and even though I know she isn't going to crash or get hurt, I squeeze my steering wheel and wring my hands over it, wishing I was blissfully ignorant of the next few seconds. My heart beats faster, harder.

"It's okay, Mel. You're gonna be fine." I already called AAA right before leaving my house. The tow is on its way. She's gonna be fine.

She dips out of view on the downward curve, so I don't see what happens next. I hear it.

BOOM. Like a bomb going off. And then immediately after, tires screeching to a halt.

When I get to the bottom of the curve, she's lifting up the hood. Smoke billows out, but the breeze quickly clears it. I pull up alongside her car and open my passenger-side window.

"You okay? That sounded like an explosion."

"I'm fine," she says without looking at me. "Thanks for checking, but I got this."

"If your engine blew, you're gonna need a tow."

"Might not be that serious . . ." She starts tinkering with stuff under the hood, then goes to the trunk and pulls out an armful of random objects, including a yellow plastic funnel. "I can handle this," she says, passing me on her way back to the front of her car. "You can go now."

"Would you mind if I waited until you're all set? Just in case you might need something. I'll stay in my car. Okay?"

"That isn't necessary," she says.

"It's also not a problem," I counter.

She sighs, still focused under the hood. "Fine, if you've got time to waste. Do whatever."

That's as close to a yes as I'm going to get from her. I pull my car alongside the ditch to park in front of her, and my phone chimes with a text.

Lucy: On your way yet?

I tell her yes, I'll just be a little late. Emphasis on little. Then I text Jenna and kindly suggest she get a ride from Autumn Mitchell because I heard she rented a limo—*have fun with that and I'll see you there!*

Jenna: Okie dokie ☺

Am I forgetting anything? I check on Melody through my rearview mirror. Her Creamsicle dress billows in my side vision, and I turn my head to see her crossing the road, chasing the funnel. Everything is happening the same way so far, nothing's changed. My tow will be here in a few minutes and then the night can move on as planned.

I've got this figured out now. I'm not going to miss my prom again.

Melody sits in her car. She leaves the driver's side door open and sits with her legs hanging out. She's texting someone. Probably to tell them she's running late. She did the same thing on night one, while we were sitting in my car together, getting to know each other. Discussing her theories on the non-existence of time. The back of my throat tightens. Am I ever going to have that version of her again?

It's only been a couple of minutes, but I'm starting to doze off. I just realized—I haven't actually slept in three days? But they weren't full days, so . . . I don't know . . . maybe a day and . . . a half . . .

Flashing amber lights jolt me awake. The tow truck. I straighten and stretch, as well as a six-foot person can inside a Honda Civic, and blink a few times rapidly, letting my contacts readjust. My eyes are drying out already, so I press them closed for a second. When I open them again, the service woman exits the truck and approaches my car, so I get out.

"Someone call for a tow?" she says.

"Yeah, over here," Melody says, but then she looks confused. "You're not from the place I called."

"I called this tow," I tell her, "but that was for you. I knew they'd come quicker than anyone else. Don't worry about paying, either, it's fine. On my parents' account. They don't mind me helping people. They actually encourage it." I'm rambling—because I'm worried. What if tonight doesn't go as well with her simply because everything was handled quickly? What if we don't become friends simply because we didn't have time to form a connection?

"Oh." She smiles slightly, then shrugs even slighter. "Thanks."

"It's JJ."

"Okay. Thanks, JJ." She starts talking to the service woman, leading her to her car.

She thinks I'm a stranger. Why do I have to give up the good I had with Melody to make sure nothing bad happens to Lucy? Why is Melody's friendship the price I have to pay for keeping Lucy in my life? How is that fair to any of us?

They finish with her car and I watch it get hooked up behind the tow. It's just starting to get dark now, and the sunset ... *whoa*. The sunset has looked different every night. The same mix of colors with the same intense vibrancy, but strewn across the sky in a slightly different array. Does that mean the days are actually different, even though they're not? So far I'd only been thinking about how this time loop has affected me personally, but now my astronomy brain can't help but wonder how it's affecting the solar system. The sun, the way the world spins to create night and day in the first place. The whole universe.

"You giving her a ride home?" the service woman asks me. "Or . . . where are you two going, anyway?"

"Prom," I say at the same time Melody says, "Nowhere together. I don't know him."

"I can give you a ride, it's not a problem. I'm already on my way to pick up my friend for our prom." I pull out my phone and flash her a few pictures of me and Lucy. "We can get her and then drop you off at your prom—I assume that's where you're going, but I've never seen you at my school before—then we'll never have to see or hear from each other again. If that's what you want. Totally up to you. But it's gotta be better than riding in a tow truck, right?" I shoot the service woman an apologetic glance. "No offense."

Melody looks away from both of us, staring quietly at her car, hitched up and useless, her brows pinched in a way that clearly indicates her mind is loud with thought even if her mouth is shut. And so is mine. There are so many things I want to say to her that I can't.

At our continued silence, the service woman hops up into her truck. "Let me know when you two got this sorted out."

"Do you believe in fate?" I say, and Melody snaps her face toward me.

"What's that got to do with anything?"

"Because fate means everything happens for a reason. And I think us meeting like this falls under *everything*. Don't you?"

Finally—*finally*—she gives me her thousand-watt grin that lights up the night.

"Why are you smiling like that?" Lucy says after we drop off Melody at the Frost Center for Fine Entertaining. We passed the mermaid fountain and kept on going. She goes to a swanky art school, but even their fancy school gym wasn't fancy enough to hold their prom. Lucy and I are on our way to Beaver Creek

High now, where we'll have a decidedly unswanky prom in an unfancy rural high school gym.

It may not be a fantasy world, but it's exactly how it's supposed to be. And that's why I can't stop smiling.

Melody is where she should be—she even exchanged numbers with me again—and I'm where I should be—with Lucy. Let her be mad I showed up with a black eye and a mystery girl. She has no idea how much worse this could have gone. How much worse it has already gone before.

"We're late," she continues, "and your eye looks awful. That's nothing to smile about. How are we going to get pictures like this? Papà wanted pictures and we had to rush out. We can't afford the photographer here."

Oh. That. Why do I keep forgetting? I turn into the school parking lot. It's so full we have to go all the way back by the football stadium to find an empty spot. We never have to park here on school days because Lucy always makes sure we're here on time, and her definition of *on time* is the rest of the world's definition of *early*.

"This'll be gone by tomorrow," I tell her once we're parked. "Like it was never there." Because tomorrow will be a new version of today, completely reset. Mostly . . . I tug my jacket closed, covering the leftover Taco Bell stain from night one. Thankfully, Lucy hasn't noticed it yet. Probably because this rancid black eye keeps pulling her attention to my face.

"First of all," she says, "nothing heals that fast. Second of all, we need it to be gone tonight, not tomorrow. Right now. And third of all, who's going to take the shots for us?"

"Chaz will do it."

"He's a terrible cell phone photographer. You've seen his Instagram."

I have, and she's right. But what she's wrong about is assuming any of this matters. We're here—together—that's all that matters. "It'll be fine," I assure her. "And we'll just edit out my eye problem."

I wish I could edit it out right now, like Lucy wants. Get it off my face. But it's a small price to pay for everything going smoothly for once. Even if Lucy is being . . . very *Lucy* at the moment.

She sighs and unbuckles her seat belt. "All right, come on. We already missed dinner. Let's hope they haven't put all the food away yet." She reaches for her door handle and I touch her elbow, snatching her attention.

"Lucy, listen to me for a sec." Big smile, even bigger than before. "It's going to be okay. We made it. We're a little late—"

"And hungry."

"Very hungry," I agree. "But we're here. This is prom! All we have to do for the rest of the night? Is *have fun*. So let's just have fun, okay?"

She stares at me for what feels like an hour before one side of her mouth ticks up and she says, "I know, I know—this is your big night."

"*Our* big night," I clarify. "Together. Like we planned."

"Okay." Her smile broadens, bright white teeth against dark-red lips. "I'm counting on you to make this night the most fun I've had in a long time."

"Hey, hey, long time no see," I say to Marcos as Lucy and I settle into the two empty chairs across from him and Chaz. Jenna is sitting with her friends at the table next to ours, and Blair is at a table on the opposite side of the dance floor—aka our gym's basketball court. They're both doing a very poor job of trying to look like they're not looking at each other.

Marcos is Puerto Rican, a talented poet and playwright, and my oldest friend in our group. He's also Chaz's boyfriend of almost four years and they're dressed to complement each other tonight, both wearing wine-red accents with their tuxes. Marcos draws his black brows together. "What're you talking about, JJ, I just saw you yesterday in English class. You miss me that much?"

My throat catches as I realize my slip. For me it's been days since we last sat together in English class, but for him it's been a little more than twenty-four hours.

The silver glitter blush on Marcos's light-brown cheeks twinkles in the low light as he turns toward Chaz. "Didn't I tell you he had a crush on me? After five years of tiptoeing around the obvious, my boy's finally coming clean."

How has it been five years already? Marcos came out to me as pansexual in middle school when he asked me to go to the Snowball Dance with him and I apologized for being straight. Fortunately, we remained friends after that, and when he started dating Chaz freshman year, it brought Lucy and me closer together. We'd met the same night Marcos and Chaz did, at our first party as high schoolers. And we just . . . clicked.

Then the summer before senior year, our friendship changed into something I'd never had with anyone else before. Physical touch that had previously been reserved for highly emotional moments suddenly became "everyday" between us. Hugs, holding hands, cuddling, just being close. I assume this started because Lucy stopped dating—for a mysterious reason she claims is no big deal—and I guess she still needed someone to provide that physical comfort she was used to getting.

I never pushed her to explain, and I never minded stepping into that role. It's become a comfort for me, too. And we make a nice foursome with Marcos and Chaz, without Lucy's significant-other-of-the-moment tagging along in our group, forcing me to either skip out on them, or be the fifth wheel. The spare tire that no one thinks about unless there's a problem.

To my left, Lucy watches the caterers clear the buffet, her leg bouncing beneath the table, no doubt sending telepathic signals that they better not forget the conversation she had with them a literal minute ago that we didn't eat yet. Gently, I rub my palm over her back, which is bare at the top in *that dress*, sending my own telepathic signal. *Everything's gonna be okay.*

Her leg stops bouncing. She leans into my touch, and her shoulders drop as she releases a long, slow breath. All of this without a word or even looking at me. It makes me wonder what the absolute heck she was thinking on night one, when she said we're no good for each other. That we're better off apart. How could she really believe that?

"I'm flattered," Marcos is saying, pulling my attention from

Lucy, though my hand stays with her. "But I'm also taken." He slides an arm across Chaz's shoulders and kisses his cheek, and then Chaz says, "Nothing personal, bub, we're just not into sharing."

"You can both shut up now," I say with a smile.

They don't, though, and I don't stop smiling, either. While Lucy and I are eating, Marcos and Chaz concoct stories for how I got my black eye. One of their ideas involves an alien invasion, another one involves a zombie bite, another has me in an audition to be a stuntman, but my favorite is the one where I chased Rainbow Brite onto a rainbow up into the clouds and her horse, Starlite, back-kicked me in the face. I would know better than to get that close behind a running horselike creature, but I give them points for making me laugh so hard I snort my drink.

"And why was I chasing her in the first place?" I ask after swallowing my last bite of chicken cordon bleu. Sounds like prime cuisine, but it wasn't great. Dry and flavorless. I've been spoiled by the steak from last night. But actually, even Taco Bell would have been better than this. The only good thing about this dinner is that coffee is available at the drink buffet. I might get through the whole night now that I'm heavily caffeinated.

"Because she's cute?" Lucy offers.

"What?" I say with semi-feigned shock. "*Lucy.* No. Rainbow Brite is not cute—not in the way you're implying. She's a child."

"Technically," Marcos interjects, "Miss Brite is way older than you. Like, pushing forty? She's a colorful cougar. Rawr."

123

"Still a no," I say, and toss a crumpled paper napkin at him. "Five years up or down, that's as far as I'll go."

"So you'd date a twelve-year-old?" Chaz says. That smirk on his face is begging to be smacked right off.

"The five years down doesn't start until I'm twenty-three, okay, we both have to be legal. Are we really having this conversation? I can't believe we're having this conversation. You guys are the worst." Actually they're the best. I love my friends. How did I get so lucky?

"My mistake," Lucy says, serious while the other two are laughing. "I thought you had a thing for blondes." Her gaze jumps to the dance floor, where Jenna is gyrating to the music that started up while we were eating.

Jenna and the prom committee really did do a good job with the decorations—even better than Whitman's prom, which felt more like a celebrity wedding reception. Our theme this year is Once Upon a Time, and the whole gym looks like it was plucked out of a fairy tale. The photo booth is shaped like a castle, complete with a drawbridge to step up into it. An ornate pair of fake-gold thrones sits proudly on the temporary stage, beside the deejay's speakers, ready for the prom king and queen to soak up their glory after they're crowned. Strings of white lights are strewn everywhere overhead, like fairies flying around between the colorful streamers. Even the floor and tables have been sprinkled with confetti-like pixie dust. Prom is in full swing.

"But maybe it's just *that* blonde," Lucy adds, still watching Jenna.

"You wanna dance?" Chaz suddenly asks Marcos. He stands

and pulls Marcos up by the hand, not giving him a choice. "We should dance now, let's go dance." They disappear in the crowd, leaving me and Lucy alone at the table.

Okay. Chaz knows something that Lucy isn't telling me. "Do you have a problem with Jenna?" I say, trying not to sound agitated, but the music is loud and I have to project my voice.

Lucy turns in her seat to face me. The overhead lights are dim, and the flickering faux candle on our table gives her face a glow, highlighting the warm undertones. She folds her hands in her lap, but her thumbs twiddle. "I don't have a problem with Jenna. I've never had a problem with Jenna for as long as I've known her. What I have a problem with is you not telling me what's going on with you two. Since when do you keep stuff like that from me?"

"I didn't tell you anything because there's nothing to tell. I offered to go to prom with her as friends because she broke up with Blair"—when was that?—"Thursday night."

"Oh. I heard it was the other way around. That he broke up with her."

"Heard from who?"

"Blair's whole sob story was posted on the student message board this morning. I had just enough time to read it before a teacher deleted it."

I never check that pointless board. "Yeah. Exactly," I say. "That's why Jenna's so upset. He cheated on her and now he's spreading lies. I was just trying to help her out . . . and I messed that up. She had to come here without me and face the rumors alone."

Lucy arches a brow toward the dance floor. "Whatever happened when she first got here, she seems to be over it now."

"I see that." She's clearly having fun, throwing it in everyone's faces that she's doing just fine without Blair. Jenna doesn't really need me, either. Whatever I thought was going to happen with her tonight? Was probably wrong.

As soon as I realize that, I also realize I don't care. She doesn't leave a hole inside me that needs filling, like when Lucy . . .

Don't think about it. She's with you now and you're here to have fun. Who knows if this night will repeat again like the others? Maybe it will, maybe it won't. *Carpe noctem.* Seize the night, whichever night I'm in, and forget about the others.

"I'm ready to dance," I say, pushing out of my chair. "You coming?"

Lucy shakes her head. "I need to let my food settle first. Go ahead."

"I can wait with you, if you want."

"No, it's fine. Go have fun. Don't worry about me."

Don't worry about me.

I'm hesitant to leave, but hovering will only make her push me away. So I slip out onto the dance floor, squeezing between writhing, sweaty bodies, just far enough in that I'm not on the outside edge. Through the crowd, I can still see her in case she needs anything.

Jenna spins, then stops her rotation when she sees me. "JJ! You made it, finally!"

Does she mean the dance floor or prom in general? Because I was sitting at the table right next to hers for a while— *Stop overthinking.* "Yeah, I made it," I say, and break out a set of jazz hands. "Ta-da!" Oh God, no, that was— Just shut up and dance.

"Are you okay?" Her thin brows draw together. "What happened to your eye?"

"This is nothing. You should see the other guy." Yeah . . . not a mark on him.

Several songs later, Jenna and I have become the center of attention. We found our sync pretty quick, and she's got some killer moves. A circle of people has formed around us, hooting and hollering and urging us on. Jenna's smile is big and bright, her laughter lost in the noise. As this song pumps out its finale, I lift Jenna by the waist and spin us a full turn with her facing the crowd. She's as thin and flexible as a willow branch. All I can see is the white sparkly fabric of her dress, like glittering moondust. Cheers ring out as she reaches toward everyone and slaps them all high fives.

We may be dorks, but at least we're dorks having fun.

When the song ends, the next one starts up slow. I bring Jenna back down until her strappy heels touch the floor. Everyone either couples up or drifts off to the sides. I check my table—Lucy's still sitting there, studying something on her phone. Not worrying that I'm dead. Not having an anxiety attack. Not out in the parking lot, in the path of an oncoming car.

Jenna turns to face me. Her loose-curled platinum-blond hair looks windblown, her pale skin above the crisscross neckline of her dress glistening with a fine sheen of sweat. Her fire engine–red lips spread wide, showing a familiar, contagious smile.

"Do you wanna—" I start at the same time she says, "I need a break."

"Okay," I say, shifting gears. "Yeah, me too. Good idea."

She nods and goes to the drink buffet, where she's immediately surrounded by her posse. Some of them shoot curious glances my way as the others are talking, as if they've never seen or heard of me. Like I'm some stranger who popped into Jenna's life rather than someone who's been going to the same school as they have for years. We just moved in different circles. As in, when I moved in a straight line down the hall, they moved in circles to get away from me.

I'm roasting. I take off my tux jacket and roll up the sleeves of my shirt, hoping the Taco Bell stain isn't noticeable in the dim light. I glance downward and . . . it's gone? Either Mom's stain lifter worked on a delay or this is another glitch. Maybe time caught up with itself and realized that stain doesn't belong in tonight's version of tonight. Or . . .

This is giving me a headache. I fill a glass with ice water from the pitcher someone left on our table while I was away.

"Aren't you Mr. Popular?" Lucy says in a joking tone. She puts her phone in her purse and she's grinning.

"Were you taking pictures of me?"

"Not exactly."

"Then what exactly?" I down the entire glass of water in three big gulps.

"Video," she says.

"You mean blackmail."

Her smile is downright devious. "All you have to do is spend the rest of your life as my servant, James Jeremiah Johnson, and no one will ever see it."

"You don't have to blackmail me for that, Lucilla Viola Bellini," I quip. "All you have to do is ask."

Her smile drops and a furious blush appears on her cheeks. She looks away, turns her whole body, but even from the side I can see her lips twibble. Great, I embarrassed her.

But I don't take it back or try to pass it off as a joke. I meant every word. And what does it matter, anyway; this time tomorrow—the next today—she might not even know I said it. *Just let it roll.*

I wipe my sweaty face and neck with a napkin and look out at the dance floor. Chaz and Marcos aren't so much dancing as they are swaying in place while they make out. One of Blair's soccer buddies and his gymnast girlfriend pass them, making gagging noises and sticking out their tongues like the PDA is a poisonous gas. As if they haven't done that themselves in the halls at school once or twenty times. Blair and Farah Justice pass them next, and Farah leans toward them, saying something that I can't hear. Simultaneously, and without breaking their mouths apart or even looking to the side, Chaz and Marcos flip her off. Farah scowls and Blair tugs her away from them.

Lucy and I both laugh, and then our faces snap toward each other. I hadn't realized she was watching, too. Just like that, the awkwardness of a moment ago is gone. The end of that slow song blends into the start of another. The opening notes ignite a familiar warmth down my spine, and from there it spreads out to every other part of my body. I'm still looking at Lucy, in *that dress* she chose to wear for me, when the warmth hits my chest like a burst of flames, in this blue vest I chose to wear for her—and I extend a hand.

"Yeah, I know, I *have* to dance now," Lucy says. "This is our song." She takes my hand and gets up, then loops her arm into mine, leading me out onto the floor.

I've slow danced with Lucy before, to this song and others. At homecoming every year, at parties, at summer festivals in "downtown" Beaver Creek, and at backyard cookouts. She always leads. There's no point in fighting her natural tendency to take charge. Our rhythm is smoother that way, in dancing, in everything. This time, she doesn't move us around much, and halfway through the song, she slides her hands up and clasps them together behind my neck, leaving me no choice but to drop my hands to her waist. They settle in the dip there perfectly, and I resist the urge to pull her close against me.

Not here, with so many people around us. They'd get the wrong idea. They'd start rumors that would be too easy to believe.

She looks up at me with those big brown eyes, staring with a sense of wonder, like she's found some precious treasure. I can't guess what she's thinking, but at least I know it's good. I stare back down at her, keeping our gazes locked, and one side of my mouth ticks up as the rest of the room dissolves around us. Colorful balloons and streamers fade to black. Formal dresses and suits become stardust and blow away. There's nothing but Lucy and me and this song.

Screw it. I don't care who sees us. If anyone asks, I'll claim I was under the magical influence of prom night. It wouldn't be a lie. I slide my arms behind her and tighten my grasp until she's right up against me. She shifts her arms so they're beneath mine now, squeezing my torso, and then she lays her head on my chest and closes her eyes. If this isn't the most perfect moment of my life, I can't imagine what would ever top it.

A bright white light flashes, and for a second my throat tightens with panic, thinking the night is going to stop right here and restart—and I'll lose this and her and everything good from tonight because she won't remember it—but when my face snaps toward the light at my left, I see Chaz holding up his phone. He got a picture of us dancing, holding each other. Bless him.

"Text that to me," I shout over the music. He gives me a thumbs-up and pockets the phone. Marcos pulls him close, and they disappear in the throng of swaying couples. Lucy looked up, too, but she lays her head on me again. Says nothing, just squeezes me harder, like she's afraid I'll slip away.

Soon, I will. We both will. Very far away from each other, on different sides of the world.

Why try so hard to keep something together that's always falling apart?

Why try, Lucy? This is why. This feeling I have when you hold me like you never want to let go. Don't you feel it, too?

This is us at our best. How can you tell me you don't want our friendship anymore?

Too quickly, the song ends and a new beat picks up into something fast with a thumping bass line. More people crowd in around us, and we break apart. Her hands get fidgety, and her mouth keeps twisting.

"Lucy?" I reach for her, but she takes a step back, bumping into someone, then taking another step, sideways. Both times away from me. "What's wrong?"

"Nothing, I"—her breath hitches—"I need to get some air. It's too crowded in here."

She's panicking. Why is she panicking? We were relaxed and comfortable a literal minute ago.

She turns and heads for the exit. I'm right on her heels, following the galaxy on her dress like I'm chasing the tail of a comet.

"JJ, stop," she says at the door. "I'll be right back. I'm fine."

"You . . . you don't seem fine. Lucy, I know you. You can hide these little tics from other people, but you can't hide them from me."

"I *will be* fine," she clarifies, her voice wavering. Yeah, that's convincing. "I'm just feeling too much at once right now, but it'll go away. It's nothing. Don't worry about me."

Saying that only makes me worry about her more.

Especially when her movements are getting more and more jumpy, like she can't stand in one place, she needs to move. But hearing that phrase again also reminds me of what else she told me on night one. She thinks she stresses me out, and that's part of the reason she was willing to end our friendship.

Afraid I might push her into that again, I raise my palms in surrender. "Okay. This is me not worrying. But if you need anything—"

"All I need is a few minutes alone," she says, and steps out.

As soon as the door shuts behind her, I text Chaz.

Me: Check on Lucy? She went outside doesn't want me to follow. She's upset. No clue what triggered this

I'm not sure where he and Marcos disappeared to, but Chaz's reply comes fast.

Chaz: On it.

Lucy is still outside when they announce the prom king and queen. It's Blair and Jenna, and no one is surprised, but no one knows how to react, either.

To awkward silence, Blair and Jenna step up onto the temporary stage, between the fake thrones and Principal Korver standing there with a mic and confusion in her eyes. Confusion over the lack of thundering applause and everyone's bewilderment, most likely. We the senior class voted them into this and now we're acting like we don't know why they won. Someone from the prom committee walks across the stage and places a gold foil crown on Blair's head, then a tin tiara on Jenna's. They stand next to each other stiffly, with far-off looks in their eyes like they're at a funeral. Then the music starts up again, something decades old and slow and obviously selected to be metaphoric about our upcoming transition into adulthood, and Principal Korver informs us that our king and queen will now lead us in the next dance.

I can't watch this. But I also can't look away. My chest cinches tight. Jenna . . .

Blair takes her by the hand and tugs her out to the middle of the floor. She places both her palms flat against his chest and he does the same to the sides of her waist, and you could probably fit two linebackers comfortably in the space between them. Farah stands at the side with her arms crossed. A few people start laughing and jeering. A few others dance along, telling the others to "shut up and grow up." But it's too easy to find entertainment in someone else's embarrassment, and the mob mentality takes over. It doesn't take long to escalate, and now people are shouting things about Jenna that are wildly untrue, that she's not good enough for him, she was never good enough for him.

Of course they side with Blair over her. Of course they believe his lies. He's not just the prom king; he's king of everyone's hearts at this school. Of course a breakup like theirs, after being the "idol couple" for the entirety of senior year, is the girl's fault for being a slut or something. God forbid a woman can be pretty without people assigning her bad motives for it. And these are the same people who were cheering her on and high-fiving her before. Following the crowd in both situations like mindless sheep.

Jenna's friends try to shout over the insults, but it's useless. No one cares. And I'm just about to step into that space between and take Blair's place as Jenna's dance partner, *just let him try something*, when Blair leans down and whispers in Jenna's ear.

Her eyes light with rage, like blue fire in the dim light. She hauls back and smacks him so hard across the cheek that his recoil knocks the crown off his head. Blair stands his ground and remains outwardly stoic, but I know from experience that had to hurt as much as the punch that gave me this black eye.

Everything goes quiet again, except for the music. Jenna lifts the narrow skirt of her dress and trots off the dance floor. The *clack-clack* of her heels starts loud and gets softer as she pushes past everyone until she's across the room, then she exits into the hall outside the gym.

Blair looks around, rubbing his cheek, swiveling his jaw like he's making sure it still works, and then he steps off, too, in the same direction.

Oh, no you don't.

I push through the crowd and follow him into the same hall that Jenna escaped to, and her friends show up a second later. Blair takes one look at the group of us, and I swear he's going to pulverize me. His stony gray eyes pin me in place and a muscle in his granite jaw ticks.

Jenna's friends call him some very choice words as they pass, then round a corner, and it's clear they found Jenna there when suddenly all of them are talking at once, their voices echoing in an amorphous cacophony. Blair presses his lips together into a firm line. And then . . . he just walks right past me, down the hall, in the opposite direction of Jenna. Whatever he was going to do or say, to either of us, he changed his mind. But still.

"What is your problem?" I say to his back.

He stops. Turns only his head. "She seems to like you, Johnson."

135

For a moment I'm stumped. I didn't think Blair even knew my name—he's the popular guy who everyone knows, not me—let alone knew that Jenna and I had any kind of anything between us. Maybe he saw us dancing tonight? But she was dancing with *everyone*. And he didn't put up any defenses at me getting confrontational. Confused, I ask, "Is that why you're being such a jerk to her?"

He turns the rest of his body to face me, then lowers his voice. "I didn't cheat."

Sure he didn't. "Even if that's true, what about the rest of it? I saw her texts you didn't answer. I heard about the story posted to the message board. I see you avoiding her tonight with Farah Justice hanging on you like an orangutan. And I literally *just* saw you manage to fully enrage a girl whose default mode is to give people the benefit of the doubt. You're not innocent, Blair, not even close."

He sighs. Yeah, being that much of a butt-maggot must be so exhausting. "She needs to hate me," he says. "I needed her to break up with me now, so it wouldn't be harder for her later."

The more he talks, the less I understand.

"Why? What happens 'later'?"

"Not that it's rightly your business, but my father and I are flying back to London after graduation. That very same afternoon. I knew my time in the States wouldn't be permanent. I wasn't supposed to . . . get attached to anything, or anyone." He shakes his head as if clearing away a nasty thought. "It's better this way. She'll move on quickly rather than trying to make a long-distance relationship work, only to watch it fall apart slowly."

136

We should cut this off now, not drag it out, if this is where it's leading eventually anyway.

I wince at the memory. Physically flinch. But Blair's still talking, so I shake those thoughts out of my head.

"I saw that destroy my parents," he says. "I won't put her through it, too."

"But you'll put her through *this*? That's just as bad. No—it's worse."

"I didn't mean for it to go this far," he says. "It slipped out of my control."

"Then you should have thought it through a little more and come up with a better plan."

Wait . . . did I really just say that? Me, Mr. Go-with-the-Flow, is suggesting a plan? This night has been full of surprises. *Every* night has been full of surprises.

Prom was supposed to be a night of harmless fun, and no matter how many times I relive it, someone is getting hurt. On night one, Lucy. Night two, me—*and* almost Lucy again. Then tonight, Jenna. I turn and walk down the hall toward her, leaving Blair to do whatever. I hear his steps continue across the tile, too many for too long to be going anywhere but the exit at the end of the hall. I don't care where he's going or what he does there, as long as he does it far from Jenna.

Unease coils in my gut. Last night ended too early to know what happened between them, but the first night, Jenna ended up back with Blair, on seemingly good terms. He's leaving now, so that isn't going to happen. Because I changed the outcome of prom by actually being here this time? As fast as the feeling washed over me, though, it slides off and away. This is for the best. It has to be. He *hurt* and *humiliated* her. She deserves better than that. Even if his intentions were good, he went about this horribly wrong.

I trip on my next step, just enough to stub my toe with a little *squeak*. Good intentions, horrible outcomes—that sounds a lot like me. But the comparison stops there. I would never do what he did.

The chatter quiets as soon as I round the corner. Jenna's leaning back against a locker with her arms crossed. Her eyes are dry, her makeup still perfect, but her mouth is twisted in a scowl. When she sees me, she straightens.

"Are you okay?" I ask her.

She makes a face at the others. It must be some silent code language they have, because without a word, her friends leave us. "I'm okay," she says. "I'm not going to let him get to me."

And I believe that, to a point. She didn't come out here to cry and complain, but she's definitely upset.

"I'm done with this night," she continues. "Me and my friends are gonna leave early, go have our own little after-prom at my place. No stupid boys allowed." Her brows shoot up and her mouth drops open. "Oh! JJ, I swear, I didn't mean you! You're not a stupid boy. I just meant we're going to make it a girls-only thing. I'm sorry if you were expecting to keep hanging out tonight. I mean, we had fun dancing and I like you, but . . ."

"But not like that," I finish for her. Story of my life.

"Honestly, I think I'm done with *all* guys for a while. I need some me time."

"Yeah." I nod. "Good plan. That'll be good for you."

"Yeah."

"And you did a good job with this," I say, not knowing how to end this conversation. "With prom. The decorations. Everything was good." *Stop saying that word.*

"Except the food."

"Except the food," I agree.

"And being crowned next to that *twit*," she adds, snatching the flimsy tiara off her head. "And . . . the disaster right after."

"Yeah." Sigh. "You're right, it's time to go. Don't look back, Jenna, just run. But maybe, you know, take those heels off first? None of this is worth a broken ankle. You gotta be safe."

She smiles at that. "Says the guy with a black eye."

We laugh together for a minute, then just sort of peter out and sigh in tandem. This is one of those good moments you never forget, something that stays fixed in your memories because there's nothing really special about what happened except how it made you feel. Like someone filled my chest with helium and I could just . . . float away forever and not care.

"The night wasn't a total loss," she says. "Now I know who my real friends are."

That's so Jenna. Able to find the silver lining, no matter how faintly it shines.

She gives me a very sister-like peck on the cheek before making her exit.

Now I remember why I wanted to try with Jenna in the first place. It's hard to not absorb her positive attitude about everything. I was wrong before. I didn't just lose an opportunity with her. I lost a chance to find happiness with someone. That's all I've ever really wanted.

As I head back to the gym, I try to keep smiling, keep my chin up, but the farther I move outside of Jenna's orbit, the more impossible that simple action becomes.

The rest of prom crawls at glacial speed. From my table, I watch everyone else making general fools of themselves on the dance floor—blackmail material, for sure, the longer the night goes on—checking in with Chaz every fifteen minutes or so. The last text he sent me said Lucy is okay, not to worry, she's just trying to sort out some things in her head. Whatever that even means, it could be anything. I've helped her deal with all kinds of garbage over the years, stuff that even Chaz might not know about, and she's done the same for me. That's what best friends do. Why did she push me away, right after she'd been holding me tight?

Marcos sits at the table, hands me a glass of punch. "Last call."

"Thanks." I take a sip, but it's way too sweet. Never mind.

"What's the matter?" he says after reapplying his lipstick. "Aren't you having fun?"

I force a grin. "I am. This is senior prom. It's our reward for surviving four years of high school. I'm having the time of my life." My voice couldn't sound more uninspired.

"That is not the face of someone"—air quotes—"having the time of his life. Is it Lucy? Because Chaz just told me she's okay."

"I know. I'm not worried about Lucy." Well. Not *only* that. "I just . . . I don't know what I'm doing wrong. Why is it so hard to find someone who wants me?"

Marcos gets that scholarly look on his face he always has when he recites one of his poems. "Maybe you've been looking in all the wrong places. Maybe, fam, it's time for you to step into new spaces. Maybe—ever think that you're just trying too hard? Because maybe, just maybe, she's closer than she is far."

"That's very rhythmic advice. But it doesn't make any sense."

Marcos shakes his head. "You really don't get it."

"No, *you* don't get it. You have Chaz. You fell head over heels for each other, like, instantly, and you've been in this . . . *perfect* relationship ever since. You don't know what it's like to not be able to get past a first date, after you waited months to even feel the urge to go on one."

"Our relationship isn't perfect," he says. "But we have different challenges than you do, so why are you comparing yourself to us? We're not wired the same way you are. Things happened the way they happened with us because we're *us*. Not you. And being you isn't wrong. It's just different."

"And makes me completely incompatible." Sigh. "I want what you guys have. Is that too much to ask?"

"No. You deserve to be happy, JJ. I'm sure you'll find the right girl—or maybe she'll find you. You never know what might happen on prom night." He grins. "All I'm saying is keep your options open."

"When did you get so old and wise, Grandpa?" I tease.

Marcos opens his mouth, probably to jar me right back, but then something over my shoulder snatches his attention.

I turn to see Chaz walking toward us, with Lucy a few paces behind. I whisper "thank you" to Chaz as he passes me on his way to Marcos. "Don't thank me just yet," he whispers back. "The night's not over."

I don't have time to ask what he means before Lucy gets close. Normalcy and energy have returned to her demeanor. She hones in on me like a missile on target. "You ready to go watch the meteors now?"

No explanation as to why she was outside for so long or why she got so upset in the first place. She's just on to the next part of our night—only Lucy and me and the stars falling down around us.

Not one argument comes to mind. "Let's get out of here."

Getting here was worth the hike up a rocky incline in the dark, carrying a heavy professional-grade telescope strapped to my back. Lucy had the forethought—of course she did—to bring a pair of shoes she could climb in without breaking or twisting any body parts. Now, at the top of Whip's Ledge, with Beaver Creek, our not-city's namesake, winding through the trees below us, I'm lying back on a thick quilt, staring up at the unobstructed night sky sprinkled with stars.

Lucy is kneeling behind the telescope with the bottoms of her bare feet facing upward next to my head. I'm not generally a foot person, but Lucy has perfect toes. Not too dainty and not too stubby. Is it weird that I think that?

When it's quiet, my thoughts go places they usually wouldn't. Like toe analysis. We're in complete isolation here. Not a sound except for the critters in the woods below.

"Wow," Lucy says, one eye squinted and the other pressed against the scope. She turns one of the dials. "I can see individual pebbles on Pluto with this thing."

"No you can't. It's not that strong."

"It's called hyperbole, JJ."

"And you hyperbolizing anything is called unheard of, Miss Logic."

She shrugs one bare shoulder, still looking through the scope. "Maybe I'm not feeling logical right now."

"Let me mark this historic day on the calendar."

"Shut up," she says, but I catch the side of her mouth upturning.

Teasing each other is just as fun as watching the Eta Aquarids fall. I've heard other people call what we have a "flirtationship." Because from an outside view it sometimes looks and sounds like we're flirting with each other, only *claiming* to be friends.

But we're not. That's just us. Other people don't understand it, and they don't have to. Like Mama says, you are your own measuring stick. Meaning I'm the one who determines what is true about myself and what isn't. Part of my truth is I don't really know how to flirt, let alone build a whole relationship with someone around the illusion of flirting with them. What would even be the point, anyway? And I'm very lucky to have a friend who understands my truth. I'm lucky to have Lucy. I've known that since the day we met.

Everything feels right finally, and we're alone. We can be us without any pressure to curb it. A sudden urge to be more play-ful comes over me. I turn and drag a fingertip lightly down the bottom of her foot.

She squeals, wriggling away from me. "Stop. I hate being tickled."

Liar. "Then why are you smiling?"

"Because tickling makes me laugh, and laughing, even involuntarily, makes me smile. It's not a good smile."

Any smile of hers is a good smile, and she really is lying about the tickling, but maybe she's just not in the mood. "All right," I say. "I'll stop."

She eyes me cautiously for a moment before deciding it's safe to turn her back on me and look through the telescope again.

"Castor," she says.

Okay, I guess we're playing the game. Totally unfair, though, because she can see a million more stars through that tele-scope. At least a million, since we're hyperbolizing.

As I look up, I yawn so wide my jaw aches. The caffeine is wearing off and the nights are catching up with me, but I can't quit this one yet. Things are finally going well. A new streak of white dashes toward the horizon. That's the tenth one since we got here, though many more have fallen that I can't see, swallowed by the moonglow. The cosmos is the closest thing to magic we'll ever get in this world.

I pick out a star. "Vega."

A few beats of silence pass. Then, "Is anything going on with you and Jenna now? Since you kind of . . . connected tonight. You gonna ask her out?"

"No. Nothing's going on. I mean nothing more than what's already been going on. We're friends. Well, no, even that's not the right word. We're more like friendly acquaintances." When she doesn't respond, I say, "Polaris."

"Bellatrix."

We're out of sync, looking at two different sections of the sky. I shift my gaze to line up with hers.

But then she pulls away from the telescope and sits cross-legged next to me, her galaxy dress flowing out all around her. In the moonlight, the stars on her dress seem luminescent. "You wanted to be something other than friends with her?"

I push up so we're sitting facing each other. "Yeah," I admit. "I did. But it's definitely not going to happen. Why does it matter now?"

"Because . . ." She starts fidgeting her hands, clasping them together and breaking them apart, opening and closing her fingers. "I—" she tries again, and her breath hitches. Then she looks up, throwing her head back, showing me her neck, and says, "Capella."

Something's clearly making her nervous. Is she going to break us up again? Does she think I think pursuing Jenna is more important than our friendship?

"Jenna's a great person," I hurry to explain. "That's it. We had fun together, but she isn't lasting. I might not even keep in touch with her after high school. Not like you and Chaz and Marcos. You guys are . . . What's that saying? *Mia cuora, mia anima, mia vita.*"

She lowers her head from stargazing, and the reflection of a meteor flashes in her dark eyes. *"Mio cuore,"* she corrects. "But the rest of it—*perfetto*."

"Then you know what I meant." *My heart, my soul, my life.*

"Yeah, I . . ." Twibble. "I know what you meant." She closes her eyes for a second and mutters something under her breath in Italian, low enough that I can't understand any of it. When she opens her eyes, she lifts her gaze toward the sky again.

"No more stars, game over." I take her hand and squeeze, place my other hand on top, sandwiching it. "I'm here. There's no one else around. You don't have to hold this in, whatever it is. Talk to me."

"Okay." She nods but then shudders. I grab my tux jacket, which was lying on our blanket, and hand it to her. She slips her arms into it and tries to tug it closed. The sleeves are too long and the rest of it doesn't fit over her chest. But she takes a deep breath in, then out, and another. She's relaxing a little.

"Take your time, Lucy. We got all night."

"No, I'm ready now. I'm sorry. This is just really hard."

"You don't have to apologize for that."

"I know, I know, I'm doing this all wrong."

"You're not—"

"If you want me to talk, JJ, then let me talk."

Right. *Be patient.* And for this, for Lucy, being patient means being quiet. I mime zipping my lips, locking them, and throwing away the key.

She shakes her head like I'm so annoying, but she does it with a smile that says *thank you*, then lets out a sigh. "I had this all planned out, everything I would say and when, but now that

146

we're here, I can't get it out. Probably because I've been holding it in for so long."

My throat goes dry. I squeeze her hand harder to keep my own from trembling.

I'm no good for you, JJ. We're no good for each other.

That isn't true.

It's something that's been true for a while.

She's ending our friendship again. That's the only thing this could be. Should I stop her?

"Wait—" I start at the same time she blurts, "I want to be something other than friends."

"You . . . what?"

She curses. "That isn't how I planned to say it at all."

My brain fails to connect anything. I'm unable to move, unable to think. "With who?"

She gives me an incredulous look. "With you!"

"Oh." It takes another second before it sinks in. Before I realize she's not pushing me away this time; she's pulling me closer. Closer in a way that we've never been. This is completely new territory for us, so I'm . . . confused. I've never gotten that vibe from her before, that she wanted me as a boyfriend. "Really?"

Her smile is tentative. "Yes, really."

Wow, um . . . I don't know what I'm feeling right now. It's not a bad feeling, though. I can tell that much. Pleasantly bewildered? Is that a thing? Or . . . cautiously optimistic?

"I'm not saying no." And I hope that sounded okay. "But why? All the sudden?"

I've never thought of Lucy in this way. No, actually, I

have . . . entertained the idea, here and there, given it a quick thought like, maybe, what if, but not often. Not enough to think it would be better than what we've already got between us, or worth pursuing. So I've never even thought to ask, or try. What we have is perfect, anyway. Why change it?

"That's what I meant to do first. Explain." She lets out a nervous laugh. "Then I got it all backward. Just . . . bear with me here. And don't tell me your answer until you hear everything."

"Okay." I smile as the initial shock of her confession starts to fall away and I think . . . *maybe*. Maybe we could try this—whatever *this* ends up being, it's got to be better than her breaking us up. "I'm bearing."

"Good. Because this is a long story. It starts the night we met, three and a half years ago."

Once Lucy gets going, she talks forever. I sit there and just listen. I know this story. I lived all of this with her, from the night we met and all that happened after that. But hearing it from her perspective is different.

That night of our first high school party, when we heard what became "our song" for the first time together. We both agreed it's so melodramatic it makes emo music sound clinical, which broke the ice between us, then led to talking for hours about things no one else understood, like how helium is such a pretentious element. "It's so stuck up," I said between sips of fruit punch. "Every time helium tells a joke, it goes right over everyone's heads."

She was already laughing now, but that was only the setup. I went on, "Like the one about atoms. I'm sure you've heard it

148

before, it's a classic. But helium tells it wrong every time. Why can't you trust atoms?"

"I don't know," she said, her eyes lighting up, focused solely on me. "Why?"

"Because they make up everything."

Then she laughed so hard, so genuinely, not caring who saw or heard her, this throaty belly laugh that some might call obnoxious and loud. It had her doubling over and snorting, and that was when I knew we'd be really good friends for a really long time.

I remember looking around the room, at all the other people talking and laughing. And kissing—already. Marcos and Chaz included, only an hour or so after they'd met. And I remember thinking what a relief it was that I'd found someone who didn't put that pressure on me to do what everyone else was doing. Lucy let me be me, simply by being her.

Now she tells me what I didn't know. She'd been hoping I would ask her out that night because she was too nervous to ask me. She waited and hoped to hear it all night, but I never did. She was disappointed—mostly with herself, for not speaking up—but she decided it was better than not having any kind of relationship at all. We clicked together too well to let it go. And then later, much later, when I'd finally opened up to her about why I don't date that often, how it takes me a while before I have those sort of feelings toward someone—and I don't know why; it just does—she figured if it would ever happen between us, she'd simply wait and see if it happened. She would wait for me to make the first move, whenever I was ready, in my own time.

Now, almost four years later, she's still waiting.

I was wrong, and so was her dad. Lucy is not impatient. She has the patience of a saint.

I open my mouth to tell her this, but she says, "Hold on, I'm not finished."

"Okay. I'm listening."

"After that," she goes on, "I thought if we ever had the chance, I would still be willing to give it a try with us. And in the meantime I really liked being your friend. I liked that we became *best* friends. But then I found out my dream of going to Italy would really be coming true. I realized that if anything other than friendship was going to happen, this was my last chance to try before there was half a world of distance between us."

Okay, but . . . "Lucy, you got accepted into that school over a year ago."

"I had to make a plan. I had to make sure this was what I really wanted. So after Macy Morris broke up with me for refusing to . . . do certain things, I stopped dating other people and cleared my head, then focused on what I should do with you. Slowly."

They broke up after Valentine's Day junior year. Macy expected their winter date to be a lot hotter than it was. After that was when Lucy started getting closer to me. Slowly, just like she said. Looking back now, it's obvious. But still I ask, "At the beginning of this school year, when you suggested we go to prom together if neither of us had a date for it . . . That was all part of this plan?"

"Entirely. Going to prom together. Wearing this dress. Coming here to watch the Eta Aquarids. Then telling you everything and . . . well, whatever happens next. And I wasn't sure this would work. You kept throwing monkey wrenches into my plans, like you always do. Chaos personified," she adds with a light laugh.

My mind jumps back to night one, when she decided it was better to push me out of her life completely. But if this was her plan all along, to take our relationship to a different place, why would she break us up? I'm missing something, and it's not like I can just ask her, hey, two nights ago when we lived a different version of today and you did this really unexpected thing that destroyed me—yeah, I know you don't remember, but can you explain it to me, please?

Headshake. "I can't believe you did all this without me catching on."

"Heh, well, I almost decided not to tell you anything after we danced tonight. That dance was perfect, and I was afraid I'd lose you if I said all this, if I pushed you too far too fast, and it made you uncomfortable."

Her words settle over me like a warm blanket on a chilly night, and the realization wraps around me like a hug. With Lucy, in this new way, I'm not uncomfortable. I thought there was a chance I might be, but . . . "I'm not uncomfortable."

"You're not," she agrees. "You're the most comfortable person I know." She snuggles against my chest, and I raise my outside hand to stroke her hair. This kind of physical closeness is normal for us, but suddenly it feels new. Every little movement feels more important somehow. "I'm glad Chaz talked me out of backing out," she says.

"Chaz knew about this?" Wait, is that why—"Did Marcos know, too?"

"Maybe. I didn't tell him, but you know how they talk."

He's dead tomorrow. They both are. If tomorrow ever comes.

Lucy pulls back to look at me. "So now that you know . . . what do you . . . think?"

I think it's . . . "Okay."

"Okay? What does that mean? Okay what?"

"I mean okay, yes. Let's give this a try."

"Really?" She practically leaps back into my arms.

I just hold her for a few minutes, a ball of heat in my gut pulsing stronger with every heartbeat, like I'm holding the sun inside me, and it's bursting with solar flares. I need this. I need *her*. Always.

We can do this. We can keep being friends and also be something other than friends. Now that I'm on that track, I wonder how I didn't jump onto it sooner. This feels very . . . right.

"JJ?" Lucy says. "What are you thinking about?"

She wants me. This beautiful, amazing girl. And suddenly all *I* want is to give myself to her. What the moon wants the moon gets.

"I was just wondering if . . . Would it be all right if I kiss you?"

She nods, biting her lower lip, suddenly shy and nervous. She's not the only one. What if I got this far just to flub it up? Just to find out she thinks I'm a terrible kisser and that ends it?

"Take your time," she says reassuringly, using my earlier words. "We've got all night."

Maybe we do. Maybe we don't. Maybe I have the rest of my life to practice our first kiss over and over and over until I get it perfect, because I might be stuck in this loop forever. But this is the only time it will be first for real, for both of us. One shot, no second chances.

I cup her jaw with both my hands, not sure how to start, buying myself a few more seconds to figure it out. My touch is featherlight, as if she might break if I hold her too firmly, and she closes her eyes. Her lips pout. I don't know if she did that on purpose, but *good God*. With that one little move, I am *done*. All rational thought leaves me and I don't even remember closing the gap between our mouths, but now I'm very, very aware that our lips are touching. The waxy taste of her lipstick is unexpectedly addictive. Maybe that's weirder than liking her toes, but I don't care.

The world tilts in a dizzying, delightful blur, and I hold her tighter to keep my balance, my fingers sinking into her round hips, and then my hands are everywhere, unable to decide what part of her I need to touch more. Her waist, her back, her shoulders, her neck—the smell of her shampoo is intoxicating, giving me a heady buzz—I want it all and all at once, so suddenly that it gives me mental whiplash, and part of me questions if any of this is even real. She's doing the same, exploring like this is the first time she's ever had her hands on me, and somehow, in the frenzy, our mouths never break apart. Everything on her is soft, but nothing as soft as her lips. I can't get enough.

The solar flares in my gut intensify, and I'm hot all over. Now I understand Marcos's love of poetry. A few verses, stanzas, whatever they're called, have spontaneously written themselves in my head in the last few seconds.

Don't get so carried away, JJ, it's just a kiss.

Right. Just a kiss.

It's just a kiss that the last three and a half years have been building toward.

It's just a kiss that, up until now, we both believed would never happen.

It's just a kiss that lasts an eternity but also keeps us frozen in this moment, like time means nothing anymore.

When we finally pull away, gasping, I actually have the thought that maybe Melody was right—time only exists in our heads. I have no idea how many minutes passed while we kissed, if any at all.

"Wow," Lucy says.

"Much wow." The poetry in my head must have gotten lost on the way to my mouth.

I'm ready for more, but she lays her head on my chest and settles the rest of her against my side, looking out at the midnight-blue horizon. "I can't believe we made wishes on falling stars last night," she says. "Were we drunk?"

"Yes, on ice cream," I say, and she laughs. "I didn't wish on a falling star, though, only you did."

"But we both wished on the moon. Well, I did. Did you?"

"I did, yeah . . ." *I wish we could stay like this forever.*

"You don't have to tell me yours, but my wish on the moon came true. It was for this. For everything I planned for us tonight to end up right where it is now." She lifts one shoulder in a barely-there shrug. "It's completely illogical to think that making the wish for it was the reason it happened. I just thought it was an interesting coincidence."

"Interesting coincidence," I say absently, "completely illogical." Living the same night three times in a row is beyond coincidence, though. "Falling stars and wishes on the moon would have nothing to do with it," I mutter.

I glance up at the stars, silently wishing this night will never end. Just like I did before.

I wish we could stay like this forever.

Surely one of them has the power to make my wish come true? I never believed in that stuff before, but now, so many impossible things have happened that I'm wavering. At least let this be the last night that repeats. If this night has to end, let me move on to tomorrow with it being the reality that sticks. Because the other nights before this, I *lost* her. What if that happens again? What if we never get back to this place we are right now?

Please! I almost shout. *Whoever is controlling this—do you hear me?* My lips tremble from trying to hold it in. *Don't take this version of tonight away. Don't take her away . . .*

My phone chimes in my pocket, and I pull it out to open a new text from Chaz. It's the picture he took of me and Lucy slow dancing at prom. Her head is on my chest, with her arms wrapped tight around me, and mine around her. Both of us oblivious to everything but us.

Before I can show it to Lucy, a scratching noise snaps my face to the side, looking for the source.

"That's odd," Lucy says. "Woodchucks don't live up here. It's too rocky. What're you doing there, little guy?"

Little? Yeah, right. I spot the fat groundhog a few feet away from us, scratching at the rock like it's trying to dig a hole. Lucy's right, this isn't natural. This is—

No, not again. Not *now*. I'm finally happy—we're both happy. Together. No arguments, no conflicts, no breaking up our friendship because of a massive screwup. This night can't possibly go this well again if I have to do it over. That's too much to hope for.

You deserve to be happy, JJ, Marcos said.

Not according to this ugly rodent. "Leave me alone!"

It pops its head up toward me, and we start a familiar staring contest.

"JJ . . ." Lucy pulls back a little. "Why are you yelling?"

"Don't!" I shout at the groundhog. What can I throw, is there something here I can throw at it? I raise my phone up high, rear my arm back, and—no. I need my phone. But I also need Lucy. I clutch her tight. "Don't take her—"

The cold black void consumes me, and my suddenly empty hands reach out, first feeling for Lucy, then feeling for anything, anyone to help me. I kick and scream. But there's nothing. There's no one. Just me and this impossible curse.

the NIGHT of the APOGEE

I wake in my bedroom, as expected, the blinding white behind my eyes taking me off guard only for a second before I get my bearings. Briefly, I notice my left eye isn't red and purple anymore, just before I sag against the mirror on my closet door, all the fight draining out of me. I can barely hold myself up. The bow tie I forgot I'd be holding now drops to the floor.

I can still feel Lucy's lips on mine. I can still feel her warm, soft body in *that dress* under my palms. But it's only ghost sensations now. It isn't real anymore. It might never be real again.

Not if I can help it.

Blue sparks appear in my side vision, and I calmly straighten, then stamp them out on the carpet. I don't know if Marty caused this time loop, but right now I don't care about the reason. Right now I just want to get back to Lucy. Only Lucy.

Tonight will be different—again. I've been given another chance—again. Maybe that's all this is, the universe balancing out all the flubs I've made in my life up to now, by giving me as many do-overs as I need to make sure this one night plays out perfectly from start to finish.

Or maybe it isn't about *me* having a perfect night at all. Maybe it's about Lucy.

She planned this out, every detail. Like her dad said, she just wants it all to be perfect. And I can help her with that. She has an itinerary in her head, and the first thing on the list is "picked up by JJ." On time. Her perfect night starts with me picking her up *on time*.

I pull out my phone.

Lucy: Where are you?

Me: Leaving soon

It's 7:31. I'm already late no matter what I do, but I can keep myself from being so late that it stresses her out and starts the night on a sour note. I fasten my bow tie in a flash. It's crooked, but whatever. That's not important. My contacts are in this time and my eyes aren't burning. Excellent. I'll call Melody's tow on the way to Lucy's, and then suggest Jenna get a ride from Autumn because I'm running late. I mean, I am, so it's not a lie. And Jenna will be fine, like she has been every other night.

I snatch the keys off the nightstand and rush to open my bedroom door. Mom is standing *right there* with her fist raised to knock.

"I have to go, sorry, I'm running late." I breeze past her and down the stairs.

"Don't forget the rules!" she shouts from the landing as I'm stepping across the living room. "And get pictures!"

The door slams behind me in my frenzy. I didn't even *see* Mama or Shayla this time. Guilt stabs my chest, but I ignore it.

I can see them another time. Tonight is all about Lucy.

She wants to *try* with me. She knows me better than anyone does, and she still wants to try. She never intended to push me away; that wasn't her plan. She *wants* me. We have to end this night together, with every step along the way exactly as she expects. Nothing, not even Melody's incident, will get in the way of it this time. Because this time, I'm going to help Melody without her even knowing.

Dead Man's Curve comes and goes with no sign of Melody's Bug. She's not here yet, and neither is the tow I called. My foot hovers between the gas pedal and the brake, hesitant to pick up speed after coasting down and around the curve. What if she's left stranded?

I have to trust that she won't be. I have to trust that everything will happen again just as it did before, and in the last two repeats, the tow I called from AAA showed up with no problems and at the right time. She'll be fine. She has to be. *She'll be fine without me.*

Tonight is all about Lucy.

I hit the gas.

Tonight will be different.

This is my fourth prom night and the third time I've picked up Lucy in *that dress*, and the effect it has on me is no different. My heart stutters and my throat catches and I have to remind myself to breathe. In "my time" I saw her less than an hour ago, but she's too beautiful not to notice. I've always thought so.

And I always will, no matter what kind of relationship we have. Even if she breaks us up—but that's *not* going to happen again.

"You made it," she says, smiling bigger than she did on any other night.

"Yeah. Sorry I'm late."

"It's not that late. We'll just have to be on time instead of early." Her lips twibble and I don't have to guess why anymore. That twibble is about her plan for later, about how nervous she is to tell me everything she's been keeping inside. About her fear of losing our friendship over it if I say no.

She has absolutely nothing to be afraid of. She just doesn't know it yet.

"You look perfect, Lucy. Everything tonight is going to be *perfect*."

"Well, I wouldn't go that far. Perfection is an unreachable standard." She's blushing. I know why she's blushing this time. In a completely nonsensical situation that shouldn't even exist, the fourth time living the same night, everything is starting to make sense. "But *grazie*. And you look good, too," she adds. "Good color choice. I like it." Her gaze stays on my eyes for a beat and her lips twibble. Again.

I was wrong the last two nights. This twibble wasn't because I was wearing glasses before, or because I had a black eye. The twibble is, and always has been, about her plan for tonight. What that has to do with my eyes, I'm still not sure. But now we're just . . . staring at each other like nothing else matters but this moment—and it doesn't. *Nothing* else matters. Tonight is all about Lucy. A goofy grin spreads across my face and then she's smiling, too, and any smile on her is a good one. We could spend the rest of the night right here, just like this, and I wouldn't care.

"What, no corsage?" Nico says, reminding me he's still in the room. Our moment is broken. "Did you forget, *coglione*, or are you just that cheap?"

Coglione. I don't have to know the exact translation of that word to know it's an insult. Every time I hear it, every nerve in me bristles. Lucy isn't the only person who has the same effect on me no matter how many times the same thing happens. Why is he such a—

"I didn't want one," Lucy says, then everything plays out exactly as before. I stay out of their sibling spat and try to act surprised when Lucy mentions her dad wants to talk.

He tells me tonight is special, but not too special.

He tells me to be patient again, after Lucy interrupts.

Then he tells me to *muoversi*. Get moving. He doesn't have to tell me twice.

After a quick hug and a *grazie*, I take Lucy by the hand and out the door. Holding her hand now does things to me that it didn't before. There are no fewer than fifteen hundred butterflies spastically flitting around in my gut, all because she got me thinking, yes, we can do this. And I wonder if to her, it's always been that way, every time. Is she feeling the same thing as I am right now? Her body language reveals nothing.

Part of me wishes she'd told me sooner. We've lost so much time, and we have so little left. But if she had admitted all this stuff years ago, would I have had the realization I had last night sooner? That I'd be comfortable giving this a try with her? Or would I have been . . .

"Ready?" I say once we're both buckled up in the car.

"More than ready. I've been looking forward to this night for a very long time."

"Me too." I feign ignorance of her real meaning and start backing out of the driveway. My hands tingle with adrenaline. My whole body feels like it's about to take flight. "We're finally here, Lucy. The night of our life."

And we're doing it right this time.

Something isn't right.

As we're finishing our dry and flavorless chicken cordon bleu dinner, and the music is just getting started, I feel a strange urge to glance at Jenna's table next to ours—and find her glaring at me, her face taut. She holds my confused gaze locked with her angry one for a moment, letting me know clearly that I'm the one she's looking at, then she turns her attention back to her friends and laughs at a joke or something. Breezy and light, her default mode. As if the exchange never happened.

Did it? Was that a glitch? Like when the Taco Bell stain appeared on my shirt, on a night I hadn't been to Taco Bell. Or is she really mad at me? For what, not picking her up? That didn't seem to bother her on any other night . . .

Though, on the other nights, I was actually running late. Very late. Tonight, I was only a little late, so I ended up arriving here with Lucy right before Autumn's limo. The limo with Jenna in it. She walked in with Autumn and her friends all coupled up, and Jenna with no one, but holding her head high as they announced her name by itself . . . and she was fine, I thought . . . until she saw me.

Thinking back, it's obvious. She barely gave me a smile. Based on what she told me the other night, I figured I'm just not that important to her. We're not even close enough to be called friends. But now I realize—in her mind, I should have gotten here *after* her, and I got here first, and she doesn't know it was only a minute before she walked in. She thinks I stood her up.

Yeah, she's definitely mad at me. No glitch about it.

Tonight is about Lucy, though. I made a choice. To put Lucy and what she wants ahead of everything and everyone else. Should I not have? But when I try to please everyone and do it all, it never works out. Except last night, everything was fine.

Well, no actually, it wasn't. It was *mostly* fine. If you don't count Lucy going outside for half of prom because she was stressed, upset, and worried.

I don't know what the right answer is anymore. I'm just guessing in all of this, as well as I can. There's nothing logical or scientific about relationships, and that puts me wildly out of my area of expertise. And if Jenna is mad at me now for not picking her up, does that mean something bad happened with Melody, since I didn't wait to see if she was okay until the tow arrived? What if it didn't show up this time? Now I'm questioning *everything*.

"What's that look for?" Lucy says, then follows my gaze before I can tear it away from Jenna. She grimaces and her brow furrows. She probably thinks I'm pining for her.

"Lucy, it's not—"

"You wanna dance?" Chaz suddenly asks Marcos. He stands and pulls Marcos up by the hand, not giving him a choice. "We should dance now, let's go dance." They disappear in the crowd, leaving me and Lucy alone at the table. Just like last night.

Except it isn't. Because now I know that Chaz already knows what I know about Lucy.

What's worse—that I just had that thought or that it made perfect sense.

Lucy turns in her seat to face me, and the flickering faux candle on our table gives her face a warm glow. She folds her hands in her lap and her thumbs twiddle. "What's going on with you and Jenna?"

This conversation feels too familiar, but I can't remember exactly how it went before. Or if we were here when we had it or somewhere else.

"Nothing's going on with me and Jenna," I say. "She broke up with Blair."

"I heard it was the other way around."

My jaw tightens. Because of Blair, not Lucy, but still I snap. "He's lying. He treated her like garbage and she refused to put up with it. She dumped him. Whatever he said on the student message board was a flat-out lie."

She presses her lips together and goes quiet for a moment. Then, "Why are you getting defensive about this?"

"I'm not." I shake my head. "It's just, I feel bad for her, that's all. He's a jerk. And Jenna doesn't deserve that, from anyone."

"True," Lucy agrees. "Jenna's very sweet."

"And there's nothing more to say about her." I catch sight of Jenna on the dance floor, having a blast with her friends. This is the part where, last night, I went out there and had a blast with her, too. Now she flicks a glance my way, scowls, rolls her eyes, and moves deeper into the crowd. Whatever, let Jenna be mad at me. It's not the worst that's happened on this night, not even close. I've still got Lucy; that's what matters.

"I'm ready to dance," I tell Lucy, pushing up out of my chair. "You coming?"

She shakes her head. "I need to let my food settle first. Go ahead."

Right. I should have known she would say that. "I can wait with you . . ." I trail off, my own words triggering a memory of what she's about to say next.

"No, it's fine. Go have fun. Don't worry about me."

Don't worry about me.

Screw that. She's the only person I'm worried about tonight. But she doesn't want me to hover and she's not ready to dance. I scan the room, taking in the fairy-tale decorations. The twinkling lights, the gauzy streamers, the blur of colors, the feeling of magic. What can we—

My eyes land on the photo booth dressed up to look like a castle.

"Come with me?" I take her hand, tugging her up.

She doesn't budge. "I just said I'm not ready to dance."

"Not dancing." I point to the booth. The photographer is currently free, with mostly everyone dancing now or finishing up dinner. "We've got pictures to pose for."

"We can't afford those."

Improvise. "Well, I didn't tell you. I've been saving up so we could get the really nice ones taken tonight. You know, something both of us could have, as a reminder of the best night of our lives, when we're . . ." My chest tightens. "Apart," I finish. "On opposite sides of the world."

A lump forms in my throat, and I swallow it back. Do I want this night to stop repeating? If it doesn't, we never have to go to that future where we live separate lives. We'll always be together on prom night. But we'll also always have to start over, with no guarantee of where it will lead. I don't want that, either.

Lucy stands, squeezing my hand for balance as she rises. "This is the best surprise."

"That's me. Full of surprises."

"Chaos personified," she says with a laugh. "But this time it's a good thing."

"That's a good one," the balding photographer says, checking the image of our latest photo on his camera. "And that's your last one, too, unless you want to upgrade your package."

Blair and Farah are waiting at the front of the line for pictures, and they both bust out laughing. "You need to upgrade your package, Johnson?" Blair jibes.

I lift my hand to reply in mime, but Lucy pipes up. "You need to upgrade your brain, *Bedford*? The one you're currently using appears to be a Stone Age model."

And this is why she's my best friend. Well, one of the

many reasons. Her default mode is to stick up for me.

She doesn't even wait to see Blair's reaction, just grabs my hand and guides me to the dance floor—where we run into Jenna. Literally. Her long blond curls smack me right in the face as she spins around, the same twirling move she was making with me last night.

"Ack—" I choke. Hair smells much better than it tastes.

"JJ!" she says, big blue eyes wide. They dart to Lucy, then back to me. "Sorry, I didn't see you guys there."

"It's okay," I assure her. "It was my fault. I wasn't paying attention."

"Yeah," she says. "It *was* your fault."

"Jenna—"

The thumping fast song ends, easing into something slow and melodic. And too soft to cover this conversation.

Everyone around us either couples up or disperses, putting a spotlight on the fact Jenna has no partner. "E-excuse me," she says. "I need a break." She scuttles past us, all the way to her posse by the drink buffet.

Last night, this was when I left the dance floor, too, and talked to Lucy at our table. But now we're both standing here, and I think I should talk to Jenna before we get too far into this night. Before she gets crowned prom queen— Oh. Right. That whole debacle with Blair is going to happen. I completely forgot. I definitely need to talk to Jenna. Now. Then the rest of the night is Lucy's. Jenna deserves an apology at the very least.

Chaz and Marcos appear in my side vision, swaying slowly. I grab one of them by the arm—I don't even know whose arm; they're dressed like twins tonight—and say, "Can you guys dance with Lucy for a minute? I'll be right back."

"JJ, we can't do three on a slow dance," Lucy starts, but I'm already walking away, leaving them to figure it out. Who says you *can't* do three, anyway? Maybe it'll start a trend.

At the drink buffet, Jenna's friends go quiet and she sips her punch. I make myself a cup of coffee, down it—ughf, that burns—then repeat the process all over again.

"Dancing fuel?" Jenna says. "Or do you have big plans to stay up all night?"

I turn to face her. "Both?"

"With Lucy."

"With Lucy, yeah." I sigh and lean against the wall by a trash can. Right where I belong, with the garbage. "I'm sorry I didn't . . ."

Pick you up like I promised.

Explain what's going on.

Treat you any better than your ex.

She waits for me to fill in the blank. Her friends pretend they aren't listening to us.

"Can we go somewhere quieter?" I say, even though we're far from the speakers. "I mean, to talk. Can we talk?"

Jenna surprises me with a grin, then turns on her heels and exits the gym. Her friends stay put, receiving some silent code from her not to follow, but I didn't get that message, so I'm right behind her.

*　　*　　*

Jenna leads me to an alcove tucked behind a flight of stairs. We're still near the gym—I can still hear the slow bass beat of the music—but it's private enough that no one will see us.

Which is good. Because a guy and girl hiding away like this on prom night has the potential to be easily misunderstood. Very strong potential, very misunderstood. Even if it were me who saw it, I'd assume the worst. Or the best? That would depend on who it is.

"I just wanted to apologize for flaking out on you tonight. I didn't mean to, but that's no excuse. And I'm sorry."

"Thank you for admitting that, at least." She nods. "Most guys wouldn't."

We stand there in awkward silence. I guess that's my cue to leave.

"What's going on, JJ?" she says, making me pause. "This isn't like you. You seem . . . off. Is something wrong? Is it—" She pulls in her bottom lip, like a new thought just hit her. "Is it Lucy? Did she have a problem with you and me?"

Me and her? As in, a couple? I'm not even thinking about that anymore, and I just told Lucy it's not happening. "No," I say honestly. "Lucy doesn't have a problem with you. Really. She thinks you're great."

"And she likes you, too?"

"She does." Except she hasn't confessed that yet, not in that sense. "I mean, she's my best friend. Of course she likes me."

Jenna smiles sweetly. "Right. Duh. Sorry, my head is a little . . ." She makes a face instead of finishing her sentence, crossing her eyes, sticking out her tongue. Back to the same adorable Jenna. "It's Blair, you know? I thought I'd be okay tonight, but he's . . . Seeing him with Farah, like I don't matter . . . like we didn't have a great thing going until he ruined it. And all the lies he's telling . . ." She swallows. "It's hard."

"You seemed to be having a good time."

"A good act, more like it." She twists her mouth.

"I'm sorry." I keep repeating that, but I don't know what else to say. On a different version of tonight, she was back in Blair's arms. Would she really take him back, after all this? Just because she's vulnerable and hurting? She's hurting because of *him*.

"Yeah. I'm sorry, too." Her voice cracks on the last word and she sniffles. When she looks up at me, her eyes are watery, like two ice-blue oceans. The first tear spills quickly, and instinctively, I swipe it away with my thumb. It's nothing but a kind gesture. But when I start to draw my hand away, she snatches my wrist, pulls me closer to her.

"JJ . . ." It's barely a whisper, her tone somehow both a statement and a question.

I can sense what might be coming but can't think of a way to stop it without physically removing myself from the situation. Like she said before—sometimes the solution is to take yourself out of the equation. I should step away. But what if I'm wrong? Stepping away would hurt her feelings. She's been hurt enough.

Jenna wraps her other arm around me, then releases my wrist and brings that hand up to my neck. Her fingers trail upward and tunnel into my hair as she lays her head on my chest. She sighs and her whole body relaxes against me.

Is this really happening? She told me she doesn't want me like this . . . Maybe I'm taking it the wrong way. Maybe she just needs a comforting hug. That's probably it. I rest my chin on top of her head and squeeze her back. "It's gonna be okay, Jenna. You're strong. You'll get through this."

She tilts her head back, the movement catching me off guard, at the same time my head tips down.

Our mouths meet, I assume accidentally, but she doesn't pull away. She uses her hand at my neck to guide us into a more suitable position, and then her lips melt against mine.

Nope, I wasn't taking it the wrong way. This is definitely happening. And like a fool I let it. My head swims. It wasn't that long ago that this was exactly what I'd hoped for with Jenna. But I don't anymore. Tonight is about Lucy. She's got it all planned out. She's going to tell me later—

I pull back with a gasp, quickly putting an arm's length of distance between us. My good sense came to me too late. I didn't signal for her to stop. This is on me. Jenna's brows wrinkle, darting toward each other, her eyes still watery from before, and I feel like I just kicked a puppy. "Jenna, I—I'm so sorry. I shouldn't have— I'm *so sorry*. This isn't what I wanted . . . with you."

Liar.

But no, I'm not. Right now it's the truth. Given the choice between Lucy and Jenna, I choose Lucy. I will always choose Lucy.

"You—" Her breath hitches. "You kissed me back."

Did I? God, I don't even remember. Did I black out?

No, JJ, you just made a colossal mistake. Because you excel at that. Congrats, buddy.

This night was supposed to be all about Lucy, and somehow I ended up under a stairwell, kissing Jenna. What? Is happening?

"I'm sorry," I repeat, stepping back even farther, out from under the stairs. Out in the open. "I'm really, really sorry. I misunderstood—"

She's on me in a flash, with her signature smack. My head whips to the side and I see stars. Then I'm staring at the floor tile, my hands braced against my thighs, waiting for my brain to settle back into its rightful place in my skull so I can see straight. Jenna's heels clack fiercely away from me, and her shout echoes down the hall. "I am so done with men!"

A few years of wonderful silence pass, and the coffee is doing nothing. Maybe I'll just take a nap right here . . .

"JJ?"

My head snaps upward, and my gaze lands on a galaxy in the shape of my best friend. "Lucy. Hey. Nothing. What are *you* doing?"

Yeah, that doesn't sound guilty.

"Looking for you. Our song is playing."

Then why is she frowning?

"What happened with Jenna?" she says, not stepping any closer. Keeping her distance. "She just stormed past me and— What's that on your face?"

"What's what on my face?" More guilt. It's becoming a theme.

Her eyes narrow. "Your cheek's all red. So is your mouth. Is that . . . lipstick?"

I wipe my mouth and my hand comes away a guilty shade of red. Fire-engine red. The same red as Jenna's lipstick. "It's not what you think."

Just keep digging that hole, JJ, it's almost big enough to jump into now.

She crosses her arms, arching a brow. "What exactly do you think I think?"

"That I was kissing Jenna."

"Were you?"

"Lucy, I can explain—"

"That's a yes." She looks like she might puke, wrapping her arms around her middle. "But you don't have to explain. You can kiss whoever you want. That's not my business."

Except it is, because she wants to be the one I'm kissing. She just doesn't know that I know that.

"You're my best friend," I say, hoping to make this right. "Everything I do is your business." I step toward her and she takes a step back. "It always has been. We don't keep secrets from each other."

As soon as the words leave my mouth, I realize that was the exact wrong thing to say. She's been keeping her feelings for me secret for years. Sixteen different emotions cross her face in the span of a second, like she can't decide which one to hold on to.

"No, we don't keep secrets," she says. "You're right. But you told me it wasn't like that with you and Jenna. I'm just surprised. I . . ."

She's not just surprised. She's crushed. And she's heading for the exit. I'm losing her.

How did I end up in this place with her again, with her leaving me?

Lucy is my moon, always in flux but entirely predictable, my steadfast and dependable companion. She keeps me from self-destructing. She keeps my chaos from spiraling out of control—usually. And for the third time in four nights since this prom loop started, she's reached her apogee. The point of orbit when the moon is farthest from the earth. When she's farthest from me. I knew this might happen again tonight and did all I could to prevent it. I tried. I even planned. And still I messed up.

Will I ever get her back? Will we ever be close again, as *anything*?

I can't lose her. Not now. Not ever.

"Lucy, wait!" I trot to catch up with her, and she walks faster, practically running. Now *I'm* feeling like I might puke. Lucy has never run from me in her life. I've done it again. I've wrecked her plan for tonight, so she's decided we're better off apart. I don't have to hear her say it this time to know.

She barrels through the door at the end of the hall, and I come to a skidding halt.

A groundhog snuck in from outside before the door closed. I'm not sure if this one is a blessing or a curse. Tonight needs to end, definitely. But what if the next repeat is worse?

I stare the thing down. "Why do you keep doing this to me—"

It sends me flailing and cursing into a cold black void.

the NIGHT of the SUPERNOVA

I arrive in my bedroom in an absolute rage. How do I *end* this!

The mirror is my first victim. *Crack!* My reflection distorts behind broken glass, the punch leaving my knuckles throbbing and bloody. Right on cue, those blue sparks coming off Marty appear in my side vision, and I lose my mind.

I grab the closest thing that can serve as a smashing tool—a giant horsemanship trophy I won last summer. With it raised high above my head, ready to come down on Marty like the Hulk on . . . anything, I let out a guttural roar of frustration and lower the trophy back to the shelf, remembering just in time that I can't destroy him no matter how at fault he is for putting me in this mess.

Instead, I have to fix him. He doesn't deserve to be fixed. He doesn't deserve anything but a burning dumpster. But I can't imagine what else could logically be causing this vicious cycle. What if fixing Marty is the only way to stop this night from repeating again?

And my best chance at fixing him is with Lucy. I pull my phone out of my pocket and check the text messages.

Lucy: Where are you?

Me: Leaving soon

Yes. I am leaving very, very soon. Right after I make this phone call to have a tow pick up Melody. I swipe my phone without thinking, going back to my call log to find the number I called for the tow truck. But that's pointless. In this version of tonight, I haven't called them yet. So it shouldn't be there.

But it is. My phone is showing I called the tow . . . twenty-odd minutes from now.

The glitches are back. Does that mean they got my call already, or is it just a glitch on my phone display? I'm not taking a chance at being wrong. Double-checking and erring on the side of being overprepared—Lucy would be proud. Scratch that, she wouldn't even recognize me like this. I tap the number and call AAA. Tell them to pick up a cream-colored Volkswagen Beetle with a black convertible top that hasn't even broken down yet. Act like I'm at the scene, describing every detail, because it's all still vivid in my memory.

"Knock, knock," Mom says on the other side of my door. "Are you decent?"

Instead of answering, I pocket my phone, grab Marty, open the door, and move past her.

"Wait, where's your tie—"

"Mom, I'm sorry, I really have to go. Now. Lucy's waiting."

And she'll have forgotten everything. Again. But I haven't. I know what she plans to tell me tonight. How do I make sure that happens *and* stop the loop? On night three we stepped into a place I never imagined we'd ever be together—and now I can't imagine us not. How do we get there and *stay* there?

"JJ, wait—" Mom calls after me. "Why are you taking your science project to prom?" She gasps, then, "What happened to your mirror!"

I'm already down the stairs, headed to the door. "I promise to follow the rules! I won't stay out all night! I'll get pictures!" Am I forgetting anything?

Yes. Keys. *Get it together, JJ.* If things go right, this is my last chance for real.

I spin to go back upstairs and Mom tosses my car keys down to me. She folds her arms across her chest, giving me one of her hard, skeptical looks. If I don't get out of here, I'll cave under that stare. It's crushed the truth out of me before.

"Thanks, love you, bye!"

Shayla's exiting the kitchen when I reach the bottom of the stairs again. Her whole face brightens and my guilt intensifies, souring my stomach. "Look at you all fancy!" she says.

An ache spreads across my chest. It feels like I haven't seen her or my parents in forever, like I'm missing things I should be part of. This is my family, and, yeah, we don't always get along, but we've always been close. Now they're distant. I see them for a few minutes and then leave, because I'm perpetually running late when this night starts. I have no control over when it stops and starts, just what happens in between.

"I promise I'll save you a dance, Shay." And I'm out the door before she can argue.

With Marty secured in the trunk of my car, I sit in the driver's seat, buckle my seat belt, and put the key in the ignition, looking out the windshield at the long driveway ahead . . . but the road in the distance shouldn't be this blurry. My contacts must be glitching again, because the night just started and my eyes are dry and burning and itchy like I've had them in for hours. I pinch-swipe them off and flick them out the window, fish my spare pair of glasses from the glove box and put them on. When I pull my hands away from my face, they're smudged in black, like they were after I pushed Melody's car into the woods.

As I reach into the cubby between the seats and get the hand sanitizer Lucy keeps in there, my mind levels up from problem-solving mode to crisis-prevention mode.

Another glitch. Another carry-over. So far they've been minor things that don't affect much, but what if one of the bigger things carries over one of these times? What if I still lose Lucy? Or someone else? This has to stop *tonight*. And for some reason, I'm the only one who knows it's happening; I have to be the one who fixes this.

But I can't do it alone. So my first step in ending this time loop is somehow convincing Miss Logical Lucy that it even exists.

Sure. No problem.

My phone chimes with a new text, and I nearly jump out of my skin. Everything has me on edge. The text is from Chaz, a picture of me and Lucy on the dance floor at prom. But that hasn't happened yet, we're not even there—

It's a glitch. But this one is exactly what I need. I rub sanitizer all over my hands until they're clean, hissing when the alcohol hits my bloody knuckles, put the car in drive, and pray I'm headed in the right direction this time. A direction that won't cross paths with Melody.

Probably not ever again. I shouldn't feel such a sense of loss at that thought, like she was someone vital in my life. Meeting her was just a weird turn of fate. Or not even fate, really. According to Melody, everything happens for a reason. *Maybe not everything, Mel.* She was only a coincidence. She was never part of the plan.

"There's been a change of plans," I tell Lucy after picking her up. We're sitting in my car in her driveway as she buckles her seat belt, wearing *that dress* that still stops my heart a little every time I see her in it. And now that I know everything behind her plan for tonight, I appreciate the dress even more.

Her jaw goes slack and she stares at me, no doubt trying to guess what I screwed up and what she'll have to do to readjust so her plan can still move forward with success. And for a moment I just stare right back, stare at her big brown eyes and those pillow-soft lips covered in dark red lipstick that I now crave the taste of.

God, I want to kiss her again. But to her, tonight, it's like it never happened. We are nothing other than friends. Which was all fine and good until she shifted the gears in my head, driving all my thoughts of her into a new direction, with just one conversation followed by just one kiss. One really amazing—

I bite my lip and hold in a groan. *Focus.* We have to stop this loop or we'll be stuck here wiping the slate clean between us for literal ever. And who knows what else bad might happen with these glitches? I have no control over that whatsoever. But there are some things I can still have an effect on, like what we do next.

"What kind of change?" Lucy says.

"We need to fix Marty. I've got him in the trunk. So here's what I'm thinking: I figure we can go to prom for a little bit, you know, just enough to show up so people aren't wondering where we are, then we sneak off to the science lab and trouble-shoot this thing."

"I . . . uhm . . . okay, hold on." She swallows. Closes her eyes. Blows out a steadying breath. Opens her eyes and speaks very slowly. "You want to ditch prom to play with our failed science project. Am I understanding this correctly?"

"Yes. Not play with it, though, we need to fix it. Tonight."

"Why tonight? It's *prom*. You've been looking forward to this for years. I've been looking forward to it, too." Her gaze softens and she looks down for a second, just a flicker of a moment. When she looks up at me again, her eyes are hard. "The project's been graded already. There's nothing left for us to do but trash it. I'm surprised you didn't already."

I shake my head. "This isn't about our grade. This is about all of us being stuck in a time loop that Marty created."

"*What?* Are you talking about?"

"Lucy"—deep breath—"I've been living the same night over and over again. This night, our prom night. Before the end of every night, it resets back to right before I leave my house to pick you up, and I'm the only one who remembers anything.

This is the fifth time now and it has to stop. I have to make it stop before something irreversible happens."

"A time loop . . ." Her teeth catch her bottom lip, and I can tell there's a battle waging in her mind. One side is saying I'm possibly high on something, even though she's never known me to indulge in anything like that, while the other side is saying: *But what if he's telling the truth?*

"That's impossible," she concludes. "You're just delirious, or something. Did you sleep last night? You look really tired. Maybe you shouldn't be driving—"

"I'm not delirious." And yeah, I'm tired, I haven't slept in days, but, "I'm not making this up. I'm not imagining things. I can tell you everything that's going to happen tonight before it happens." As soon as I've said it, I scramble to think of something. "I knew you were going to wear that dress, put your hair up like that, half-up and half-down, and wear dark red lipstick that matches your nails."

"Telling me you knew what I would look like *as you're looking at me* isn't convincing."

All right, then . . . "I can't see your toes now, but I know they're painted the same color as your fingers."

"That doesn't mean anything. I always match my fingers and toes. You've seen that."

Okay. I didn't want to make this stressful for her by bringing up certain things, but she's leaving me no choice. "You picked out that galaxy dress for me."

Her lip twibbles, but she doesn't relent. "Not hard to guess that, either, Mr. Astronomy. You're my partner tonight. You'll be with me for hours. I wanted to wear something I knew you would like looking at."

Anything she wore I would've liked looking at, because she's the one wearing it. And now? With that kiss still fresh in my mind? She could wear a garbage bag and I'd break out in a sweat.

At my silence, she shakes her head, likely assuming she's won the argument. "I can't believe we're having this conversation. You and me, of all people. You're suggesting something that isn't at all possible. Completely illogical. Beyond the realms of natural law."

Great, now I've got her putting up defenses. I need her on my side—we're a team. Me and her against the universe. Time for my last resort.

"Yes. I agree with all of that." I pull my phone out of my pocket and open to Chaz's text that came through early. The photo of us is still there and it's time-stamped a couple of hours from now, on today's date. I flash it toward Lucy, and her eyes widen. "Completely illogical," I say. "But there it is. This is from night three, a couple of nights ago for me now, when we danced at prom."

She takes my phone slowly, staring at it like she's afraid it might explode. "Did we . . ."

My stomach drops. If she asks about what we did on the bluffs—

"I mean, didn't we dance the other nights, too?" she corrects.

"No," I say, my shoulder dropping. Relieved she didn't ask what I thought she was going to, but also, if she's asking about the other nights, then she's starting to buy into this possibility.

Her gaze pops up from the phone to me. "Why not?"

"Oh. There were . . . issues. The first two nights were kinda bad. So was last night. Really bad. The third night wasn't, though, the night that pic was taken. It was actually mostly good, almost perfect." I try a smile, but she's not interested.

"Really?" she accuses. "Because it looks like you have a black eye."

"I do. Did. But that was nothing compared to the other stuff." I take the phone from her and slide it into my pocket.

"Why, what happened?" she says quietly, like she's afraid to hear the answer. If I know Lucy, her mind is already trying to sort it out, hypothesizing all the possibilities. The worst one, I doubt she'd ever guess. So I won't tell her that I messed up so badly she had an anxiety attack in public and had to be taken away in an ambulance. And, oh, by the way, I wasn't there with her all night, and she got so steaming mad about the whole thing she ended our friendship. What good would that do either of us? Zero.

"It doesn't matter," I tell her. "It's all in the nonexistent past. And I know what to do now so the bad stuff won't repeat. I've already prevented one disaster tonight, before I even picked you up." That's assuming Melody is okay. I took care of it, though, right? Just because I didn't actually see her or the tow this time and I wasn't the one to drop her off at her prom doesn't mean something bad happened. She's fine without me. We were never supposed to meet.

"What disaster?" Lucy says.

"It doesn't matter," I repeat, then put the car in reverse and back down Lucy's driveway. "All I want to do is stop this thing, stop living this same night over and over, but I need your help. So will you help me?"

We sit in tense silence as I drive down the deserted country road.

"JJ," Lucy says calmly. Too calm? "You're going the wrong way."

"What, no I'm not. This is how we always go to school from your house. I could drive this route with my eyes closed."

She sighs. "We have to pick up Jenna, remember?"

No, I didn't remember. I forgot to tell Jenna to get a ride from Autumn, too, so now I *have* to pick her up. Probably for the best, anyway, so she won't get mad at me. So I won't have to pull her aside to apologize. So we'll never kiss.

Yeah, we definitely have to pick up Jenna.

But to Lucy, I say, "You're right, I forgot."

I pull into the nearest driveway and turn us around.

"If you've lived this three times before, why did you forget? You should be running on autopilot."

Because this is me we're talking about. I excel at forgetting things and/or screwing them up. But in my defense, "Every night, something slightly different has happened. I've never been to Jenna's house. She got a ride from Autumn Mitchell the other nights, in a limo. You rode in it, too, the first night."

Lucy looks out the window at the passing trees. "Because you were running later than you thought you were? Like usual? Because you're terrible at keeping track of time?"

"Yes." The problem wasn't just me, but I'm not about to tell her all the sordid details. Instead I go with: "You know me too well."

"I do." In my side vision, I see her turn away from the window. "You weren't that late tonight, though."

I flick her a quick glance and a smile, then put my eyes back on the road. "I know how important punctuality is to you. It took me a few tries, but I figured out how to get here quick."

She reaches over and takes my right hand off the steering wheel, holds it tightly in hers. "There's hope for us yet."

Maybe it was a slip, but I caught it. She said *us*.

Jenna lives in the same upper-crust development that Melody does, even on the same street. It didn't register the other night when I dropped Melody off, because Jenna's address wasn't on my mind. And I never thought of Jenna as upper-crust, to be honest. She's so down-to-earth I always assumed she was on the same crust level as me and Lucy. Not lower-crust. We're like in the middle of the middle-crust. We have everything we need, but not everything we want.

Jenna and Melody and anyone else in this neighborhood could have whatever they want.

Lucy insisted on waiting in the car, so I step up to the house—mansion?—alone and ring the doorbell, wondering why Jenna goes to Beaver Creek High, an average public school that no one outside of this county has ever heard of, when she could go to a place like Whitman Academy that's won presidential awards for educational excellence, or whatever their claim to fame. She's definitely smart enough to and apparently also rich enough.

Some middle-aged guy answers the door in a crisp button-down shirt and trousers . . . with a *crease*. I'm suddenly very aware my tux is incomplete—no tie—because this has to be her dad, and what is he expecting from the person picking up his daughter tonight? Someone of the same crust, at least. Someone who wears a tux with a bow tie.

Or someone British, like her ex-boyfriend, because Americans are good at assuming all Brits are refined. If only he knew the real Blair Bedford.

"You must be JJ," he says, extending a hand.

The strength of my handshake reveals my plummeting confidence. "Yes, sir."

"Mr. D is fine. No need for that 'sir' business." His gaze drops to my hands as I release my weak grip, and he frowns. "Where's the corsage?"

"Oh, this was really last-minute. I didn't have time to—"

"It's fine, JJ," Jenna says, stepping up from behind him, her white dress sparkling with every step as her heels clack against the polished hardwood flooring. "Don't let him scare you."

"Hey, I'm not scary." Mr. D turns toward her with a smile and kisses her cheek. "You look beautiful, sweet pea. What time do you think you'll be back?"

Jenna looks to me for an answer, shocking me into a moment of silence. She made it pretty clear on night three she didn't want anything other than a night of fun *at* prom. But then she kissed me on night four ... Either way, there's no after-prom for us. There's no anything for us. And especially not tonight—I'm planning on bailing not long after we get there. Even if I wasn't, there are no guarantees on anything. I've learned that much, at least.

"Uh ... I don't know," I stammer. "It depends. You never know what might happen."

"What's that supposed to mean?" Mr. D's frown deepens and his brows draw together. He crosses his arms. I know a Dad Look when I see it. Not that different from a Mom Look. "Jenna said the two of you are friends, correct?"

"Yes!" Jenna and I say in unison. "Bye, Daddy," she adds, ushering me out the door. "Don't wait up."

Walking to the car, I tell her, "You look nice." My voice sounds stiff, though, like I didn't really mean what I said, and Jenna pauses, cocking her head slightly. I meant it, she's as pretty as always, but ...

Can she feel it? Is it noticeable that I'm not interested in her the same way I was before? Now we're just two people who know each other from school and can get along, offer genuine compliments, even help each other out if needed, but that's it.

"Thanks," she says, shaking it off. "You, too." Then she sees Lucy sitting in the front seat of my car and stops short. "I guess I'm sitting in the back?"

"Is that okay? Lucy gets carsick if she's not up front."

Jenna smiles big, overly cheerful. "Of course that's okay!"

That's overcompensation. She's already regretting this. If the night repeats again—and I'm doing everything to make sure it doesn't—I won't pick her up again. She can have the limo. I'll just have to make sure she gets to prom first, or I get there second. Whichever.

I open the rear passenger door and it takes her a minute to get settled inside, as if she's forgotten how to sit. Once I'm inside, too, and turning the ignition, I pop a glance to the rear-view mirror. Jenna's looking around her like the walls of my car might eat her.

"This is . . . cozy." She nods and beams another super smile.

"Would you have preferred something fancier? More spacious?" Lucy says, with what I call her "red flag" tone. She's not angry yet, but all it will take is Jenna making one more veiled insult about something she holds dear. In this case, my car. Which she also considers *her* car. She goes on, "I heard Autumn Mitchell got a limo. I bet she'd be willing to pick you up. You have her number, right? Aren't you guys friends kind of?"

Oops . . . I forgot I told her about that.

"Kind of, yeah," Jenna says, her Barbie-like grin still plastered in place. "But we only know each other casually, like, we're friends with the same people? We aren't really that close. I wouldn't want to impose. This is fine. It smells nice! Like Chanel. Is that what you wear, Lucy?"

Melody's perfume. It's back. This is worse than the limo comment. I fumble with my seat belt a few times before clicking it into place.

"No . . ." Lucy locks a hard stare onto me, the facial equivalent of her "red flag" tone, then turns her head to look at Jenna. "I don't wear perfume. I thought that was yours."

Before Jenna can reply with the obvious question—*if it's not my perfume and it's not Lucy's, then who else was in here, JJ?*—I throw the car into drive, tires squealing, and they both let out a little gasp as the sudden forward thrust presses them back into their seats. "Sorry," I say. "My foot slipped." *Change the subject.* "So, Jenna, I've been meaning to ask . . . why didn't you go to Whitman Academy? Don't they have a writing program there?"

She takes the bait and starts word-vomiting a response.

I've tuned her out, though, and press the gas pedal down farther when we hit an open stretch of road. The faster we get to prom, the faster Lucy and I can slip away from it and fix the original glitch that started this whole thing—our broken science project.

"That was the worst chicken cordon bleu I've ever had," Lucy says, and pushes her plate away.

"It's the only chicken cordon bleu you've ever had," I remind her, and push my plate away, too, then down the last of my third cup of coffee. "And I knew it would be bad. You know what we should have done? Stopped at Taco Bell on the way here."

"Yes, we should have." Lucy laughs. "That sounds so much better. We don't need this pretentious poultry. If this night repeats again, you have my permission to take me to Taco Bell."

The music has started up, covering our conversation with a deep, thumping beat, and Chaz and Marcos have left us already. Now that Lucy's had some time to digest the idea of the time loop, she won't stop talking about it. And this is good. I need the wheels in her head turning at top speed if we're going to figure out how to stop it.

"On the second night, I almost did take you to Taco Bell." I think back. It was after we dropped off Melody and Lucy wasn't cool with the idea of poaching. It was late. We were both really hungry. Then she said, *I can be spontaneous, too.*

Sure she can. That's why she planned out what would happen on prom night a year ahead of time.

"So why didn't you?" She takes a sip of water.

We ate at someone else's prom, someone you might never meet again. I got punched. You almost died. "The night stopped," I say instead. "I jumped to the next repeat."

She thinks on this. "Same time every night?"

Huh. Now I'm the one taking a moment to think. "No, actually. See? This is why I need you to help me. I hadn't realized until now it was a different time each night."

"It isn't a set loop, then. If there's no order to it, it's a chaos loop. And if it's a chaos loop, you're screwed. And if you're screwed, we're all screwed. You won't be able to predict everything that happens from one repeat to the next."

"Yeah. I'm already seeing that."

"Something really bad could happen and you wouldn't be able to stop it, because you won't know it's coming."

"I know. That's what I'm trying to prevent." Among other things, like having to watch our relationship ping-pong between friends and not-friends and something-other-than-friends.

"If someone died one of these nights, do you think they would come back to life when it resets?" Her jaw drops a little.

"Has that already happened? Did someone—"

"No," I assure her. Although I don't know for sure if she got hit by that car on night two and came back okay the next night, or if the loop reset right before impact.

I force my thoughts onto what I *do* know. "There are also these weird glitches that keep popping up."

"Glitches?" Lucy straightens and leans closer to me. "Like déjà vu in *The Matrix*?"

"Kind of, yes. Little repeats that jump from one night to the next, while everything else resets." I let out a yawn so wide my eyes water. This coffee isn't strong enough to fight four sleepless nights. "So like, on night one, for example, I had worn my contacts, and by the end of the night, my eyes were burning, right? And then—"

"That always happens," she interrupts. "I don't know why you bother wearing them. Anyway, what happened with this glitch?"

"Wait, wait, back up a sec. Lucy, I wear contacts on special occasions because you told me I look better without my glasses. Am I wrong for wanting to look good?"

"No. I . . ." She leans back in her chair and focuses on her hands in her lap. "I didn't know what I'd said had that effect on you."

"You're my best friend. I value your opinion more than anyone's."

She looks up at me. "But you made yourself endure physical discomfort because of an opinion I should have just kept to myself. I don't even remember why I said it, because I think you look good with glasses, too. You always—" She clamps her mouth shut.

"I always what?" Bring out the worst in her? Make her say stuff she doesn't mean?

"You always look good, JJ. That's what I should have said."

This shouldn't shock me into silence, after all she told me on night three, but it does, and I just stare back at her, still processing the fact that she really does like me *like that*.

Twibble.

It's not time for this yet. We'll get there eventually. Be patient.

I look around for something to help me change the subject, get us back to talking about the time loop, and I catch Jenna stepping off the dance floor as the music slows. This time, instead of with me, she danced with Trevor Pickett on the most recent fast song, one of her friends from the school paper staff. He maneuvers his wheelchair up to his girlfriend for the slow song, and my gaze follows Jenna all the way to the drink buffet, where her friends crowd around her. On the other night, they kept glancing at me, but tonight they have no reason to, because I haven't done a thing with Jenna since we got here, good or bad. And she doesn't seem to care either way.

"What's going on with you and her?" Lucy says, snapping me out of my thoughts.

Sigh. "Absolutely nothing. I thought I needed to help her get through tonight, but she's fine. She's been fine every night"—almost—"no matter what happens."

Lucy nods. "That's very typical of you."

"What is?"

"You have good intentions. You just don't always know how to use them. It's not a problem, though, not for me anyway."

We're too opposite. And it only creates problems.

My head spins. This is definitely a chaos loop—and Lucy's part of the chaos. Every night, she has been something different. Always herself, but a different version of herself. She's usually predictable, but ever since this loop started, she's done nothing but surprise me.

"Look at those two," Lucy says, and I follow her gaze to Chaz and Marcos making out on the dance floor. "They're so in love they're completely oblivious to the rest of the world."

I remember this.

"Not as oblivious as they seem. Keep watching." I lean closer to her so I can keep my voice down. "Carson Spires and Mia Howard are going to pass them soon and make faces at them. Then Blair Bedford and Farah Justice are going to pass and Farah's going to say something we won't be able to hear. Then Chaz and Marcos both flip her off."

Lucy laughs but keeps watching. It all plays out exactly how I said it would.

"Why are you the only one who remembers everything?" she says.

"I don't know. Maybe because Marty was right next to me in my room when he fritzed?"

"Yeah . . ." Lucy nods slowly. "That has to be it." She doesn't sound convinced, though. "We should go work on it now."

"Hang on, this is when—"

Our song starts playing. I stand and offer my hand to Lucy,

but she won't take it. She's never refused this song before, not once in the last three and a half years. Last night this song even prompted her to search for me. "What's wrong?" I ask.

"What if we run out of time? We don't know when this version of tonight will stop."

"One dance, Lucy. Then we can go save the world. Promise."

Still, she protests. "You already had this dance, why do you need it again?"

A million reasons, but I settle on: "It's not just for me. It's for you, for both of us. This is *our* song, and we will dance to it at *our* prom every time we're here together. I'll make sure you get this dance every night for the rest of my life if I have to, if this loop goes on that long, and it'll be the best part of our prom every time."

Her cheeks redden. "Fine, be that way." She takes my hand and we step out, then settle into each other on the dance floor, surrounded by swirling colors and blending sounds. It's different this time. She's distant, not holding me as closely or watching me as intently. She's got too many other things on her mind.

We can't end this dance the same way as before, with her so overwhelmed she has to get away. So instead of just swaying with her to the music and enjoying the feel of her—definitely doing that, but also—I talk. A lot. I talk all the way through the song to keep her thoughts off everything she's worrying about.

It's not just empty talk, though, not for us. I tell her jokes she's heard a hundred times before but that I know she'll laugh at. That's how we started, strangers at a party freshman year, making a comment about this song and then talking all night about stuff that only we understood, telling jokes that only we found funny.

"Are you cold?" I say. "We could go sit in the corner, it's always ninety degrees."

She rolls her eyes, but I count it a win. If she was truly annoyed, she'd do worse.

And when the jokes have run dry, I sing along to our song in the whiniest lovesick voice I can muster. Now, when it ends, she's smiling big and throwing her head back with her throaty, snorting belly laugh that I love.

It worked. I have to remember this for next time, if there is a next time.

There'd better not be a next time.

Lucy tugs me off the dance floor, still smiling. "We're going now. You promised."

"Okay, okay, let me just send Marcos a text so he and Chaz don't wonder where we are." I pull out my cell phone as we're walking and bring up my contact list. Right under Marcos's name is Melody's.

Another glitch. I didn't meet her, let alone get her phone number tonight. But it's an opportunity to make sure she's okay that I can't pass up.

Me: Do you have a sec to talk?

Please answer please answer please answer please—

Melody: Who is this?

Relief floods me so strongly I get light-headed and my knees weaken. We reach our table and I steady myself against a chair.

195

Melody is okay. Jenna is okay. Lucy is okay. We're all okay.

    Me: Sorry wrong number

"All set?" Lucy says. Her eyes are shining and her lips don't twibble. She's got a vibrant energy about her, determined to solve this impossible thing, whatever it takes.

"Yes, everything is perfect." It's the perfect night to end on.

"Perfect," Lucy says, opening the door to our physics classroom. "It isn't locked. Luck must be on your side tonight."

"No such thing as luck," I remind her.

"Figure of speech," she volleys back, like I knew she would.

As we step in, I flip the light switch and the room wakes up. I peek at Mrs. Ruano's desk, hoping in her haste to get to the weekend, she didn't just forget to lock the door, but also left her gradebook lying around? Suddenly the idea that I might never know what grade she gave us on our project makes my stomach churn. Or that could be the nasty chicken cordon bleu, but either way, we worked hard on Marty. He's a piece of trash, but still. He's an A-worthy piece of trash. But her gradebook isn't there, and the drawers of her desk are locked.

Lucy sets Marty on our table in the back like it's a workstation, then goes to the actual workstations along the walls and starts collecting tools. Her enthusiasm tugs a smile out of me, but the effort of that one little action exhausts me. Everything exhausts me right now—because *I'm exhausted*.

I climb up onto the blacktop table next to ours, the one where Carson Spires sits on the days he decides to actually show up for class, and lie across the length of it with the front side of me down, then cross my arms and rest my chin on my folded hands, watching Lucy work.

"When Marty fritzed," she says, unscrewing the main panel, "what did you see exactly?"

"Blue sparks. Just like when your hairpin fell in. Vibrations, too. I think."

"Hmm . . ." She pops the panel off. "First thing I guess is finding that bobby."

My eyelids droop, sleep threatening to pull me under. What if I fall asleep and wake up in the next repeat, though? What if I blow my chance for Lucy to help me fix this? I force myself to stay awake, force myself to talk, my brain scrambling for a topic that feels worth the effort. It takes only a moment to find one. "I've been thinking," I start.

"Dangerous," she teases.

"Funny." I toss her a smirk, then continue. "When you made your first wish the other night—last night for you—the wish on the falling star, about going back to see your mom before she left your family so you could convince her to stay and you could have a second chance . . ."

She keeps working, but her movements slow. "What about it?"

My groggy thoughts bump against one another, trying to form a single coherent one. "On night three, we were talking on the bluffs, and you reminded me you didn't really believe the wish would come true, anyway. So. If we can get Marty to stop glitching and fritzing and work the way he's supposed to, do you want to give it a try? See if we can make your

197

wish come true? Not as a granted wish, I mean, but through science?"

Now she stops, staring down at the device, her hands frozen in place and her chest rising and dropping slightly faster than it was a minute ago. "Was that all I told you on the bluffs?"

No. Not even close. You spilled three and a half years' worth of secrets and then we shared a kiss I really wouldn't mind experiencing again.

"Was there something else you'd planned to tell me?" I ask innocently.

Just say it. Just ask me and I'll tell you YES all over again. But only if you say it.

"Nothing, no." She goes back to tinkering.

I guess in this version we stay platonic friends, nothing else. And I need to remind myself that isn't a bad thing. "So do you want to try?"

"To go back in time and change the past?"

"Yeah."

"Maybe." Her lip twibbles. "Do you?"

"There are plenty of things about my past I wish happened differently, sure." But that isn't why I wanted Marty to work. It was for something weirdly reminiscent of what's actually happening. To be able to go back in time, after Lucy moved to Italy, and spend a day with her whenever I wanted. So it would be like she never left.

"But I don't know," I mumble through a yawn. "I think I'm better at winging my way through life. I'd probably just screw it up worse on the second try."

She nods, her smile cunning. "True."

"Gee, thanks." I laugh, and it devolves into a monster yawn that pops my jaw and leaves me light-headed. My eyelids flutter. Then close. Then . . .

"JJ?" Lucy's voice breaks into a fuzzy dream I already can't remember. She shakes my arm. "Hey . . . wake up."

I rub my eyes and sit up on the table, groaning at the ache in my neck, then blink a few times and run a hand through my hair. Lucy hands me my glasses, which must have fallen off. It's too bright in here. My eyes take a minute to adjust. "How long was I asleep?"

"Long enough for me to fix Marty."

Just like that, I'm alert. "You fixed him?"

"Yeah, it was easy once I got the bobby out and uncrossed the wires, then replaced the—" She presses her lips together and looks down, like she's embarrassed for getting into the details. Or maybe she remembered we might be short on time. "I mean, I can't know for sure it'll work."

I hop down off the table, glancing at the clock on the wall. It's after ten. Prom is almost over, but if we're still in the science lab with Marty, then we're still on night five. Nothing reset. "You think it's safe to test him now?"

"I don't know if it's safe, but I think we should try. Before it gets any later. I didn't want to wake you up, though, you were so tired . . ."

"I'm glad you did. It would have been a waste to get this far only to sleep my way into the next repeat. And no offense, Lucy, but I don't want to have to convince you about this all over again. Once was hard enough."

Her mouth twists. "Well, you might still have to."

"If that picture of us doesn't glitch into the next night, I don't know how I will."

"Just be patient with me," she says. "I know I can be . . . difficult."

"We both can. It's kind of our thing." I offer a smile like it's an olive branch.

She takes it, offers an apologetic smile of her own, then picks up Marty, and we head out the door. In the quiet hallway, sounds of prom echo faintly past us, drifting like ghosts. Thumping beats, pops of laughter and cheers, all the stuff I'm missing that I can't remember why it mattered so much. I expected this to be one night of fun. *The* night of fun. The night of my life. But no matter how amazing it might have been, it would only be here for a few hours, then gone forever. Time never stops, even when it's stuck in a loop.

A strange sense of grief washes over me as we pass our lockers, which will belong to other students in the new school year, an endless cycle of beginnings and endings within these walls, and I'm not sure what exactly I'm mourning. My prom? My childhood? The planned night Lucy and I were *supposed* to have and never will?

Is what we got instead better, though? Maybe. Maybe not. I don't know anymore. Every night has been a clash of expectations and surprises, a mix of good and bad.

My chest tenses and my gut flutters with nerves. I'm either going to fix everything now or fail more spectacularly than ever before. That's how the universe seems to be operating lately. One extreme or the other; nothing on the spectrum in between.

We push out the main entrance of Beaver Creek High, into the cool night air and the darkened parking lot, heading toward the football field. It's the only space wide open enough to safely test Marty. There's nothing explosive inside, but going by our history with him, Lucy isn't entirely confident he won't explode.

I'm inclined to think he very likely won't, that the sparks were just from the metal hairpin reacting to the electrical charge. The chances of an explosion, even a small one, are slim to none. But this is a classic case of Lucy being Lucy. Overly cautious and overprepared, always.

Weaving through the parking lot full of cars, I catch a flash of sparkling white in my side vision, then whip my head toward it.

Jenna.

Strike that. Jenna and Blair.

They're standing beside his behemoth truck, Jenna with her brows furrowed and arms crossed, Blair's jacket draped over her shoulders and a fake tiara on her head. His cheek is still red from Jenna's smack, and he gestures as he talks, his face almost contorted like he's in pain. Pleading? This is the talk I prevented them from having on several nights. And maybe the talk they *did* have on night one, before Lucy's crash. Before I found Blair consoling Jenna at the hospital.

I'll never know if it was Jenna's worry over Lucy that brought them back together that night or the fact that they talked and worked it out. Or both. I should have taken Jenna's advice from the start—sometimes the solution to your problem is to take yourself out of the equation.

Jenna and Blair are not part of my equation. Or vice versa. I should have never been involved.

I don't realize I've stopped to stare until Lucy turns ahead of me, raising her voice to cover the distance between us. "Hey, what's the holdup?" She still doesn't see them. But they definitely heard her.

Jenna and Blair turn toward us slowly. Blair's face goes from supplicating to aggravated in less than half a second.

"JJ." Jenna flashes a tight grin. "Hi. Uh. What are you doing out here?"

In a brilliant stroke of genius, I say, "Nothing. What are you doing out here?"

"None of your business," Blair says, not angrily but with a terse edge, like he just wants me to go away. And I can't be annoyed with his brush-off, because that much I understand. This really is none of my business. Nothing about their relationship has ever been any of my business.

"Actually, never mind, I can see what you're, uh, doing," I stammer. "I didn't mean to see it, but I did. I'm . . . sorry for interrupting." And I'm very confused. Why would she consider taking him back? Or even listening to him right now?

Whatever. Why do I still care? Jenna can do what she wants, and apparently she is.

I turn away from them and head toward Lucy. But then Jenna says, "Wait," and her heels clack across the asphalt. When I turn again, she's right by me.

"What, Jenna?" I don't mean to sound so clipped, but she's got me stumped. I feel like I don't even know her anymore. Did I ever?

"I just want to explain," she says in a hushed whisper. Blair is a few feet from us on one side, and Lucy is a few feet from us on another side. I guess she doesn't want either one of them to hear this. "I know this probably looks bad, after everything we talked about yesterday, and everything that happened tonight, and with the crowning and . . . well, I'm sure you saw. But then he—he talked to me, the way he used to. He apologized. He said he couldn't stand to see me hurt anymore because of him. He told me the real reason he pushed me away, and it wasn't right, I know that, and I'm not getting back together with him. But I don't want the last things we ever said or did to each other to be . . ." She sighs sharply. "He's not a bad person, JJ. He just didn't know what to do, and he made the wrong choice. Don't we all sometimes?"

I nod. Who am I to say someone doesn't deserve kindness after making a huge mistake? Isn't that basically the definition of my relationship with Lucy? One epic failure to the next, for years. And she's still putting up with me.

Until she didn't, said she couldn't anymore.

That's way in the past now, a past that doesn't really exist, a slate wiped clean by this loop. Except it's still in my memory, even if no one else remembers, stuck there like smoke, the acrid scent clinging to everything on me. My clothes, my hair, my nostrils. Every breath I take, it's all I can smell. *I'm no good for you, JJ. We're no good for each other.*

I shake it off. Just for a moment.

"He doesn't deserve you, Jenna," I tell her honestly. "But I hope everything works out, for your sake."

"Thank you." She smiles and then walks back to Blair, says something to him I can't hear. He opens his truck door for her and helps her up into the passenger seat. As I catch up to Lucy, I hear the engine rumble and then get quieter and quieter until it disappears.

"What was that all about?" Lucy says, heading for the football field again.

Instead of answering her, I ask, "Why are we friends?"

That stops her just short of the entrance to the field. She looks up at me in the dark, the moonlight reflecting in her big brown eyes. "What kind of a question is that all the sudden?"

"I just . . . I don't know what you see in me. What makes me worth all the stress I cause?"

"Whoa, whoa, whoa." She lets out a humorless laugh. "What stress? You think you stress me out? Where is this coming from?"

"On the first version of tonight, you told me we stress each other out too much. You said—"

"Stop, JJ. Whatever I said, I was wrong. I was probably just . . . mad, or something. We both know my temper isn't the best sometimes."

I shoot her an "oh, really?" look.

"Okay, more than sometimes. But that isn't the point. Listen to me." She sets Marty down on the ground and takes my face in her hands, tilting my head downward, forcing me to look right into her eyes. "You don't stress me out. You're *an outlet* for my stress. You help me channel it away, even when it's at its worst."

"I know." What she's saying is logical, but based on other things she's said, on other versions of tonight—from other versions of herself—it makes no sense.

"Do you, though?" she presses. "Do you really understand how much that means to me?"

"Yes. I do. Lucy, you told me." My chest heaves as I try to take in a full breath, but I feel like I'm one lung short. "You told me everything."

She blinks rapidly, my response throwing her off, her expression turning uncertain. "What are you . . . talking about?"

"I mean you told me everything you'd been holding back. You told me why you stopped dating people after Macy Morris dumped you. You told me you've wanted to be with me, as something other than friends, since we met at that party. You told me you planned out this whole prom night so we could be together, from picking out that dress to having our own private after-prom under the stars and everything in between."

Her eyes close, her face pinches, and she turns away. Drops her hands from me.

"But I don't get it," I say. "Because on the first night, you—"
What are you doing, JJ?

205

Her eyes snap open, and she locks them onto me, razor sharp. "I what?"

I've said this much. I might as well keep going. "You ended our friendship. I screwed up bad that night and you said that's it, no more chances. You said you needed time and distance from me, possibly forever. You said we're no good for each other. It was you then, the same as it's you now. So why was I worth forgiving for all those years and then suddenly not? Why was I ever worth forgiving at all?"

"JJ, I don't know why I did what I did before." The crushed tone of her voice cracks my heart wide open. "All I know is I wouldn't do that right now. I can't even imagine doing it."

I want to believe her, but, "You still haven't told me why. *Why* wouldn't you now?"

"I . . ." She bites her trembling lip and releases a shaky breath. "It's just a feeling. There's no logic to it whatsoever. It's hard to explain."

"Can you try? Please," I whisper.

Her hands fidget before she clenches them tight and then opens them again, shaking them out. "When I'm with you, everything is light, even if it's heavy. When I'm with you, my own darkness isn't scary. When I'm with you, I don't feel flawed, even though I am. Very, very flawed. And it's really hard for me to say that out loud, to admit that I make a lot of mistakes, when I demand perfection from myself and everyone around me. But when I'm with you, I feel . . . flawless."

The crack in my heart starts to stitch itself back up. "Even when we argue?"

"Even when we argue." She laughs softly. "I told you it wasn't logical. But you know . . ." Her expression turns dour. "I've wondered the same thing. My temper, my perfectionism, my tendency to argue—those are the top three reasons people break up with me. So why are you still friends with me, with everything I put you through? The nitpicking, the unrealistic expectations, the constant worry. How can you stand me?"

For a moment I just stare at her, absorb the way she looks in this moment, with the breeze ruffling her galaxy dress, making the stars on it flicker in waves. And her hair cascading over her shoulders in loose dark curls that gleam red in the moonlight. The way her deep brown eyes shine briefly when a meteor flashes across the sky. We're missing the Eta Aquarids tonight, but we're gaining something much more magical.

The truth.

And some of it is ugly. But she's been completely honest with me, so I owe her the same.

"Lucy . . ." I step closer to her, rest my hands on her shoulders, then let them fall slowly down her bare arms. By the time I reach her hands, goose bumps have prickled across her exposed skin and she shivers. I remove my jacket and give it to her, without a word. She takes it and puts it on, without a word. "Here's the thing. You do stress me out, because I worry about you all the time. But I worry because I care, and I care because . . ." I hesitate, then let out a nervous laugh. "It isn't logical."

"That seems to be the theme of the night, so go ahead. Just tell me."

"Okay." Deep breath in. Out. Again. "When I try to imagine a world without you in it, I can't. When I try to remember my life before I met you, it's like it didn't exist. *I* didn't exist, and so when I met you, it was like . . . um . . . when a star forms. Things came together at just the right time in just the right way, to create something from nothing. Lucy, my . . . my biggest fear? Is losing you. Then a few nights ago, my worst nightmare came true. I lost you—not because you were taken away from me. But because you *chose* to push me away. And almost every night since, I've lost you again, just in different ways. I don't know how to stop this from happening over and over and over."

Lucy squeezes my hands and I notice they're trembling. "Why would I . . . Why was I so upset at you?"

"The why isn't important now." Not important enough to upset her all over again. "Ever since then, I've been stuck in this time loop that shouldn't be possible, and I'm starting to wonder if any of it is even real. That maybe my brain is tricking me into believing we'll be together in this loop forever, reliving a night where we always start out as friends, because it's trying to protect me from the truth—that I don't actually have you as a friend anymore. So it's made up this imaginary place for me to exist, because I don't actually exist without you."

God. I sound like Melody. What if she was right all along? Time only exists in our heads. *What if all of this is just in my head?* If that's the case, then this crude time-travel device won't do anything to stop it. So I have to believe it's real, and that Marty will work, because what's the alternative? A whole lot of *nothing.*

Lucy inches closer, wrapping her arms around my torso and squeezing. "This is real," she says, craning her neck to look up at me.

"How can you say that for sure?"

"Because I know I'm real. If I wasn't, I couldn't do this." She pushes up on her toes and curls one hand behind my neck, and her lips meet mine.

For her, this is our first kiss. For me, it's our second, and it came about in a completely different way, but it affects me just as strongly. Within seconds, I'm struggling to breathe evenly. I'm savoring the taste of her lipstick and getting drunk on the smell of her shampoo. I'm holding her tighter and tighter because, even smashed against each other, we aren't close enough.

I could kiss her a million times and this feeling would never get old, this feeling like my whole body and mind have been shot like a rocket into the sweetest oblivion.

When she finally breaks away and we both gulp for air, she lays her head on my chest then says, *"Mio cuore, mia anima, mia vita." My heart, my soul, my life.*

"Ti amo, Lucilla." *I love you.* "I realize now . . . I think I've loved you for a long time. I just didn't recognize that's what it was until you . . . you made me see it."

She looks up at me, and I think she's going to kiss me again, but then her brows dart toward each other and form a deep wrinkle. "Your eye . . . You look like you just got punched."

I touch my finger to it and wince. It's swollen and tender, throbbing. "I did get punched—a couple of nights ago. It's a glitch."

"And it's bleeding." She kicks off her heels so she's barefoot, bends over and picks up Marty, then trots onto the football field, shouting over her shoulder at me. "We've got to stop this. Now."

I follow her across the grass that's still soft from yesterday's rain, and my phone chimes with a new text. I'm honest-to-God afraid to look at it after just getting my black eye glitch, but curiosity wins. It's from Chaz. I tap it open and find a picture of me and Lucy on the dance floor at prom—my mouth open like I'm yodeling and Lucy's head bent back the way she does when she's belly-laughing. That was from tonight, but I don't remember Chaz snapping a picture of us. Maybe he did and we didn't notice? Or maybe he didn't and it just appeared on its own . . .

Either way, this chaos loop is getting tangled out of control, and our best chance at preventing something catastrophic is in a fickle science project with improvised wiring.

A string of new texts from Chaz appears right after the picture.

> Where are you? Prom's almost over and I lost Lucy
>
> Found her. GET HERE
>
> She's convinced you're dead. Are you?
>
> PICK UP YOUR PHONE

That was when Lucy passed out on night one. She isn't with Chaz now; she's with me and she's fine. Just another glitch, but it still got my heart pounding, like post-traumatic stress that's been triggered. I never want to see those texts again. If this works, I won't have to.

Lucy sets Marty in the very center of the field, on the fifty-yard line, right over the beaver's head painted in the grass. "All right," she says. "You ready?"

I pocket my phone. "No."

"Me neither."

She flips the switch, and Marty whirs to life, then she grabs my hand and we take off running toward the goal posts like we're going for a game-winning touchdown. Maybe if we run fast enough, we can fly right off the earth, ride a comet to the stars, and live the rest of our days on the moon, just the two of us.

Forty yards.

I glance at Lucy. She's breathing hard but smiling, like a child running through a sprinkler in summer, her gaze focused straight ahead. She doesn't see me see her.

Thirty yards.

I glance up, almost losing my balance and tripping. Meteors flash around us, several of them all falling at once, like dripping fireworks. It's unreal. This can't be real. I lift my free hand toward the sky, as if I could catch them in my palm.

Twenty yards.

A small, dark figure moves in my side vision, the side Lucy isn't on. I whip my head toward it but see nothing in the shadow of the bleachers.

Ten yards.

Nothing has happened. Something should have happened by now.

Beaver Creek.

We reach the end zone and drop. Crouch and turn, waiting.

And waiting.

And wait—

KABOOM!

Marty . . . just went supernova. In a glorious explosion that shouldn't have been possible—there was nothing inside him that could make such a magnificent fireball. Yet there it is. We stare at each other, her wide eyes and dropped jaw mimicking mine, then look back at the smoking remnants of our only hope.

That was our *only hope.*

"What now?" Lucy says.

"I don't—" All rational thought disappears when a groundhog totters out onto the field.

"Is that a woodchuck? Oh no, it's going toward the fire. Get away from that!" Lucy hops up and starts making noise, waving her arms and moving toward it, trying to get the thing to run off scared. But it doesn't.

The groundhog looks right at me, then at the dwindling blue flames and growing billows of smoke, then back at me, and actually shakes its head. As if to say, *Silly boy, did you really think that would work?*

"Fine," I say, throwing my hands up. "You win. Game over now. Please just *stop.*"

Lucy has drifted several yards away in her attempts to save the devil from its own hell, and then suddenly she leans over like she's catching her breath after a hard run. We did run, but she was fine a minute ago.

"JJ? I can't—" She sucks in air, loudly and distorted, like her lungs just stopped working.

Because they probably did, for no reason at all. Lucy's glitching.

Panic seizes me, gauging how large the gap is between us. I can't lose her again. What if I don't get her back next time? Or ever? *I can't lose her.*

"Hang on!" I shout, jumping to my feet and sprinting toward her.

Lucy swivels to face me, her expression riddled with confusion, clutching her chest, and then she drops to her knees.

How am I going to get her back after this?

I still don't know, but I have to try. "I'm coming!"

Absolute terror fills her eyes. She outstretches one arm, reaching for me as I run closer, her other hand planted in the grass for support. Her fingertips brush mine and I squeeze.

But I squeeze nothing but air. See nothing but black. Hear nothing but my ragged breaths and pounding heart. Feel nothing but cold emptiness, inside and out.

the NIGHT of the TOTAL ECLIPSE

The blinding white behind my eyes doesn't faze me this time, though it takes a second to regain my balance after running, then floating, to now standing still. I stare at my reflection in my bedroom mirror, still breathing hard, my limbs still buzzing with adrenaline, Lucy's name caught in my throat. The unfastened bow tie hangs loose in my hand. The black eye is gone. My contacts are in, no glasses. No taco stain on my shirt.

Everything reset, but something feels off. Something isn't happening that should be.

As soon as I think it, my memory fills in the gap. No blue sparks in my side vision.

Marty should be fritzing, but he isn't there. At all. His explosion on night five made him unable to reset on night six, tonight. Six nights of this . . . not even a week and I'm spent.

How many more repeats? Infinite? If this is immortality, I don't want it. Let me just die.

But Lucy . . .

I check the texts on my phone. Everything from prom night has been wiped, except:

Lucy: Where are you?

Me: Leaving soon

I don't know what to do anymore. I just want this to end.

"Knock, knock," Mom says on the other side of my door. "Are you decent?"

"Yes, come in." I fasten my bow tie as Mom enters the room and her reflection approaches mine in the mirror.

"You're a pro at that," she says. "I thought I might have to help you with it."

"I've been practicing."

"Good! You look so sharp." Her blue-gray eyes study me from beneath her side-swept bangs. "You feeling all right?"

No. "Yes. Why?"

"I don't know, you seem . . . too somber for prom night. Like you're going to a funeral. Is everything okay between you and Lucy?"

Not at all. "Everything's great. Why would you think it has to do with Lucy?"

She doesn't get a chance to reply, because Shayla comes blazing into the room. "Look at you all fancy!" she squeals, and this sad sort of choked laugh escapes me. I love my baby sister so much, and I haven't seen her enough. I miss this little human tornado. "Dance with me, JJ."

She grabs my hands and starts doing her jump-skip-fairy-sprite-forest-dance thing, humming the song she probably just

215

made up, while I stand in place, twirling her around me a few times, then sweep her up into my arms, and she begs me to toss her onto my bed. I do as I'm told, and this is way more fun than going to prom.

This is also going to make me late.

Unless . . . I don't go to prom this time.

As soon as the thought hits me, I've decided that's what I need to do tonight. Or rather, not do. And I wonder why I didn't think of it sooner. I can avoid every mess that happens at prom by just avoiding *prom* altogether.

"Can I wear a tux to my prom, too?" Shayla is saying as she drags herself—and my blankets—across my bed. "But a pink one? With roses embroidered on the sleeves? And sequined high heels? And a giant rose corsage on my wrist?"

"Of course you can," Mama says, entering the room. It's been a few nights since this happened, but I remember it and I'm ready. "You can do whatever you want, baby girl." Shayla jumps off the bed, shouts in victory, then runs off down the hall and thunders down the stairs.

As expected, Mama whips out her phone. "Can I get a few pictures before you leave?"

"Yes!" I say excitedly, shocking both my parents into wide-eyed looks. "Take all the pictures you want." I immediately strike a pose, and she laughs and gets to work.

"Look at him, Danni, our little boy is all grown up." Mom's voice cracks like she's about to cry. She thinks I'm all grown up? Yeah, right. Would a mature adult get himself trapped in a time loop on prom night? A chaos loop, at that.

Chaos personified.

"Mom, I'm still your little boy tonight. Come 'ere." I pull her up against me and we take a picture together. Then she takes the phone from Mama and I get one with her. Then we all cram our faces into a selfie, and since I'm holding the phone this time, I tap a bunny ears filter onto all of us. Too bad these pictures won't last beyond tonight. We look ridiculous. I love it.

"You'd better get going now," Mama says, taking the phone from me. "Don't keep Lucy waiting. You know how she is."

"Yeah, I know how she is." She is the person I need right now.

"Remember the rules," Mom says.

"I remember. No drugs, alcohol, speeding, getting anyone pregnant, or being a juvenile delinquent." When Mom crosses her arms, I add, "And have fun."

Shock flits across her face, but only for a moment before it goes stern again. "Not too much fun . . ."

"Be safe, JJ," Mama adds.

"I will. Promise. And I won't be out all night." Because who knows how long this one will be?

As I skitter down the stairs, my phone chimes with a new text.

> Lucy: On your way yet?
>
> Me: Yes I'll be there in twenty. Ish
>
> Lucy: Twenty?!
>
> Me: Have to make another stop first
>
> Lucy: SIGH
>
> Me: ☺

While I've got my phone out, I text Jenna and suggest she

get a ride from Autumn Mitchell, because I won't be making it to prom after all. I start to type *something came up* but then remember that's exactly what Blair told her in their text conversation she showed me on Friday. So I go with—

Me: I'm sorry things didn't work out as planned

I'm sorry.

I'm sorry.

Jenna: No worries. ☺ Hope you're ok. Talk Monday?

If Monday ever comes?

Me: Yeah. Talk Monday

On my way out to my car, I call the tow and arrange for them to take care of Melody. That's it. Done. I'm taking the rest of the night off. Just me and Lucy and no prom. If I feel like going to prom again tomorrow night, I will, but for now, I need a break.

And I need my best friend.

But first, I need Taco Bell.

"Why does it smell like Taco Bell in here?" Lucy says, buckling her seat belt in my car.

I pull a paper bag from the back seat with the bell logo on it, just long enough to show her, then put it back. "Our dinner."

"We're supposed to have dinner at prom."

"We're not doing our 'supposed to' tonight. We tried that, multiple times, and it didn't work out so well."

She stares at me like I've grown a third arm. "What are you saying?"

I put the car in gear and start backing down her driveway. "I'm saying let's skip prom and go straight to the bluffs. Just you and me. The whole night. We can eat Taco Bell and watch the sunset, then watch the stars come out and fall down all around us. We can just be . . . us. This night will be the night of *our* life, no one else's, done *our* way."

"You want to skip prom." She shakes her head. "You've been looking forward to prom for years! For as long as I've known you!"

"I don't care about prom anymore," I tell her. "Prom is like any other school dance we've been to. Right? I'm more excited about what happens after. So let's just get to the after part."

She goes quiet. I can practically hear the wheels spinning in her head as she recalculates her plan for the night.

When I turn onto her road the opposite way I would if we were going to school, she doesn't try to stop me. That was easy. But then I remember, she thinks I still have to pick up—

"What about Jenna?" she says.

"Jenna's fine." She'll be fine without me, just like Melody. She has always been fine without me. "She knows I'm not going. I didn't tell her why, though. That's our secret."

Twibble. "And Marcos and Chaz?"

"Tell them what we're doing instead of prom and I guarantee you they won't have a problem with it. Go ahead. Text one of them. Doesn't matter who, they'll both say the same."

She's quiet again as she pulls out her phone and starts tapping the screen. She knows I'm right; she just doesn't know why.

"Well?" I ask when she's done.

"Chaz said have fun and we can all get together tomorrow. They'll fill us in on anything we missed that's worth talking

219

about." She doesn't sound surprised. More like, pensive.

I flick another glance at her and then my eyes are right back on the road. There's an intersection ahead. One way takes us to Whip's Ledge. The other, nowhere. Straight ahead goes to prom. "Any more arguments?"

"No." She sighs. "But there will be if you didn't get me a chicken burrito supreme."

"You really think I would forget your favorite item on the menu?" I say through a grin, and take the turn toward Whip's Ledge.

A few minutes later, we pass a tow truck driving in the opposite direction, away from the Frost Center for Fine Entertaining. There's no one in the passenger seat, but in the rearview mirror, I see a cream-colored Beetle with a black convertible top is hitched to the back of the tow, getting smaller and smaller as it's pulled away.

Melody really did make it to her prom like I hoped. But she'll never know the guy who helped get her there, night after night, was once her friend. As far as she's concerned, I don't exist, and she's fine without me.

And I have to be okay with that.

"Are you okay?" Lucy says through a snorting laugh, not even trying to hide how hilarious she finds my pain. And by pain I mean spilling the last bite of my taco onto my white shirt. I tried futilely to catch the drip before it landed, resulting in dropping what was left of the taco in my hand onto my pants.

"I'm fine." I wipe at it with a napkin, which just spreads it into a colorful blob. "My tux, on the other hand . . ."

"Rented?"

"Unfortunately. Extra charge to remove stains."

She busts up laughing again, snorting loudly with every breath. "I'm sorry."

"You sound like it," I say with a laugh of my own starting.

"JJ, that always happens when you wear white! You should know better. Maybe it's time you invested in a bib. Do they make them in adult size?" The visual of this, I assume, sets her off into a belly laugh so hard she tips over until she's lying on the blanket beneath us, completely on her side. Her shoulders are shaking and her mouth is open so wide her eyes have squinted shut.

"This isn't even that funny." I'm lying. I'm laughing with her. "You're just drunk on processed chicken and cheap guac."

"At least it's all in my stomach where it belongs!" she squeals.

This is the Lucy I love. Skipping prom just to be with her was the best idea of my life.

If I could have this version of tonight over and over again forever, I would take it. But there's no guarantee something bad won't still happen—tonight or any other night after this—just because it's been good so far. And the glitches . . . they're getting progressively worse.

As Lucy pushes herself up to sit, her image is distorted and jumpy, like a YouTube video with a slow internet connection. She doesn't notice, which makes no sense, either. Sometimes

I'm the only one who sees a glitch and sometimes I'm not, like when Lucy saw my black eye appear last night. Even the chaos is in chaos.

"Look at that sunset," she says, sobering, her voice all breathy with wonder. She scoots up next to me and lays her head on my shoulder, staring out at the pink-orange-purple horizon, and folds her legs at her side, covering them with the flowy skirt of her dress. I stretch an arm across her back, brace her bare shoulder, and hold her in snug. The smell of her shampoo floods my senses, and instinctively I melt. She relaxes against me, too, and we're quiet for a while, just watching. Up here, on top of the world, the view is nothing short of magic.

"What are we going to do?" Lucy says. The sun disappears and darkness comes quickly. "When I'm in Italy and you're in Texas and we're both busy with a new school and new friends and . . ." She pauses. "And we don't have this anymore?"

"If there was a way to keep us here with each other forever, Lucy, I'd do it right now."

Except . . . I already did. I just didn't think it would really happen.

I wish we could stay like this forever.

My wish came true, but only for me. She doesn't know she's already stuck here with me on this same night over and over and over. Forever. Or until the glitches overtake reality and we all disappear, swallowed into the dark side of an eclipse.

If it's a chaos loop, you're screwed, Lucy said. *And if you're screwed, we're all screwed.*

The world is probably going to end and it's all my fault. For wanting her to stay.

I still want her to stay. Why is that so wrong?

"We can't keep our lives from moving forward in different directions," she says. "And I don't want to, anyway."

"What? You just said—"

"I just said 'what are we going to do?' Not 'we shouldn't even go there.'"

"Okay, I'm officially confused." The first meteor flashes across the midnight-blue sky. "You're contradicting yourself."

Lucy pulls away to go to the telescope, and the side of me she'd been up against mourns the loss of her warmth. A chill skates across me and I shudder.

"That's because I want both," she says. "I want to stay here and I want to go. And I don't know how to get both things that I want. The only way is to choose one and sacrifice the other. I'm not giving up Italy, so . . ." She places one eye against the telescope and turns a dial.

"So you're giving up me."

"Not you," she clarifies. "Just the everyday closeness I have with you now."

"Italy is worth it?" That's a jerk thing to ask and I shouldn't have. But it's out there now, hovering between us.

"Italy is . . . a second chance for me, in a way."

"There are no second chances, though." At least there weren't until I got stuck with a limitless number of them. But what good have any of them done me?

"Not a second chance, no, you're right. Not doing the same thing again with a different outcome. More like a fresh start?" She turns another dial, then angles the scope upward a bit. Her bare, painted toes wiggle as she readjusts her position. But her nail polish is a metallic blue, instead of the dark red that matches her lipstick. Another glitch, and that one is just a random wrongness, no connection to anything else that happened. Everything is out of whack.

She goes on, unaware anything is amiss, even though the stars on her dress are literally dancing before my eyes, swirling around like they're caught in the pull of a black hole. "What I mean is I need to get away from my old life and start a new one. One where it doesn't matter what my mother is doing that she shouldn't or not doing that she should, because I'll be far away from her and uninvolved either way. But that means I'll be far away from the things and people I want to be involved with, too. Like you. And this. I don't want to lose the good stuff, but I don't see any other way to move forward from the bad stuff. We have to . . . split apart. Live our own separate lives. This would happen eventually, I knew that. I just didn't want to believe it."

The longer she talks the more dejected she sounds.

Have I completely thwarted her plan for tonight? Bringing her here early has her focusing on different things, pushing her thoughts in a different direction. Toward hopelessness.

Lucy wants to move forward, and she can't until we're out of this loop. I've trapped her and she doesn't even know it. I want her to have what she wants, but . . . I also want *her*. And she said she doesn't want to lose us, either. She just thinks she doesn't have a choice.

I have to stop this. Maybe if I stop it, there's still a chance we can work something out and be together. Maybe I can go to Italy, too—I never even considered that before, so I don't know if it's even an option. But I won't know for sure until we're out of this loop, and we can't get out of this loop until I figure out how to stop it, and the only way to stop it is to reverse whatever started it. How did this whole thing start?

"JJ?" she says with concern, still looking through the scope, then her voice lightens. "Did you fall asleep on me?"

"No, I'm . . . thinking."

"Dangerous," she teases.

Another meteor flashes overhead. Has the answer been right in front of me this whole time? It isn't logical, but I'm out of logical answers. Maybe it's time to think more illogically about this, so far outside the box that the box isn't even in the picture anymore. The night before prom, Lucy and I both wished on a star.

Well, no, that's wrong. My wish was on the moon.

I wish we could stay like this forever.

I try to recall more of what we said that night, and it comes back in fuzzy little jagged pieces. In my time, it was almost a week ago.

Ice cream . . . the star game . . . soft, warm, cozy . . . *you're chaos personified . . .*

Did you see that? There's another one!

Lucy had first made a wish on a *falling* star. She wished that

225

the time-travel device would work so she could go back and keep her mom from leaving their family. If the opposite of that came true—that it *wouldn't* work—that would explain why Marty kept fritzing.

And if her wish on a falling star came true, but opposite, and my wish on the moon came true, but more literally than I intended, then the only way to stop this loop is to reverse my wish—by wishing it again but this time on a falling star, knowing the opposite will come true.

The answer hits me like a kick to the gut, and my chest stutters with erratic breaths.

I have to wish us apart, permanently, and I have to really want that wish to come true.

Never. That's impossible. I look up at the sky and declare firmly, "I won't do it."

"Won't do what?" Lucy says.

I turn my face toward her, and she's looking right at me. She's so beautiful. My moon . . . I'll find another way. There has to be another way—

The rocky ground beneath us suddenly rumbles like an earthquake, shaking so violently that the telescope rattles, bounces, and falls over. Lucy yelps in surprise and scuttles toward me.

"What's going on?" she says, clutching me.

"I don't know . . ." But that's not entirely true. As the ground starts disappearing in chunks, replaced by holes that lead to who-knows-where, I understand it's a glitch—the worst one yet; the world is crumbling apart—and I understand that any second now, a groundhog will appear. I scan the area, whipping my head around until . . .

"There you are."

We stare at each other and the thing waves its little rodent hand at me as if it's casually saying hello.

"I can't," I shout. "Please. Don't make me do this!"

The ground under us disappears, and Lucy drops out of my arms, screaming my name. The cold black void consumes me. I can't stop this from happening, so I just relax and let the universe have its way with me. Another repeat is coming, and it has to be the last one.

My final second chance.

the NIGHT of the ETA AQUARIDS

My reflection comes into focus in my bedroom mirror. Then blinks out of focus. Then becomes clear again. What...? It isn't just the mirror. Everything in my room is glitching in and out. The world is unstable, falling apart, but I'm steadier now than I have been in days. Because I finally know what to do.

I just don't want to do it.

Make a wish on a falling star and the opposite will come true. It did. I firmly believe that's what happened. Lucy wished on a falling star that Marty would work, and the opposite came true. He fritzed and fritzed until he blew up. Then we wished on the moon.

I wish we could stay like this forever.

My wish came true, in a way. Which means so did Lucy's. And I remember, she told me that already, on night three. Her wish on the moon was about prom night...about *me*. For her plan to succeed—and it did. Well, one time, at least.

None of this is logical. It's all I have left, though.

I check my phone.

Lucy: Where are you?

Me: Leaving now

228

Leaving . . .

My hand holding the bow tie clenches into a fist. How am I supposed to wish us apart? And truly *want* that wish to come true? How am I supposed to want Lucy to leave me, when that's the thing I've been dreading since she told me her dream of going to Italy will be a reality?

But now I know more about why she wants to go. It isn't because of the great school, or to meet her extended Italian family, or even to taste the authentic food. Or rather, it isn't only about those things. She needs to start over. She needs a new life. She needs to move on.

Without me.

"Knock, knock," Mom says on the other side of my door. "Are you decent?"

"Come in." I fasten my bow tie. With a few flicks of my fingers, I'm done. Perfect.

Mom's reflection steps toward me in the mirror, and everything happens the same way. Shayla runs in for a quick dance. Mama insists on a Vogue photo shoot. They don't seem to notice things are blinking in and out all around them, not even the glitches on their own faces. If I'm wrong, if this doesn't work, this is probably the last time I'll ever see them. The world can't possibly survive like this into another repeat. I squeeze my parents tight, kiss the tops of their heads. "I love you both."

"You'd better get going," Mama says. "You know how Lucy is."

"Yeah. I know how she is. She's perfect."

My parents exchange a look, then Mama ushers me out into the hall. "All right, time to go. Have fun."

"But not *too* much fun," Mom adds.

"I know, I know." I spout off all the going-out rules as I practically tumble downstairs. My feet feel too big and my bones feel too light. Uncoordinated and awkward. My whole body is an odd mix of despair and hope, volleying back and forth, unable to grasp just one and go with it. I think I know what I'm doing now, but didn't I think that on the previous nights, too? Wasn't I so sure I had it?

And none of it worked.

What if I don't have it this time, either? What if I only think I do?

Even if I'm right, what if I can't do what I think I need to?

In the car, with my seat belt buckled and the engine running, I call AAA about Melody's about-to-be-broken-down car, then send a text to Jenna to let her know I'm running late and she might want to hitch a ride with Autumn Mitchell in the limo she rented. Knowing everything Jenna's going to face later tonight, making sure she gets the luxury ride she wants and deserves is the least I can do.

Jenna: Okie dokie. ☺ See you later!

Me: See you later

With a smile, I turn off my phone and stash it in the glove box. No distractions while driving. But also, after I pick up Lucy, I won't need my phone the rest of the night, however long this one lasts.

The road is glitching so bad I almost veer off into a ditch, more than once. Going down Dead Man's Curve is especially harrowing, but somehow I make it through in one piece. Melody is already there, and so is the tow truck. I don't have a reason to stop this time, but I stop anyway. One last goodbye.

"Everything okay here?" I say through the window.

"We've got it handled, young man, but thank you for asking," the service woman says, then goes back to her truck to get it ready to hitch Melody's Bug.

The forest behind Melody is a blur of tree trunks and new green leaves, some of them not fully formed yet, blinking in and out of existence. She stares at me, her brow wrinkled, like she's trying to figure me out. Like there's something familiar about me.

"Something wrong with your gas pedal?" she says finally.

"No, um." I start to ease off the brake, then immediately push it down again. "I hope the rest of your night goes better."

"Thanks," she says warily. Because I'm a stranger. "You can go now. I don't need your help. Really."

"I know you don't." I ease off the brake again, pulling away. "You never did."

Melody will be fine without me, and so will Jenna. I know that for sure. Lucy will be, too. She's strong—a lot stronger than I am. It isn't her I'm worried about if we split.

It's me.

Lucy has always held me together and kept my chaos in control. She isn't perfect, I know that, but we are perfect *together*. We are a well-oiled machine made of broken parts. Without her . . . I'm just broken.

The world is broken tonight. I'm not sure I'll be able to save it, or me, or any of us.

At Lucy's house, my talk with Signore Bellini feels more final than it did on the previous nights.

"Papà, hurry up, we need to go!" Lucy shouts from the living room.

Her dad sighs. "Lucilla not so patient sometimes."

"That's okay," I tell him. "She's not the one who has to be. I am."

He raises his bushy brows, nodding as if he's impressed. I can't even take credit for that, though. I learned it from him. I'm sure he has more to teach me, too. This better not be the last time we ever see each other. But even as I think it, his kind features blur and jump from another glitch. The walls move in and out like they're sighing, taking their dying breaths. Signore Bellini pulls me into a tight hug and it's a struggle not to let tears fall.

"*Grazie*, Papà."

"For what?"

"Everything," I say. "But especially for bringing Lucy into my life."

"*Prego.*" He pats me hard on the back a couple of times, then releases me. "Now, *muoversi*, before she come in here and drag you out."

I flash a grin, then quickly sober when Lucy steps into the hall, turning both our heads in her direction. The stars on *that dress* shift like they're alive. Like swarming bugs. The whole world and everyone in it has become one big glitch. "Ready now?" she says.

"Ready."

We step out to my car. We get in. Buckle up. Lucy smiles because she doesn't know what I've been through—what *we've* been through—over and over already. She doesn't know I know everything she hasn't told me yet. She doesn't know that I love her . . . have always loved her, will love her still when this is over, whatever happens.

She was right—she is rarely wrong—and I should have put my faith in that, even when it meant losing her. No matter how hard I tried to prevent it, this was going to happen eventually.

It's something that's been true for a while. I just didn't want to believe it.

The sun is sinking, about to relinquish the final hours of this day to the moon, to the night, for the seventh time in a row. For years, I looked forward to prom, knowing I'd have only one shot at making it the best night of my life. I've had a week of best nights of my life now. I should be ready. I said I'm ready.

But I'm not ready for this at all.

By the time we pull into the Beaver Creek High parking lot, I'm on the verge of a breakdown. I try to keep myself in check, keep my breathing even and my jaw relaxed, so Lucy doesn't pick up on it and get upset. But everything that's happened over the past week comes tumbling down on me, and I can't hold myself up under the weight of it. I park us way in the back, by the football field, even though there are plenty of open spots closer to the building because we're not late. I need a moment away from people, just me and Lucy.

A limo pulls up by the front entrance, and Jenna and Autumn and her friends get out of it, then they all snap pictures of one another with their phones before disappearing inside. More cars pull in and people get out, no one in any hurry.

The sun hasn't set yet. Prom hasn't officially started. We're here early. Normally, Lucy would be elated by this—on another version of tonight, she was—but now her silence says otherwise.

I can't even look at her; I'm too ashamed. She might never live past this day. Never graduate. Never go to Italy. Never do all the things she plans to do with her life—she has so many plans, always a plan for everything, at least ten steps ahead. And her fool of a best friend took it all away with one selfish wish.

"JJ," she says, "you're . . . not okay." She takes the car keys from me, drops them into the console between us, and then holds my hand with both of hers. "What's going on?"

"I messed up. Worse than I ever have before."

"What did you do?"

"I can't explain." I shake my head. My lips tremble. I try to keep it in check and my jaw aches with the effort. "It doesn't make sense. I just . . . I'm so afraid I'm gonna lose you tonight."

"I'm not going anywhere." She tugs my hand toward her. "Come 'ere."

Slowly, I lean over, farther and farther until my head is resting on Lucy's shoulder, our hands still held together between us. Without a word, she reaches her other hand up and holds it against my head, cradling it, pressing it even tighter against her. She tunnels her fingers through my hair and lightly strokes my scalp. We've been here before, at different times with different problems over the years. My best friend knows exactly what to do. Some of my tension releases in a long exhale, and when I breathe in again, all I can smell is her shampoo. Not one trace of Melody's perfume in here.

It's just us.

"Whatever happened," she says, "I'm sure you thought you were doing the right thing."

"Good intentions don't matter. I did everything wrong. And I think I know how to fix it, but I don't know if—if I can."

"That doesn't make sense."

"I know." I push myself as close to her as I possibly can in this awkward position, nuzzling against the warm dip between her neck and shoulder, snaking an arm across her soft waist, seeking out every cozy spot on her I can find. This is my safe place. Anywhere with her. "Why do I always screw everything up?"

Her chest heaves and she sighs. "You don't. Not always. Not even a lot."

"You're too good to me. I don't deserve you giving me the benefit of the doubt. I don't deserve *you*, period."

Oddly, she laughs at that. "Considering how much you put up with from me, I'd say it's the other way around. I don't deserve a friend as good as you."

I lift my head to get a better look at her. Her dark red lips twibble, and this time I know why. I know exactly what she's thinking, with me practically curled up in her lap and my face only an inch from hers—all the things she plans to tell me later. But we might not have a "later" tonight. And even if we survive past this night, we might not have a "later" of that kind at all.

"*Ti amo*, Lucilla." More and more each day. Night. Whichever. Both.

"*Anch'io*," she says.

That means "me too."

"*Le parole non possono descrivere il mio amore per te.*"

I can't even attempt to translate that one. All I know is *amore* means "love" and *mio* means "my." My love?

She must read the confusion on my face. "You're my best friend in the whole world. Of course I love you."

Oh. I draw back a little. "I didn't mean—"

Lucy's phone starts ringing from her purse, playing our song. We both have that set as our ring tone. The only way I know it's her phone and not mine, other than the fact mine is shut off and locked in the glove box, is that my phone plays the chorus of our song and her phone plays the verse. They complement each other, just like she and I do. She fishes her phone out, forcing me all the way back into my own seat, and answers it.

"No, Chaz, we're here," she says, then huffs. "What, did you forget how to text?" She pauses, listening to his response. "Weird. Yeah, we're fine. We're coming." She ends the call and gives me an exasperated look. "Chaz's phone is acting up. He couldn't get a text through and said he had a bad feeling, like we were in an accident or something."

Glitch. I bite my lip. "Weird."

"That's what I said." Her face is distorted from the glitches. She's still the most beautiful person I've ever seen. "Okay," she says, her tone suddenly lighter, "time to forget your troubles and focus on where we are and what's happening *right now*. This is prom! This is what we've been waiting for! All we have to do for the rest of the night? Is have fun."

Did she really just use my words from a previous night? Lucy doesn't talk so cheery like that. Lucy doesn't usually have to convince me to have fun. This loop is officially out of control.

Dinner is gross, as it has been every night before this, but I savor every bite. It's the best worst dry, rubbery chicken cordon bleu I'll ever eat.

"Taco Bell would have been better than this," Lucy says when we're done.

"Agreed." I toss back the last of my coffee.

The music starts up, and Chaz and Marcos slip away onto the dance floor. With the glitches, prom looks even more magical this time, everything blinking in and out, all the colors twisting and swirling together. Whatever song is playing is unrecognizable, completely garbled. Jenna gets up from her table beside ours, and I instinctively look up at her movement. She gives me a cheesy grin as she steps out to the dance floor.

"You wanna dance?" I say to Lucy, knowing her answer already.

"No, I need to let my food settle first. You go ahead, though. Have fun. Don't worry about me."

Yeah, right. "It's fine, I'll wait with you. There's actually, um . . . something I wanted to talk to you about while we have a minute here, alone." Though it's not exactly private and it's not exactly quiet, with the music blasting so loud I have to practically shout to hear myself.

"Is this about whatever upset you before? Your screwup?"

Yes. One hundred percent. "No, it's about you."

"Oh?"

"The other night—I mean, last night, when we made those wishes on the moon . . . I have to confess something. My wish was about you. About us. I wished that we would never have to be apart. I'm . . . you know, I'm not looking forward to you going to Italy. I'm happy for you—ecstatic for you, honest—but I don't ever want to be without you close, as a . . . as a friend. So it's just hard. To think about. Not knowing what's going to happen or not happen. Or whatever." I try to pass it off as something lighter than it is, but her face doesn't soften. She's not stopping me, either. I should have made a wish to be able to read her mind. "Anyway I know your wish was to reverse the one you wished about your mom on the falling star, so I thought you should know mine. It's only fair."

Her mouth twists. "I have to confess something, too."

"Yeah?"

"I didn't wish for a reversal. My wish was about us, too. I wished—" She presses her lips together and a furious blush blooms on her cheeks. "Well, I don't want to jinx it by saying it out loud. Then it won't come true."

238

She doesn't have to tell me what it was. She already told me on a different night. But: "Since when do you believe in things like jinxes and wishes?"

"I don't," she insists. "It's just a saying. A figure of speech."

"You mean like all those other 'figures of speech' that you 'just say'? Like, 'don't push your luck,' or 'fingers crossed'?"

Her nostrils flare as she presses her lips together for a moment, processing. Then, "It doesn't mean I believe in them."

"Why shouldn't you?"

"Did you really just ask me that?" Now she laughs. She thinks I'm joking. I can't blame her, though. Before this loop started, I would think I was joking, too. But now I know better.

"I bet if you made another wish tonight," I tell her, "on a regular star this time, it would come true."

She starts to laugh again, then stops herself short, staring at me as her eyes go a little wider. "Wait, you're serious. Why are you serious?"

"Because I finally realized the truth—that some of the best things in life aren't logical. They can't be explained, except maybe by magic. Things like . . . love." I heard her admit it once before already; the way she feels about me isn't logical, but she strongly believes in it. And it's the same with how I feel about her. Nothing about it makes sense, and yet, it exists. It's real. Is believing her wish on a star will come true that much of a leap?

"Magic," she deadpans. Her eyes dart to my empty paper cup. "What was in that coffee?"

"Nothing. Never mind." I get up from my chair, shaking my head. "I'm gonna go dance. Will you be ready in a few?"

"Yeah," she says, her gaze calculating. "I'll be right here."

I meet Jenna on the dance floor.

"JJ!" she exclaims, the glitches flapping her hair around like it's caught in a tornado. "You made it." She laughs for no reason and continues her energetic moves, facing me.

But I'm not in the mood for this. I think I just need to say, "Goodbye, Jenna. It's been a trip. Every night with you has been great— Well, no, except for the slaps. But the rest . . . Actually, no, mostly not. What I mean is I don't . . . This isn't . . . We're not . . ."

With every word her brows pull closer together. "What are you talking about?"

"Blair's not cheating on you," I blurt, and that stops her dance moves. I go on, "This is the last night, but it might end before he can tell you. So you need to know. It's all an act, the same as you're acting right now, pretending everything is okay. When it's not. You're hurting. And I know you're hurting because of him, but he's got some things to tell you, so just . . . listen, if you think you can stand it. You don't have to do anything but listen. And then see what you think. Okay?"

"I . . ." She swallows. "I took myself out of the equation. That solved the problem."

"It didn't, though. Not permanently. Splitting up was only—"

Everything stops. *Oh . . . my God . . .*

"Only what?" she presses.

"Temporary." My head spins. "It's all temporary . . ."

As long as time keeps moving forward, anything that happens is temporary. Even the things that have happened within each repeat have changed from night to night, because time was still moving forward until it looped back to the start. Circumstances can always shift again, at any time, back to what they were, or into something completely different. Maybe even something better that I never would have imagined . . .

The best nights of my life might still be ahead of me. Maybe the best nights of *our* life are still ahead of *us*, Lucy and me both, even if we're apart. Maybe hanging on to something good is preventing something better from coming along. I'll never know unless I get there.

And the only way to get there is to stop this loop.

"I'm sorry, Jenna," I say, turning away from her, "I have to go. I have to do something. Now."

I weave past people off the dance floor, quickly deciding against taking Lucy outside with me. If I'm right, and I get this night to stop, I'll see her soon enough. Tomorrow. I head for the exit far from our table where Lucy is still sitting, obliviously checking her phone.

But someone stops me before I can open the door. "JJ, wait."

It's Jenna. She followed me? I turn to face her, and the glitches have turned her mouth into a blur of fire-engine red.

"What's going on?" she says.

"Nothing, it's fine. Don't worry. Everything is finally right. I figured it out. I have to make a wish on a star."

"Oh." She pauses. "Okay . . ."

"I have to make a wish on a *falling* star," I clarify. "There are a ton of them out there tonight, so it shouldn't be hard." My throat tightens and I try to swallow past it. "The hard part is the wish itself."

"There are falling stars out tonight?" she says with this odd sort of excitement in her tone. "How magical! We should all go out and make wishes on them, all together. Our one final act as seniors before graduation. We could wish for whatever we want to come true after high school!"

"It doesn't work the same with falling stars, though," I try to explain, but she's already trotting off toward the stage.

Within a few seconds, the music cuts out and Jenna's voice replaces it through the speakers. "Attention, everyone! Can I have your attention? We're going to do something very special tonight, all of us. Listen carefully!"

Oh *no*. What is she doing?

She's doing what Jenna does best. Spreading her optimism. She wants everyone to get a magical wish tonight. It's so Jenna. But what if it messes up what I need to do to stop the loop? What if all the wishes get tangled up with one another and confused?

"All right," Jenna says through the microphone, "is everyone clear on what we're doing? Any questions?" She pauses for a response, and the room is quiet. "Okie dokie, let's go!"

She steps off the stage and heads to the exit. The crowd follows her, though it's so jumbled and glitchy I can't tell if people are going along with it because they want to or because they think they have to. Everyone has become an amorphous blob rather than individuals. I can't pick out Marcos and Chaz, or anyone who's at a distance anymore.

Suddenly, Lucy is right by me. *That dress*, even though it's glitching, gives her away. "Where is everyone going?" she says.

"Out to wish on a star, and I'm doing the same thing."

I can't see her expression clearly, but her tone is rife with shock. "You're kidding, right? You have to be kidding."

"I've never been more serious about anything in my life." I start walking, and reluctantly, she keeps step with me.

"This is ridiculous," she says.

"No, this is all part of the fun. The magic of prom night." I playfully nudge her with an elbow, calm and carefree on the outside while my insides tighten into knots. "Just go with it. *Carpe noctem.*"

She sighs a sigh that in Lucy Language means "fine, but you owe me for this."

I already owe her, for this and everything else. More than I could ever repay.

Thank you for showing me that every new day is a gift. No matter where it leads us.

She'll be fine without me.

And I'll be fine without her.

I have to be, for both our sakes.

I can do this. I can let her go. All the way to the moon if that's what she wants.

The room starts falling apart around us. Streamers flutter to the floor. Light fixtures drop and explode into shards and sparks. The speakers on the stage crumble into dust. But no one is fazed. I'm the only one who can see it. Once Lucy and I are out of the building, weaving through cars across the parking lot, we follow the blob-crowd toward the football field. Lucy shudders. Goose bumps have popped up all over her bare arms.

I remove my tux jacket and hold it behind her so she can slip into it.

"Thanks," she says. "So . . . what are you going to wish for? What do you want to come true more than anything?"

What I want is her, always. What I want doesn't matter.

"Come on, Mr. Spontaneous," she presses.

"That whatever you wish comes true." How's that for improvising?

"Nice try." She smirks.

We step onto the clay track that surrounds the football field. Everyone is spreading out. Meteors streak across the sky, too many at once, jumping and skipping and lighting up the night. Some of them land on the ground, then fizzle out. The sky is literally falling.

Lucy squeezes my hand as we find an empty spot on the grass and plant our feet.

"What about you?" I ask her.

She hesitates. Then, "I wish—"

"Wait, don't make the actual wish yet!"

"What— I wasn't, but . . . Why?"

"Not on a falling star," I say. "Remember? Or the opposite will come true."

She laughs. "You don't really believe that."

"Right now I do." I believe all of that. I will never not believe that again.

After another expected sigh, she says, "Okay, I guess we're doing this," and she looks up. Everyone is looking up. But I keep looking at her.

Stars fall all around her, blazing. Her hair glows red in the light like fire. She's tilted her head far back, searching the sky. And to my left, movement catches my eye, a dark figure standing out starkly against the brightness. I turn my face in that direction. The groundhog is back, the only thing free of glitches and staring at me, expressionless.

Time's up.

"I wish . . ." Lucy starts, and finishes it silently like a proper wish.

In my head I think it—feel it, believe it: *We'll be fine without each other. We can move forward. We can live separate lives. We don't always have to be together.*

And I voice the opposite on every falling star in my vision, still gripping her hand tight.

"I wish we could stay like this forever—"

The Eta Aquarids ignite the world. Everything goes blinding white, then angry red, then just . . . disappears.

A familiar weightlessness lifts me up and away, and this time, the void isn't cold, dark, and empty. It's warm and glittering with stars.

the NIGHT of the RETROGRADE

White flashes behind my eyes, and then I'm moving—really fast. Instead of Lucy's hand, I'm gripping a steering wheel.

I'm in my car. I'm *driving*.

And I'm about to hit a groundhog running across the road, desperately trying to save its life. Acting the way a normal groundhog would. This can't be the same one as before.

I swerve around it and slam on my brakes, tires squealing, heart pounding, and the car comes to a crooked stop, dangerously close to a ditch. This isn't a repeat. I'm not back in my bedroom an hour before sunset. It's dark, a heavy mist hovering above the asphalt and the fields on either side of me.

Maybe the night didn't repeat—dare I hope? But the world didn't end, either.

Where am I? And what day is it? *What just happened?*

The clock on my dashboard reads 5:22. Every repeat started right after Lucy texted me at 7:30 p.m. What's going on? I pull my phone out of my pocket—and notice the taco stain on my shirt. Not only is it there, and obviously so, but it's crusty and stiff. The display on my phone . . . this better not be a glitch.

It's Sunday, 5:23 a.m., the morning after prom.

I immediately open up my text messages to see what carried over, if anything, and the elation I felt a second ago turns into dread so quickly and fiercely that I actually gag. No picture of me and Lucy dancing at prom, with a black eye or otherwise. And all the messages from the first prom night are back. Every single one of them, from Chaz, from Jenna, from Lucy . . . all in order, playing out the worst night of my life down to the last minute.

> Don't worry about me.
>
> Where are you? Prom's almost over and I lost Lucy
>
> Everyone is looking for her and for you and I hear sirens.
>
> PICK UP YOUR PHONE

Everything that happened on night one was real. Night one was the only one that stuck. The cosmos are back in motion, finally moving forward again, but not without a retrograde first. Why did it have to go all the way back to night one? The *worst* one. When Lucy *chose* to end our relationship.

When I look up from my phone, I realize what road I'm on. This is where I was after I left the hospital on my way back home, trying to get there before my parents woke. I promised them I wouldn't stay out all night. But instead of moving ahead, straight down the road that will take me home, I turn the car the rest of the way around and go back toward the hospital, speeding like I promised I wouldn't. Like I know I shouldn't. Like I might die if I don't get there fast enough, because the black hole is in my chest again, and seeing Lucy is the only way to fill it.

At the same time, I hope I *don't* see her. If she's still there, or was ever there, then night one really was my only reality.

The night she broke off our friendship.

The night we spent completely apart until *everything* fell completely apart.

The night she never got a chance to tell me all the things she'd planned to tell me.

The night we should have had our first kiss, but it never happened. *It will never happen.*

The night of my biggest screwup. My worst fear.

The night I lost her and couldn't get her back. Over and over again.

What if I *still* can't?

I've accepted that possibility, I have, but I didn't think I'd be facing it again so quickly . . . I haven't even had time to adjust to my new viewpoint yet. This is skin I'm not used to wearing.

As I turn into the ER entrance, I think back, all the way to that party freshman year, and then think forward from there. The only thing I've wanted since meeting Lucy was to stay together in some way. For *my* benefit. I let that singular goal of our relationship control how I reacted to her last night. Even though things aren't always the best between us, even though we're like the gears of a broken machine, sometimes moving in sync and other times groaning under the pressure until we snap, then pop back into place, being with her was always better than being without.

I still believe that. The problem is, she doesn't. Not this version of Lucy on this night.

Our breakup probably really was inevitable, then. No matter

how unbelievable it seemed to Lucy on a different version of last night that she would ever push me away, it was going to happen eventually, because I may be her outlet for stress sometimes, but I'm also the one causing it. Lucy was right; she is rarely wrong. She needs a break from me. When she pushed me away, I just didn't want to accept the truth. Instead of giving her the space she needed, instead of giving it any thought first, I went with my gut reaction like I always do and held on to her tighter. That didn't solve a thing.

The waiting room of the ER is empty now, the emergencies of the night before taken care of. I wish I could put a Band-Aid on our relationship and know it would be fine again with a little time and healing. But I don't know if it will. Nothing right now is certain. Nothing *ever* is. Everything is temporary.

The receptionist recognizes me, asking right away if I'm back to see Miss Bellini. Any lingering hope I had that Lucy wasn't really here flickers out and dies like a candle at the end of its wick.

"Is she sleeping?" I ask, my voice raspy and my throat raw like I've been crying. I did cry that first night. I might cry again. My eyes burn.

"Probably," the receptionist says.

Be patient.

"I—I don't want to wake her, then. Can you just give me an update?"

Everything is temporary.

The receptionist checks her monitor, clacks a few keys, then says without looking at me, "She's been stable all night. Should be checking out as soon as the morning charge nurse clears her. You're welcome to wait."

We'll be fine without each other.

"No, that's—" My throat catches. "That's all I wanted to know. Thank you."

I grab a handful of tissues from the box on the reception desk and walk out, one thought hovering over me like a thundercloud about to let loose a flood.

Sometimes the only solution to your problem is to take yourself out of the equation.

"What's your problem?"

Shayla's voice cuts to me from across the room. I blink, groan, and roll over in bed to find her staring at me from my bedroom doorway with her arms crossed.

"You didn't help with the horses this morning. You missed church. You missed lunch. You planning on sleeping the rest of your life?"

Even though I'm physically exhausted from living seven nights of the same thing, six of which shouldn't have existed—possibly didn't?—and emotionally drained from giving up the one person I cherished more than anything in the world, I'm happy to be home, to have my little sister around to tease again. "Yes," I say, smirking. "This is my life now. Professional sleeper. Don't crush my dreams . . . literally."

She rolls her eyes, grumbles something, and disappears into the hallway.

"Shay, wait! Come back."

Slowly, she reappears, a scowl twisting her mouth. "What."

"Don't you wanna know what prom was like?"

She considers this for too long before finally nodding, then sitting on the edge of my bed. I regale her with all the good stuff I can remember. The decorations. The fancy dresses, hair, and suits. The music. The *magic*.

Shayla's attention span is limited, though, even when talking about one of her favorite things, and she's out of my room before I've finished. Okay, whatever, fine. She'll have her own prom soon enough—and that thought brings a smile to my lips. She will get to have her own prom, because time will keep moving forward. Did it ever really stop?

I'm still not sure. All those repeated nights definitely felt real at the time, but now . . . I don't know . . . how could they have been? Did I only imagine what I thought prom would be like if I was there? Imagine all the details? The *kisses*? On night one, I never saw Lucy's dress, only the straps that peeked out from under her hospital blanket, and her shoes under the chair. From that, did I imagine what she would have worn— something she picked out just for me? Imagine that she's wanted to be something other than platonic with me this whole time? Because deep down I wanted her to *that much*. Even if I hadn't totally understood my own feelings yet . . .

Maybe it really was all just in my head. Maybe I blacked out from the stress of losing her, and that was my brain's way of coping.

My phone chimes with a text. I snatch it from my nightstand and blink until the screen comes into focus. Still Sunday. It's going on three o'clock.

> Jenna: I'm sorry I smacked you like that last night. So much awful stuff happened at prom and it all built up and I shouldn't have let it out on you. It's too much to text. I'll tell you all about it on Monday if you're still okay with talking to me.
>
> Me: I'm sorry too. I should have been there. But a lot of awful stuff happened to me too. Talk to you about it tomorrow after you tell me how amazing you did on your math test
>
> Jenna: ☺

I don't get a chance to put my phone down before another text comes through. So much for taking a day to myself to wallow in misery.

> Chaz: You there?
>
> Me: Here
>
> Chaz: What happened with you and Lucy at the hospital after I left last night? She won't tell me.

Strange. Lucy has no reason to be tight-lipped with Chaz. If she's not telling him she ended our friendship . . .

> Me: Is she home now?
>
> Chaz: Yeah I just left her house.
>
> Me: She said nothing about me?
>
> Chaz: Not one word. She still mad?
>
> Me: I don't know

But I'm about to find out.

                    *   *   *

As I approach Dead Man's Curve on the way to Lucy's house,
everything that happened with Melody on night one comes
rushing back. If night one is the one that stuck, the only one
that was real, then I still have her as a friend. She ended the
night by giving me her phone number. I haven't tried contact-
ing her yet, but there's no reason I shouldn't. If Lucy has ended
us for good, a new friend to help me get through that loss, help
fill the void a little, wouldn't be a bad thing.

When I reach the bottom of the curved incline, a cream-
colored Volkswagen Beetle with a black convertible top is being
dragged away by a tow truck. I pull up alongside the ditch and
park, then take out my phone.

> Me: Hey Mel ☺ Just checking to make sure you were real . . .
>
> Mel: Hey hi! Yeah. LOL. I'm real. What you up to?
>
> Me: On my way to Lucy's house. My friend I told you about.
> She had a—

My finger hovers above the screen as all the bad memories
steal my attention. I shouldn't be referring to her as my friend
anymore.

> Me: an accident last night at prom. And it was my fault. I
> need to apologize
>
> Mel: OMG what happened?
>
> Me: Long story. Will fill you in later. Anyway I saw the tow
> truck taking your bug and just wanted to let you know it's
> all good
>
> Mel: Great! Thanks. But sorry about Lucy. ☹

                            253

Me: Me too. I better go. Sorry to cut it short

Mel: It's OK we can talk later.

Me: Yeah. Maybe tomorrow? Let me know when you have time

Mel: Whenever ☺ But don't keep Lucy waiting. Today is yours JJ don't waste it. Go create your own fate.

"Wait out here on the porch," Nico says from inside the doorway to the Bellini house. "If she says you can come in, then okay. But I wouldn't count on it." He grins before shutting the door in my face, clearly enjoying the fact Lucy hates my guts right now. I expect that from him, but this time seeing it actually hurts, doesn't just annoy me, because I deserve it.

I sit on the porch swing and wait. It's cooler today, with a chilly breeze that bites right through my thin T-shirt. The sun is hidden behind a patchwork quilt of gray clouds. It's probably going to rain again. The mud in our horse paddock won't even have a chance to fully dry first. Spring in Ohio can be pretty abysmal, but sometimes . . . it's pretty, period, with blue skies and cheery birds and flowers blooming. Those are the days I cling to, the ones that give you a taste of summer, the ones that make the dreary days worth getting through.

As long as time keeps moving forward, summer will eventually return.

The front door opens and my heart stutters for a second, hoping it's Lucy. But it's not. It's Signore Bellini, and his face is stern. Not the warm welcome I usually get from him.

"JJ," he says. "Why you here?"

Simple question. But the answer isn't.

In another reality, Lucy confessed her feelings for me on the bluffs. In another reality, she wore *that dress* and we kissed, more than once. In another reality, I told her about the time loop, something she believes with every fiber of her being is impossible, and she helped me try to stop it. No one else would have, but she did. In another reality, we skipped prom for a Taco Bell dinner, just us, and we talked about things only we know of each other. In another reality, we danced to our song for the last time . . .

Actually, the answer *is* simple. I'm here because she's my best friend, and I love her.

Whether we are friends, not-friends, or something-other-than-friends, I will always love her. In every version we lived the past seven nights, no matter what happened, I loved her, in this way or that. It was the only constant.

I can't tell her dad that, though. Not before I've had a chance to tell Lucy first. "I wanted to see how Lucy's doing, after . . ."

"She no good." I open my mouth to ask what happened, but he raises a palm to stop me. "Physically, she is fine. Mentally, no good. Sad. Quiet. Isolating herself. Very upset."

"I don't know what to do. Papà, what should I do?" My voice catches, almost cracking. My fear of losing her is trying to take control again. I won't let it. I can't let it win. I *do* exist without her; it's just going to be hard. I force myself to breathe. To ignore my gut reaction of panic. To slow down and *think before doing*. I don't always have to go with my gut. I don't always have to improvise on the fly. *Be patient.*

I start with, "What did she say when you told her I'm here?"

"She did not say she want to see you, and she did not say she not want to see you. She say no words since you left last night."

No words. That's what Chaz said, too. I thought he meant she wasn't telling him just that one thing about us, but she's not talking to *anyone* about *anything*.

"You think you can help, I let you in," Signore Bellini says. "You think you make it worse, go home. She need patience, like I tell you before. Can you give her that?"

I nod. "I think so." A few nights ago, I couldn't. I didn't. But now, I know I can try.

"*Va bene.*" He jerks his head toward the door, a small smile touching his lips. "*Muoversi, polpetto.*"

"*Grazie.*"

Normally his nickname for me, *polpetto*, would make me smile right back. It literally means "meatball," and somehow that's a term of endearment. But my throat remains tight and my jaw remains clenched as I walk in, cross the living room, and head upstairs. This house is as familiar to me as my own, but today I feel like a stranger, aware that one wrong move will get me kicked out. Possibly forever.

And if that happens, it's Lucy's choice. Whatever happens is her choice, not mine.

Her bedroom door is open, but I knock on it anyway. "Can I come in?"

She doesn't answer, but I hear the mattress shift and then her feet padding across carpet right before I see her. For the past week, I've seen her in the same dress, the same makeup, the same hairstyle. Stunning, every time. Now, even though she's in leggings and an oversized sweatshirt, her face scrubbed rosy clean, her eyes puffy, and her hair wild . . . I smile at the sight of her. She's a mess. This is the private version of Lucy that only a few have ever seen, and I'm one of those privileged few.

Today she will get the me she should have had all along.

She frowns at my smile. Glares, even. Then turns and sits on her bed in heated silence.

I sit on the floor next to the bed.

Her toes are still painted dark red, the same as her fingernails, remnants of a night she had planned out for a year that, in this reality, never happened. What was supposed to be the best night of our life never happened.

And like Melody said, *everything happens for a reason*. So maybe the same is true of what was supposed to happen but didn't.

"Do you believe in fate, Lucy?"

Her brows knit together, and her plump lips press into a firm line. She wants to ask me what I'm talking about, but she's too stubborn to break her silent treatment. Her willpower wins, and she says nothing.

"Okay, you don't have to answer that," I say. "I know the answer is no. And you know I don't believe in it, either. Or at least you knew I didn't, until today."

The curiosity burning through her has to be reaching blazing temps. But she stays quiet.

"What I mean by fate right now specifically is, uh . . . when bad things happen, they might lead to better things that wouldn't have happened if not for the bad. Does that make sense?"

Her lip twibbles, and she offers a nod so slight I almost miss it.

"When you told me what you told me last night . . . When you said—" I slouch and sigh, the memory of it like a physical weight and I'm shaking under the strain. It's time to let it go.

I sit up straighter, square my shoulders, and look her right in the eye. "You were right. We stress each other out. We always have. For almost four years, you've been my number one concern. For almost four years, I've been nothing but a person-shaped ball of stress around you, coiled up tense and ready to fend off any little thing that would possibly hurt you, and when I'm not around you, I'm constantly worried about what might happen to you that I won't be there to help you with. And even more so recently, knowing we're going to be on opposite sides of the world soon. Lucy, I don't want us to be apart. It's my worst fear. Because I . . . I"—*breathe*—*just say it*—"I love you. I don't mean platonic love. I mean romantic love."

Her big brown eyes widen bigger and rounder than I've ever seen them before. Nothing else on her moves, not even a twibble.

"You were right about us stressing each other out," I continue. "And I was wrong to deny it. You were right to break us up. And I was wrong to try to keep us together. But you were wrong, too, about us being no good for each other. I'm a better person now than I was before I met you. There are a lot of parts of me that still need fixing, though. I'm not perfect. I'm a work in progress."

"I'm not perfect, either," she says quietly.

She spoke. Maybe there's hope for us yet, but I'm afraid to hope even a little.

"And that's why our relationship hasn't been perfect," I say. "We haven't always been perfect friends to each other. But you know what? I don't want perfect, Lucy, if it means I can't have you. I want *you*. We're both in pieces, in different ways. Sometimes those jagged edges don't line up, and we grate on each other—okay, a lot of times—but when they do line up . . . it's seamless. There's no one else out there who fits together with me as well as you do."

She clutches the edge of the mattress and swallows hard, lips trembling.

"If you think we shouldn't be friends or anything else, and that we need time and space from each other, maybe forever, that's your choice, and I will respect it. I'm not here to tell you what to do or try to change your mind. I just . . . wanted you to know the truth. That I worry because I love you, and because I love you, worrying isn't a burden. It's a privilege. And I'm sorry. I'm sorry for a lot of things, but mostly I'm sorry for not telling you any of this when you needed to hear me say it. I was afraid of losing you. *Mio cuore, mia anima, mia vita.* I couldn't imagine my life without you in it, and that scared me into holding on to you so tightly I smothered you. I'm sorry," I repeat, realizing I've gone on too long. Time to wrap this up. "If

259

I had another chance, I wouldn't let my fear get between us. I would have said to you last night what I'm saying to you now—that it's okay if we aren't always together. We can be apart if you need us to be. But you and I both know there's no such thing as second chances. So all I can say is I love you and I'm sorry."

Lucy's silent again, and I'm pretty sure that's it. We're done. She let me say my piece, and it changed nothing. I don't regret telling her, though. I only regret telling her too late.

This is her choice. It's not up to me to choose what's best for her, even if it means losing *my heart, my soul, my life*. We'll be fine without each other, eventually. Right now? Not so much.

Slowly, with my body feeling like it's suddenly tripled its weight and my gaze fixed on the scuffed white toes of my Converse, I stand and head out of the room, into the hall. *I respect your decision, Lucy. I trust you to do the right thing for you. I still love you. Always, no matter where we go from here.* I get as far as the top of the stairs—

"Wait," Lucy says behind me, her voice soft and pleading. "Don't go."

I turn to face her. God, she is so beautiful. The most beautiful mess I've ever seen.

She takes a tentative step toward me, her hands held in front of her, twiddling her fingers like she always does when she's mildly anxious. "If you can believe in fate, just this once, then maybe I can believe in second chances. Just this once."

My knees go weak. I brace myself against the wall. "What are you saying?"

"I'm saying . . . let's start over." She holds out her right hand. "Hi, I'm Lucilla, but you can call me Lucy. What's your name?"

I grab her hand and shake. Then hold it between us. She doesn't let go, either. "I'm James. But you can call me JJ."

"JJ . . . that's cute, like you." A smile tugs up into her cheeks. "So, JJ, I went to my senior prom last night. It wasn't the fun night I thought it would be. In fact, nothing went according to plan. It was an absolute train wreck, but at least I looked good when they found my body in the wreckage."

My laughter releases in one loud pop, and my tension along with it. "I don't doubt that."

"Would you like to see the dress I wore? I know we just met, but something tells me you might like it." Her expression turns conspiratorial. "I might even model it for you."

This is the Lucy I fell in love with, that I'm falling in love with all over again.

I don't have to feign surprise when she shows me the galaxy dress—it was real?

If that was real, then how much of the other stuff was real, too? For now I can only hope, and every new day is a gift. So I don't need to rush anything. We've got time. *Be patient.*

We spend the rest of the day talking and laughing, getting to know each other more deeply than we ever have before, and it really is like starting over. A slate wiped clean by the truth. Who knows what might happen from here . . . Will we go separate ways, very far apart, to other sides of the world, like I feared? And if we do, will we stay in touch? Will we, by then, have become something other than friends?

Or maybe something I can't even think up right now. Something completely unexpected.

All those nights that repeated, I thought each one was another second chance to do things right. But they weren't. The real second chance was this, today, after the loop stopped. Just like Melody said. *Today is yours.* Not yesterday. Not last night, no matter how many last nights there were. Today.

Today is yours. Don't waste it. Go create your own fate.

ACKNOWLEDGMENTS

This book was very fun to work on but happened to come about during some very turbulent times in my life. You would not have this book in your hands now if not for the following people:

Thanks to Laura Bradford for continuing to prove just how lucky I am to have you as my agent. This book—and quite literally *everything* that I write—would not exist without your support and guidance. You keep me going through it all. You help me sort out my wackadoodle story ideas that hit me at 2 a.m. You push me to do better. Thank you to the moon and back!

Thanks to Emily Seife for digging into this story and helping me shape it from the very start, since before I even had a complete manuscript written yet, and all the way until it was ready to print. I appreciate your editorial care, how you helped me figure out the best way to tell JJ's story—over and over and over again. Working with me probably felt like a time loop itself, like the revisions might never end. I know it can't be easy to work with an author who just doesn't "get it" sometimes and who can admittedly be stubborn. Thank you so much for all your hard work and patience with me. Thanks also to everyone else at Scholastic who worked on this book, from edits to design and beyond. I may not know all of you, but I sincerely appreciate you!

Thanks to this wonderful group of fellow writers who helped me at different times during the process, providing valuable feedback and, at times, much-needed emotional support: Jen, Kelly, Victoria, Judy, Cathy, Joyce, and Tara. I couldn't have done any of this without you.

Thanks to Dahlia Adler at LGBTQ Reads for everything you do. I can't say that enough. Thank you, thank you, thank you!

Thanks to my second family at Entangled Publishing for being the most lovely group of coworkers I could ever ask for. Books are my favorite thing in the world, and I'm extremely lucky to have a career making books with you folks day in and day out. Liz, Stacy, HR, HH, Judi, Candy, Jess, Curtis, Hayden, Holly, Bree, Debbie, Robin, Nina, Brenda, Alethea, Erin, Katie, Rebecca, Riki, Meredith, and in case I forgot anyone . . . ALL of you are the best! Thanks also to all the authors I work with at EP—you remind me every day why I love editing books as much as I do. You're all so wonderful, so creative, and a joy to work with.

Thanks to my former coworkers at Kohl's who have stuck with me even though I don't clear out fitting rooms and merchandise pretty things with you anymore. You are more than just former coworkers—you are my friends. There are too many of you to list, but thanks especially to DJ, Sarah C, Sarah B, Kristy, and Elizabeth for your friendship and support. I love you more than a Lowest Prices of the Season sale with a 30 percent off coupon and Kohl's Cash.

Thanks to Mama and my sister, Dianna, for reasons too numerous and too personal to list, and for always being there to pick me up when I fall. Thanks to my Italian family and my Italian American upbringing, which had a strong influence on this particular story. Lucilla Bellini came to life because of you. So did my unwavering addiction to pasta and pizza.

Thanks to Joe, my ex-husband. We were married when I started this book and divorced when it was all done. Our life together didn't work out how we planned, but you were always supportive of my writing career, since before I could even call it a career, and I will never forget all you did to help me, how you never let me give up on my dreams no matter how tough things got. This book (and the one before it) exists because of you, too, and I'm grateful for that.

Thanks a million to my son, for putting up with a scatter-brained, overemotional mom who's constantly trying to meet one deadline or another and probably "makes" takeout for dinner more often than they should, but thank you especially for giving me hugs whenever I need them. It seems overnight you became a six-foot-tall teenager, but you'll always be my baby.

Eternal thanks to Melissa Linville, my dear friend whom this book is dedicated to. My last conversation with you feels like only yesterday, when you were asking about this new book I was writing and how excited you were that it would be published so you could buy a zillion copies and tell everyone you knew about it. You were my champion, my confidant, my cheerleader, and you were gone far too soon. Ten years of friendship was not nearly enough. But the effect you left behind is lasting. You will never be forgotten and you will always be loved. I'm glad for the time we did have together. I'm very lucky to have been one of those who knew you. Thank you for your contagious optimism and teaching me that every new day is a gift. I wish the time loop in this book were real, so I could spend one more day with you again and again and again. Miss you so much . . .

And last but never least, thanks to all of you who read JJ's story from start to finish and ended up here, reading this page. Thanks double if you read my first book and came back for more. It's because of you that I'm able to do what I love for a living—tell stories, write fiction, make books—and I've got so many more stories to tell. I hope you'll be with me for those, too. *Grazie, grazie, grazie!*

ABOUT THE AUTHOR

Lydia Sharp worked a number of different jobs, everything from retail management to veterinary medicine, before turning their passion for stories into a career. They are now a romance editor and write YA novels with lots of kissing and adventures. Lydia lives in northeast Ohio with an ever-growing collection of owls. When not completely immersed in a book, they binge on Netflix, pine for Fall, and host mad tea parties in Wonderland. Follow them on Twitter at @lydia_sharp for updates.